THE ADVERSARY

The
Defining
Curse

RANDY C. DOCKENS

Carpenter's Son Publishing

The Defining Curse

©2022 by Randy C. Dockens

Published by Carpenter's Son Publishing, Franklin, Tennessee

Published in association with Larry Carpenter of Christian Book Services, LLC
www.christianbookservices.com

Edited by Robert Irvin

Cover and Interior Layout Design by Suzanne Lawing

Printed in the United States of America

978-1-952025-68-6

About This Book

The story of the curse on Jehoiachin is one of history, mystery, and debate. The premise of this book is based upon three things: (1) the curse administered by the prophet Jeremiah to King Jehoiachin, the king of Judah, in Jeremiah 22:24-30; (2) Jehoiachin being brought out of prison with favor by the son of Nebuchadnezzar who reigned over Babylon after his father's death in 2 Kings 25:27-30; and (3) a book by Steven M. Collins, who wrote *Parthia: The Forgotten Ancient Superpower and Its Role in Biblical History* as to how this powerful kingdom rose from the descendants of Israel's exiled people who did not return to their ancestors' homeland. What is presented here is one possibility as to how all of this could have come about, Scripture remain true, and how all of prophecy can still come true.

Contents

foreword

Even though Nebuchadnezzar is one of the most well-known Babylonian kings, there is a great deal that is not known about him and his reign. This statement holds true for the prophet Daniel as well. While there is a lot we know about the prophet's character, steadfastness, and visions, there is little known about his day-to-day life.

The event that ties these two famous and enigmatic characters together is the curse of Jehoiachin, which was delivered by the prophet Jeremiah. Some have tried to downplay this curse. Others have tried to overplay it. Yet I feel there are clues in Scripture and in historical records that can help us piece together a plausible scenario that links these characters. While there is much poetic license in this novel about the life and families of Daniel, Jehoiachin, and Nebuchadnezzar and how their lives were intertwined, I feel it is very much in line with what we do know and could very possibly have occurred as told here.

What I desire to bring forward in this novel is that God's prophecies always come true. He has a reason for everything he says and does. While many have tried to explain away the curse Jeremiah issued to Jehoiachin, I want to provide an alternative that puts it in another light, one many have not considered. Rather than somehow discounting Jeremiah's words, I think there is a way to believe exactly what was prophesied, grasp the ramifications it implies, and see how much *more* alive Scripture becomes when we treat its words as factual and take an honest look at what unfolds.

CHAPTER 1

The Curse Revealed

Mikael sat at his favorite spot. He leaned back, placing his hands behind him on the large boulder on which he sat as he gazed across the bubbling brook in front of him at a flying creature coming toward him. The winged creature diverted its flight to land on the limb of a tree on the other side of the brook; the tree was in full bloom and covered in hundreds of tiny yet beautiful white flowers. *What was it Adam named such a creature? Oh, yes. Bird.* Mikael realized he had never before seen a flying creature of such magnificent beauty. Its feathers were a flaming red in color which morphed into orange and then into a brilliant yellow as its feathers formed its long, flowing tail. It stood out like a beacon against the pure white of the flowers now surrounding the majestic creature.

The bird at first seemed to ignore him as it looked from one side to the other in quick, staccato head jerks. Then the creature seemed to look directly at Mikael, giving a trill and producing a sound so melodic Mikael stopped breathing for a few seconds.

"Master," Mikael whispered in awe. "You really know how to astound."

Mikael whistled in a puny attempt to make a return call to the bird. He had to laugh as the bird just cocked its head back and forth a few times as if in confusion.

"Oh," Mikael said. "My sound is not good enough for you? Is that it?"

The bird flitted its head back and forth as if answering his question.

Mikael laughed again. "Well. I see I'm not up to your standards."

The creature gave its melodic trill again and flew over Mikael in a high arc.

Mikael smiled. Everything here in Eden was so wonderful, beautiful, peaceful. He shook his head. His Creator could really create.

This was one of the reasons he loved coming to this dimension. There was always something new to behold. It seemed the Creator was constantly creating something unique and wonderful. But he knew this beauty was not just for him and his fellow angels to enjoy when they had time to come here. One day, those in the righteous part of Sheol would be brought here. He wasn't yet sure how that would happen. But his Master had said it would take place, so Mikael knew it would. The timing was up to the Master. Mikael looked around again and smiled. He had been to Sheol when it was first created. While beautiful, it did not compare to Eden. This paradise was so much more wonderful. In Sheol, the feeling was foreboding even while beautiful. Here, there was such peace and beauty— almost beyond comprehension.

Mikael looked back into the sky while watching the path of the bird as it headed for a grove of trees on the other side of the grassy meadow behind him. It was then Mikael noticed Raphael in the distance, turning a three-sixty, then focusing on him and striding toward him in an almost militaristic, determined cadence. As Raphael neared, Mikael sat up straighter.

"Hello, Raphael. Anything wrong?"

Raphael displayed a serious, determined look. "Mikael, come at once. He's done it again."

"He? As in?"

"Lucifer," Raphael said with a tone that essentially said: *Who else?*

Mikael stood, now also quite serious. "What did he do this time?"

"He's gotten the prophet Jeremiah so riled, Gabriel says he's about to put a curse on King Jehoiachin."

Mikael's eyes widened. "What kind of curse?"

With a slight shake of his head, Raphael replied, "Gabriel didn't say. But it can't be good."

"Well, curses usually aren't."

"Of course," Raphael said. "I just mean . . . "

Mikael put his hand on Raphael's shoulder with a small smile. "I know what you mean, Raphael. So, what's the plan?"

Raphael gave a shrug. "Not sure there is one. Gabriel is going down to observe. I thought you might want to join him."

"Definitely."

"You know," Raphael said as he looked down and then back at Mikael. "I don't understand why our Lord allows him to do all of these things."

"Our role is not to question, Raphael, but to obey."

"Yes, yes, I know," Raphael said. "But look at all he's done so far. First, he rebelled in our dimension when he had a position that any other angel would have gladly traded positions for. Then he deceived Serpent and Chavvah, manipulated both Serpent and Adam to actually rebel against our Creator, almost annihilated the human race before our Lord saved Noach and his family by destroying the wickedness Lucifer had brought to the earth, and almost created another coup at Babylon with Nimrod and his wife attempting to create a superhuman with the power to control the earth!" Raphael took a deep breath. "Now he's trying to get Jeremiah to reverse the promise our Master made to King David. I mean, he just doesn't stop. Why?"

Mikael put his arm around Raphael's shoulders and gave him a light pat. "Remember what the Master said in the beginning. It's all about choice. There is no love without choice. There is no freedom without choice. But there are consequences—some immediate, others delayed." He smiled. "Don't worry, Raphael. Our Creator will make it all right in the end." He gave a firm pat to Raphael's shoulder. "He promised it, so it has to come true."

Raphael nodded. "I know you're right, Mikael. But it's hard to see everyone suffer so much. And all for the vain ego of one." Raphael stiffened his stance. "But you're right. Our job is to serve, not solve the problem. That is the job of our Creator. We do our part, and he will definitely do his."

Mikael smiled. "That's the spirit. Now let's go meet Gabriel."

They teleported to the angel dimension and searched to find Gabriel. After a short time they found him conversing with several other angels.

Gabriel held up his hand in greeting. "Mikael. Good. You're here." He nodded at the three angels with him. "I was just telling them of my plans."

Mikael looked at the three and gave a slight nod of recognition. He returned his focus to Gabriel. "Do we need to bring a contingent of angels?"

"I don't think so," Gabriel said. "I thought the three of us could go and first evaluate." He nodded toward one of the angels with him. "I've told Quentillious of the possibility of that need, just in case."

Quentillious bowed to Mikael. "With your permission, though, certainly. You are, after all, the Captain of the Lord's Host."

Mikael gave a slight nod. "Thank you, Quentillious. Yes, prepare a contingent, just in case." Mikael looked to Gabriel and then back to him. "Hopefully, that is as far as we will need to go in this instance. But we should be prepared for battle if the need arises."

Quentillious nodded. "Very good, my captain." He and the others turned and left. Mikael, Raphael, and Gabriel remained.

Mikael looked at Gabriel. "Raphael told me about Jeremiah. What has him so worked up?"

"As you know," Gabriel began, "Jeremiah has had to put up with so much abuse from the royal household ever since the death of King Josiah. He has been an extremely faithful servant of our Lord despite being placed in prison many times for speaking the truth of Yahweh."

Mikael nodded. "Yes, I'm sure that has to weigh heavy on him. It's like speaking to a brick wall. Yet several of the kings, including Jehoiachin's father, were almost as bad, weren't they?"

"Indeed, they were," Raphael interjected. "Several of them suffered greatly for their refusal to follow our Master's directions that he provided them in the Law of Moses."

Gabriel nodded. "That's very true. Their actions have had great consequences to their subjects as well. Not only physically, but spiritually. I think the latter is what is weighing heavily on Jeremiah's heart."

"And we're going there to change his mind?" Mikael asked.

Gabriel shook his head. "Not exactly. I think Ruach, the Lord's Spirit, is the one leading Jeremiah in this direction."

"What?" Mikael turned wide-eyed. "Why would he do that?"

Gabriel gave a smile. "His ways are above ours."

Raphael looked from Mikael to Gabriel. "Wait. Gabriel, I thought you said Lucifer was behind this."

Gabriel nodded.

Raphael squinted. "And Ruach is also behind this?"

Gabriel nodded again.

Mikael held up his hand. "Hold on. Lucifer *and* Ruach together on this? That doesn't make sense." He shook his head. "That doesn't make sense at all."

"Oh," Gabriel said, "Lucifer is never on the side of Ruach." He smiled. "But Ruach can still use Lucifer's plans to his own advantage without Lucifer knowing it."

Mikael rubbed the back of his neck. "Yes, that's likely true." He looked at Raphael and then back to Gabriel. "So, what are *we* to do?"

"Observe," Gabriel said.

Mikael started to reply, but Gabriel held up his hand. "But be ready for more action if the need arises."

"Okay," Mikael replied. He didn't know what else to say. From experience he knew Ruach was never completely straightforward, but always had a plan, and that plan always worked out as designed. Mikael knew his job was to serve, and that was what he was willing to do.

Raphael developed a confused look. "I don't get it."

Mikael smiled and patted Raphael's shoulder. "Remember our conversation just before teleporting here."

Raphael sighed, then nodded. "We are his servants."

Gabriel smiled. "And we obey."

"All right, then," Mikael said. "Let's go observe."

All three disappeared from their dimension and entered the time dimension.

CHAPTER 2

Jeremiah's Pronouncement

Mikael and his two fellow angels reappeared on the portico of the palace that went along its wall from the side where one could observe the temple. Mikael stopped and looked at the complex Solomon had originally constructed; he sighed. He remembered the beauty of the temple when King Solomon first built the structure. Its white plastered walls shown brilliantly when the morning sun's rays grew higher and over it. The gold—part of each of the two pillars' capitals in front of the temple and along the eaves of the roof line—would reflect the sun's light, making it look like a sparkling jewel within the city itself. He always thought that befitting the worship of his Creator: the brilliance of the temple representing the Shekinah glory of the Almighty penetrating into the world from the center of Jerusalem.

But now . . . now the scene was a stark contrast. Over the years various kings had stripped the beloved, beautiful structure of its brilliance and wealth to pay off some despot to prevent his hordes from invading, or to gain their favor in some way rather than trusting in the One for whom this structure was created. Despite the effort that King Josiah, Jehoiachin's grandfather, had made to restore the temple from so many years of neglect, the structure was a far cry from its original glory: gold had been chipped off the capitals of the pillars and many parts of the roofline, and even from the temple doors themselves. The magnificent bronze basins Solomon had made for the priests to wash before entering the structure to perform their temple duties were now disassembled, the major one removed from its base of twelve bronze oxen, and the oxen now gone, likely melted down to pay some royal debt. Sacrifices were still being offered, but now on an altar that was a replica from a pagan altar King Ahaz had seen in Damascus and remade here! Ahaz had moved, to the north side of the temple, the magnificent altar King Solomon had created for conducting atoning sacrifices for Israel.

All Mikael could do was shake his head. Israel had started out so wonderfully and apparently was going out with disgrace. Now he wondered if the nation would even have a future. If Jeremiah went through with what was predicted, what was the future for Israel as a nation—or even as individuals?

Mikael felt a hand on his upper arm. This brought him out of his thoughts.

"Are you all right, Mikael?" Raphael asked.

Mikael nodded but then tilted his head slightly from side to side. "Yes. And no." He gave a weak smile. "It's just sad to see how far Judah has fallen."

Raphael nodded. "I think I hear Jehoiachin around the corner on his patio."

As the three angels rounded the end of the portico it turned into a large patio overlooking other magnificent buildings of the palace. Mikael couldn't help but sigh seeing how magnificent the palace had been maintained—but the temple itself almost in shambles in comparison.

*****

Jehoiachin, reclining on ornate pillows at a low-lying table, was eating some fruit, cheeses, and bread. A few other royals were dining with him. On either side stood two servants with large date palm fronds waving them to stir a breeze for the king and those at the table. Jehoiachin looked to be only about eighteen years of age; those with him were not much older. They were engaged in discussions eliciting a great deal of laughter.

A servant entered and bowed. "I beg your pardon, my lord."

Jehoiachin threw a date at one of those at the table and the others laughed harder. He looked over at the servant, seemingly annoyed. "Yes, Abijiah. What is it?"

"The prophet Jeremiah is here to see you."

Jehoiachin pounded his fist on the table. "Why do you interrupt my afternoon pleasure with my friends with such news?"

Abijiah bowed again, lower than before. "I'm sorry, my lord, but he was insistent."

"Yes, I'm sure he was. He always is." He threw up his hands. "Well, since you've already spoiled the mood, might as well make it complete. Show him in."

"Oh, Coniah, your majesty, this could be fun," one of his friends said. "I think he's quite amusing."

Jehoiachin rolled his eyes. "Yes, you would, Hananiah. You were always the strange one."

The man cackled with laughter. "True, Coniah. So true."

Jehoiachin threw another date at the man. "But you're not the one he prophesies against." He shook his finger at him. "Your tone would change if he was actually prophesying against you personally."

The man gave a dismissive wave. "Oh, it can only bother you if you actually believe his drivel." He laughed again. "Otherwise, it's just entertainment."

In a matter of minutes the servant returned with a bearded man, somewhat tall and thin, wearing a tunic and sleeveless cloak. The servant bowed, turned, and left.

Jehoiachin looked up and forced a smile. "Well, Jeremiah, to what do I owe the pleasure?" He gestured toward the table. "I would invite you to sit, but I fear your visit is a quick one." He plopped another date in his mouth. "Is this one of your deliver-an-insult-and-leave scenarios?"

"Jehoiachin, your majesty, it is with heavy heart that I come."

"Oh, is that so? All of your insult delivery getting to you these days?"

{ Mikael could see Jeremiah's demeanor physically change. It was evident he had not come here willingly to deliver his message. Ruach was most assuredly behind this. Jeremiah was about to give a message he truly did not want to deliver. }

"Your majesty . . . Coniah . . . "

Jehoiachin laughed. "Coniah, now, is it? We're getting down to a personal level, are we?" He stood and came over to face the prophet, raising his arms slightly. "Okay, Jeremiah. Let's get personal. What's on your mind?"

"Ruach, God's spirit, has troubled me greatly these last few days."

"I have some medicine for indigestion," Hananiah inter-jected. He belched and then laughed. "I use it often." The others at the table snickered.

Jehoiachin gave him an irritated stare. Hananiah shrugged, giving a silly smile.

Turning back to Jeremiah, Jehoiachin said, "And just what is your troubling news?"

"It is your actions, and your heart, my lord. Yahweh wants you to come back to him."

Jehoiachin shook his head. "Yeah, I bet he does." He gestured toward Jeremiah. "Isn't that what my grandfather did? And look what that got him."

{ Mikael saw Jeremiah's shoulders droop. It seemed this was not going the way Jeremiah had hoped. }

"Coniah," Jeremiah said, voice low. "Your grandfather, Josiah, acted before consulting with Yahweh for his course of action."

"Oh, I see," Jehoiachin said sarcastically. "It's all about you in the end, isn't it, Jeremiah? My grandfather, my father, and I didn't come to you for advice before acting." He turned in frustration and then turned back, shaking his index finger at Jeremiah. "You're only feeling left out." He laughed. "You're as vain as the rest of us."

Jeremiah sighed. "I'm trying to help you see things from Yahweh's perspective."

Jehoiachin's eyebrows raised. "Oh, is that so? And what is the Almighty's perspective?"

"There are consequences to a king's actions that go beyond those of his own life. There are still consequences to the actions of your great-great grandfather, Manasseh, that have not as yet been enacted. Your grandfather, Josiah, postponed those because of his heart turning to Yahweh. Yahweh can do the same for you."

Jehoiachin's face turned stony. He pointed toward his own chest and spoke with firm voice. "My great-great grandfather repented and came back to Judah stronger than ever and did great things. *What* are you talking about?"

Jeremiah shook his head with a sigh as though he was trying to help a confused child. "The sins of Manasseh were very grave and set things in motion that cannot be delayed indefinitely. There is a chance Yahweh still can if *you*, yourself, repent." These last words were said with a pleading tone.

"Well, I think we are quite all right, thank you. My father has things under control."

Jeremiah shook his head as his eyes began to water. "No. No, Coniah. He most certainly does not." Tears began to run down his cheeks. "Yahweh has shown me his fate. It's . . . it's not pretty. His death will be brutal, and his body will not even be buried like a common work animal. There will be no dignity in it."

"What?" Jehoiachin raised his hand as though he was going to slap Jeremiah across his face, but he paused and closed his fingers, wagging his index finger in Jeremiah's face instead. "Such disrespect deserves your death, Jeremiah. But I won't take your life . . . if you just go." He pointed in the direction Jeremiah had entered. "Go now!"

"And our fate?" Hananiah asked.

Jehoiachin turned in frustration and saw the grin on Hananiah's face. He gave Hananiah a hard stare, shook his head, and turned back to Jeremiah.

Jeremiah's gaze turned to Hananiah. "You feel you are like this beautiful cedar beam which King Solomon had placed here from Lebanon." He pointed at a huge beam running from one end of the patio to the other. "But just as its beauty crumbles in the fire, so will yours."

"Oh, oh," Hananiah said. "A riddle." He clapped his hands together rapidly. "I love riddles."

"And what about *my* fate?" Jehoiachin asked. "Do you have more insults to fling?"

Jeremiah's gaze settled back on Jehoiachin. "It's not good, I'm afraid—unless you repent."

Jehoiachin's face grew red. "I will not repent to you."

Jeremiah shook his head as more tears came. "Not to me, Coniah. To Yahweh."

"Oh, please! You deliver this unjustified news to me, and I'm supposed to repent to a vindictive God." He shook his finger at him, then lowered it. "And you can stop calling me Coniah! Your words show you do not have the right to be that familiar with me."

"I . . . don't want to tell you this, Co . . . I mean Jehoiachin. But Ruach compels me to deliver his message."

Jehoiachin gave a sarcastic bow. "Oh, by all means, unburden yourself. That's what you've wanted to do ever since you arrived, isn't it?"

Jeremiah shook his head. "No," he said, barely whispering. "It's the last thing I want to do. But here is the message from El Shaddai, the Almighty, whose words cannot be thwarted. 'Jehoiachin, you had the chance to be like your grandfather, but have chosen to be like your father and great grandfather instead. Their sins were many, as are yours. Therefore, you will bear the consequences of all the years for which they have not been atoned. Even if you were a signet ring on my finger, I would still cast you off to signify you no longer have an inheritance with me. You, your mother, and those you love will be taken captive by the very man you feel your father has under control. He will rise up and carry you away, never to return to this land of Yahweh. None of your sons will ever reign on the throne of David in the land of Judah. What you did not want to happen will most assuredly come to pass.'"

Jehoiachin's face grew beet red. "The audacity you have to speak to me that way! To show you that I still have mercy, I will let you leave. But you must leave now, or you will never see if your words come true. Do you hear me?" He pointed. "Go!"

Jeremiah bowed as tears, which were running down his cheeks, dripped onto the patio floor creating two small pools of moisture in the dust. As he righted himself, he uttered a final sentence: "I'm so sorry, Coniah."

Jeremiah turned and walked away.

Jehoiachin turned in frustration several times as he returned to the table.

Hananiah laughed. "Well, that was priceless."

Jehoiachin picked up a date and threw it at the young advisor as hard as he could. "Shut up, Hananiah!"

CHAPTER 3

Lucifer's Input

Raphael turned to Mikael. "So what happens now?"

"What, indeed?" They heard the words spoken from behind them.

All three turned quickly.

"Lucifer!" Raphael exclaimed. "Why are you here?"

A broad smile came across the dark one's face. "Oh, and miss this priceless moment?" His expression quickly turned to one of deep concern. "And what will happen to David's kingdom now?" His smile quickly returned. "It's all such a mystery, isn't it?"

Mikael's eyes widened. "You think you have thwarted Yahweh's plans?" He shook his head. "You're delusional."

Lucifer continued to smile but was now also shrugging to go along with it. "We shall see. I do believe, though, he doesn't go back on his prophecies." He looked from one of them to the other. "That is true, isn't it?"

"Oh, stop being condescending, Lucifer!" Gabriel said. "You most assuredly know the Master never goes back on his promises." He shook his finger in Lucifer's face. "But don't think you've won this. I'm sure he's way ahead of you on this."

Lucifer's eyebrows went up. "Oh, yes. Yes, of course. I'm sure you're correct." He chuckled. "But I think he's scratching his head right now. And he said *I* was impetuous." He shrugged again with still another chuckle. "Maybe he *can* paint himself into a corner after all."

"You wish," Raphael said. "The only person in the corner is you, and you just don't know it yet."

"Oh," Lucifer replied, "I think the only one in the corner is dear Jehoiachin there. In the corner of the chessboard of history."

They all turned back to look at the young king in waiting. Jehoiachin was fuming as he returned to the table. He had another date in his hand but was tapping it on the table mindlessly. Others tried to comfort him, but that just made him more angry. After a couple of tries, everyone left him in his funk while they carried on in conversation without him.

Lucifer went on.

"And Nebuchadnezzar is the one who currently has him checkmated in one direction. And I'm right there in the other direction. And who put me there?" Lucifer donned a large grin. "Yahweh himself."

Gabriel turned back to him. "Your pride will be the end of you, Lucifer."

"Yes," Raphael said. "You'd better watch out for the chess pieces behind you. You can be taken off the chessboard as well."

"Thank you for going with my analogy, Raphael. But I don't think yours works as well as mine. Mine is factual. Yours is fantasy."

"Well," Mikael said. "As you yourself have said: time will tell."

"Yes it will, Mikael." Lucifer placed one hand on Mikael's shoulder and one on Gabriel's. "It's been fun. Let's do this again sometime. Have to run now, though. See you soon."

Lucifer vanished.

"Ugh!" Raphael said. "That one really gets on my nerves."

Mikael patted Raphael's shoulder. "I know, Raphael. But sometimes you just have to let it all go. You know he is prone to say things as fact when we know, if his words are different from those of Yahweh, whose words will prevail."

"I know, Mikael. But . . . " Raphael looked from Mikael to Gabriel and then back. "I can't help but think he has a point. How can both promises from Yahweh be correct?"

Gabriel shook his head. "I don't know, Raphael. But we must believe Yahweh has all things under control."

"Absolutely," Mikael said. "Lucifer makes it seem as though Yahweh did something rash here, but we know that is not his character. He may get upset at something, but that has never made him do anything irrational."

Raphael stood in thought for several seconds. "You're right. Just because I don't understand it doesn't mean our Creator doesn't have it all planned. But still . . . "

Mikael cocked his head. "But what, Raphael?"

"But I want to understand how King David has been promised to have an eternal kingdom—and how Jehoiachin will not be part of it."

Mikael nodded. "Me too, Raphael. Me too. It is quite the conundrum." He looked at Gabriel. "Maybe Ruach will explain it to us."

Gabriel chuckled. "We can ask. He isn't always straightforward in his answers, though."

Mikael thought back to his other dealings with Ruach. Gabriel's statement was definitely true. "Well, let's go ask, anyway."

Gabriel and Raphael nodded. Mikael turned for one more look at Jehoiachin, who still seemed in quite the foul mood.

The three angels disappeared.

CHAPTER 4

Ruach's Announcement

The three reappeared in the angel dimension and headed together to find Ruach. On their way, Mikael saw Quentillious, who, once he saw the three of them, headed in their direction. Apparently, he had a message.

Quentillious gave a slight bow when he reached them. "My captain, is everything all right?"

Mikael lifted the corner of his mouth and shook his head slightly. "Not really, Quentillious. How are things here?"

"Everyone is on standby for your orders. We have performed practice skirmishes to be sure our skills are honed." Quentillious suddenly had a worried look on his face. "I . . . I hope that was appropriate. I mean, under the circumstances . . ."

Mikael smiled and placed his hand on Quentillious's shoulder. "Yes, Quentillious. That was exactly what you should have done."

Quentillious gave a nod and seemed to relax his stance. "Everyone performed admirably," he added, eyebrows raising. "Do you need us back on Earth?"

Mikael motioned for Quentillious to walk with them as they restarted their quest to find Ruach. "That's what we're finding out now. Have you seen Ruach?"

"Not since just before our practice skirmishes." He pointed and said, "There. Heading in the direction of the throne room."

When they reached the split in the walkway, they headed in Ruach's direction. In the distance, Mikael saw Azel and Uriel approach. As he got closer to the large angels, he noticed something like heat waves radiating from a hot surface next to them but also looking as though in humanoid form. *Ruach. Good*, Mikael thought. *We've been able to find him quickly.*

Ruach always presented some difficulties to Mikael. Being God's Spirit, Ruach was noncorporeal and looked translucent, his body producing only an outline that caused one's view of him to look like a distortion of that person's view and not a clear distinction of a person. Mikael smiled to himself. He often missed seeing him until Ruach was right next to him, startling him when Ruach would touch his shoulder. That was the other thing. Ruach could put his hand on Mikael's shoulder, and Mikael could feel his touch. Yet if Mikael tried to do the same, his hand would go directly through Ruach. Apparently, because Ruach was of a higher dimension, he appeared as spirit in their dimension.

Ruach, Azel, and Uriel turned when they saw Mikael and his three fellow angels approach. Azel and Uriel gave a nod. Mikael nodded in return and addressed Ruach.

"I'm so glad I found you, Ruach."

"You have something to report?"

Mikael cocked his head. "Well, yes. But mostly I wanted to ask you a question."

Ruach appeared to nod. *Of course Ruach already knows this. He knows everything.* It often struck Mikael as odd how

Ruach, although knowing all, did not reveal all but made others find the needed information on their own.

"And what is your report?" Ruach asked.

"Jeremiah did deliver his curse, as predicted."

Ruach nodded. "And you want to know why and how the promise we made to King David will still come true?"

"Yes, my Lord," Raphael interjected. "How can it now come to pass? Lucifer looked so smug about it. He seems to think he has won the upper hand."

"Oh," Ruach replied. "I fear it is far worse than that."

Raphael's eyes widened as he glanced from Ruach to Mikael and then to Gabriel.

"What could be worse?" Gabriel asked. "Are you implying our Creator's words can be nullified?"

"Lucifer believes so," Mikael said. "That's what he implied to us. But that's impossible." He glanced at the faces of the others to see if they believed this as well. "Isn't it?"

"Don't worry, Mikael," Ruach said. "We're pretty good at impossible."

Mikael chuckled. "Indeed, my Lord."

"Lucifer's confidence can be exploited—but also should not be underestimated."

Mikael was unsure what that meant. That was the other thing with Ruach, and even with Yahweh. Rarely were their answers direct. Their words typically had dual meanings so that they were true for one's present circumstance but also true in general; the latter meant one could apply them in many similar circumstances. Yahweh's words were timeless.

"I take that to mean you want us to do something," Mikael said. "As always, we are at your service."

"Even as we speak," Ruach continued, "a lot is at play in the time dimension. Jeremiah's prophecy against

Jehoiachin's father, Jehoiakim, is in play. The Babylonian king, Nebuchadnezzar, wishes to punish him for his insolence in refusing to pay the tribute debt he imposed upon the kingdom of Judah. Nebuchadnezzar will put Jehoiakim in shackles to bring him back to Babylon. Yet Nebuchadnezzar will then receive word that his father, Nabopolassar, has died suddenly, and that he must return to Babylon immediately to take possession of the throne. Because of the necessary haste of this, Nebuchadnezzar will unshackle Jehoiakim, leave, and allow Jehoiakim to remain in Jerusalem—with just a warning."

Mikael's eyebrows raised. "Well, that's good, isn't it?"

He noticed everyone looked from Ruach to him and back. They seemed to think the same.

Ruach didn't answer his question but kept talking.

"This will surprise Lucifer. He thought he had other scenarios in motion." Ruach placed his hand on Mikael's chest. Mikael felt the warmth of the touch flow through him to his core. Oh, how he loved this touch. "You, Mikael, will need to counter Lucifer's next move and put the right course of action into play. That is the only way to achieve Jeremiah's prophecy and the Almighty's decree simultaneously."

Mikael's stance stiffened. "Absolutely, my Lord. Anything. What do you wish me to do?"

"Prepare for battle, Mikael."

"We are prepared, my Lord," Quentillious interjected. "Our captain has already seen to that." He paused, then continued. "But . . . what are we preventing Lucifer from doing?"

Mikael looked back to Ruach. That was his question as well.

"You are to help Jehoiachin take the step Jeremiah has prophesied to him. Lucifer wishes to make Jeremiah's prophecy come true, literally, by having him destroyed and eliminating all hope of the ultimate prophecy coming true."

"And you want the prophecy to be fulfilled a different way?"

Mikael saw Ruach nod—or at least that is what it looked like he did.

"The prophecy will be fulfilled just as Jeremiah has stated, but in a way that will keep the prophecy to King David intact as well. Lucifer has influenced Nebuchadnezzar to send a mercenary army against Jerusalem to fulfill what time did not allow him to do personally. Jehoiachin must be protected for the prophecy to be fulfilled."

Mikael nodded. "We will see to it."

Ruach went on. "You must prevent Lucifer and his followers from influencing Jehoiachin to attack in revenge of his father's death. He must do what every king rejects at his very core."

Mikael's eyes widened as he spoke with a tone of disbelief. "You want him to . . . surrender."

"Yes, Mikael. Jehoiachin must surrender and be taken captive. The salvation of his people—both in his present and in his future—depends upon it."

CHAPTER 5

Battle Preparation

Quentillious stood at attention when Mikael turned to face him.

"Prepare the angels."

Quentillious gave a nod and moved quickly to carry out his commander's orders. Mikael turned back to Ruach. "So, what are we in for?"

"A full-scale war, I'm afraid. Lucifer feels he has the upper hand and wants to keep it at all costs."

Raphael looked from Mikael to Ruach. "What exactly is he hoping to accomplish?"

"Ensuring the prophecy of the curse," Gabriel interjected.

Raphael looked confused. "By ensuring Jehoiachin is removed from Jerusalem?" he asked.

"No, Raphael," Ruach said. "By ensuring he is removed from the earth. You see, Lucifer is not happy with just the curse itself. He wants to ensure Yahweh's promise to King David has not even a sliver of a chance of coming true."

"But . . . " Raphael looked from one to the other as if wondering if he was the only one missing something. "Josiah has another son as well."

"Yes, Raphael," Ruach said. "That is a story unto itself. But for now, Lucifer was taken off guard when Nebuchadnezzar left Jehoiakim in Jerusalem at the news of the death of his father. So Lucifer has incited him to send a mercenary army against Jerusalem. This army will fulfill Jeremiah's prophecy. Yet Lucifer has two tactics at work. He will try to get the mercenary army to kill Jehoiachin as well or, if that fails, will attempt to incite Jehoiachin to try and revenge his father's death. His hope is that, in so doing, Jehoiachin also will be killed."

"And we are to prevent that?" Mikael asked. "Is that it?"

"You need to keep Jehoiachin safe when his father is attacked, prevent Lucifer's angels from persuading Jehoiachin to take revenge, and prevent his army from inciting the mercenary army. They have orders to wait for Nebuchadnezzar to arrive but, if provoked, may not follow those orders.

"I'm afraid this will be a long battle, my friends."

With those words, Ruach vanished.

Raphael shook his head and looked at Mikael. "Now what?"

"Well . . . now we prepare."

As Mikael turned to address his legions, the others fell in line behind him. He could see all the angels congregating at the Altar of Stones, so he headed in that direction. When he arrived, the angels parted, leaving a path for Mikael and those with him to pass through the throng. Quentillious was just finishing his preparatory speech to all the angels.

". . . while our captain may ask a lot from us, it is only at Yahweh's bidding that he does so," Quentillious said with raised voice, addressing all angels. "We are Yahweh's messengers, and we obey the tasks given us."

Many angels raised their arms in agreement and lifted shouts of approval.

Once Quentillious saw Mikael arrive, he stepped back and motioned for Mikael to address the angel army.

Mikael unfurled his large and majestic wings, which were almost invisible when folded, and rose so all could see and hear him.

"My friends," he began, "Quentillious is right. Much will be asked of you. But we will be victorious because we are messengers of the Most High. His will is our bidding."

The angels shouted their approval again.

"In many respects, this will be similar to the battle we fought when we protected Noach and his family. Yet this battle may last a good deal longer. Therefore, we will fight them in waves. When one legion gets tired, the next will take its place. Your job is to prevent our adversary from being able to incite the mercenary army which has gathered around Jerusalem. The waves will be in this order: Gabriel's legion, Raphael's legion, then Uriel's, and last, Azel's legion.

"Remember, the Adversary's army can only affect humans if they are near them to implant thoughts into their minds. Therefore, keep them occupied and defending themselves against you, and they will not be able to influence." Mikael gave a broad smile. "Even more true if you are able to incapacitate them."

The angelic throng gave a united roar of approval.

"Follow the commands of your legion leader. We won't be able to defend all enemy influence. It's important to know when and when not to do so. Your leaders will know the crucial times to prevent such influences." Mikael paused to ensure all were listening. "This is especially true for any of Lucifer's angels getting near Jehoiachin."

Mikael looked down and pointed. "Quentillious will appoint a leader in each legion to lead in the wave attacks as we fight those in the palace itself." He focused on the throng of angels which had gathered and spoke with a commanding voice. "You have trained for this, you have succeeded before, and you will succeed now. Yahweh is depending upon us, and we cannot fail him."

A thunderous roar rose from the crowd, all agreeing with Mikael's message. Mikael waited for the noise to die down.

"As you know, even our foes are immortal. We cannot kill them, but Yahweh has given us the power to incapacitate them with our swords. As we did during the Great War, you will separate those we incapacitate from their swords and then guard them so they cannot rejoin the battle. I have asked Quentillious to have one-third from each battalion be responsible for this effort. Do not be discouraged if you are chosen for this effort, for it is just as noble and important as being within the fray of battle. It is you who will help turn the tide to victory."

A roar went up from the crowd once more. Mikael heard a chant: "Yahweh! Yahweh! Yahweh!"

He smiled. This was the attitude he hoped to see. The battle was ultimately not about victory, not about them, but about their Lord and Master.

Mikael saw a bright light descend to the Altar of Stones. Before them stood Yahweh himself. He saw something like a wave retreating from the altar backward as each angel genuflected before their Lord and Master. Mikael lowered himself to the ground and did the same.

He felt a hand on his shoulder followed by a warmth that penetrated through him. "Rise, Mikael."

He did so and looked into eyes so mesmerizing it was like looking into eternity itself. How he loved this one. It was beyond his understanding how Lucifer could have rejected him, a being who exuded such love for those he created.

Yahweh addressed the throng before him. "Arise, my sons."

As each angel rose, they lifted their arms and yelled shouts of praise. Yahweh raised his arms and the throng quieted.

"My angels, my children, my messengers, thank you for your service to me and to the Godhead. I'm afraid Lucifer has become even more emboldened as his time on Earth has continued. The future of mankind and my plans for my creation are in the balance. I know you will be victorious, but, as has been stated, much is being asked of you in the coming days. The battle will be long, but I will give you strength. Maintain your focus, follow your training, and continually remember whom you serve. Ignore the taunts and threats that will be hurled your way. They are made to distract you. Don't let that happen, and you will succeed."

The angels roared in approval once more.

As they continued their praise, Yahweh turned to Mikael. "The main point is that Jehoiachin must do what all kings are never prepared to do. He needs to surrender himself to Nebuchadnezzar. Yet this must be his choice and not one clouded by the confused thoughts Lucifer will hurl his way. Jeremiah will talk to the Queen Mother, Nehushta, who will try to talk reason to Jehoiachin. Yet others will advise him differently. You must let them talk among themselves and not be encumbered by demonic influence."

Mikael nodded. "Yes, my Lord. I will do as you command."

Yahweh smiled. "I know you will."

Yahweh turned, but Mikael called back to him. "My Lord. Will Lucifer ever recant?"

A saddened look came across Yahweh's face. "Pride has blinded him to his true potential. Unfortunately, failure only emboldens pride rather than softening it." He shook his head. "He has made his choice. Our job now is to offer opportunities to those he wants to bring down so they can decide which side they will ultimately choose."

"And in this case?"

Yahweh patted Mikael on his upper arm. "In this case, we must allow Jehoiachin the chance to make the right decision."

Mikael nodded as Yahweh turned and then disappeared as a beam of light retreating upward from the Altar of Stones.

Mikael turned back to the great army. "My friends, gather with your legion commander for final instructions. Then we deploy."

CHAPTER 6

Jehoiakim's Demise

Nehushta stood at the patio balcony looking out at the advancing army in the distance.

{ As Mikael arrived, he noticed she had a hugely worried look on her face. He felt sorry for her. She would be losing a husband today. He wondered what was going through her mind. Did she believe in Jeremiah's prophecy? Did she hate him for it? Or did she know, and accept, the consequences of her son's actions and refusal to repent? }

She turned when she heard someone behind her. "Jehoiakim, I fear for your safety," she said to her approaching husband and king.

Jehoiakim, dressed in full battle gear, came to her, held her shoulders, and looked into her eyes. "It will be all right." He smiled. "In spite of what that grumpy old prophet says, you will not lose a husband today. You'll see. Yahweh will not allow his city to be taken."

Nehushta looked down and then back at him, her eyes wet. "I hope so. But . . . " She shook her head and tried to hold back tears. "No, I won't think it." She nodded. "You are right. I trust you."

Jehoiakim smiled. "Good. Now I must go and defend our city against this mongrel heathen horde Nebuchadnezzar has sent against us."

As Jehoiakim turned, he stopped. He watched as Jehoiachin approached, also dressed in full battle attire.

"What are you doing, Coniah?" Jehoiakim asked.

Jehoiachin cocked his head. "Going with you, of course."

Jehoiakim shook his head. "No, my son. Not this time. You must stay here. Just in case . . . " He glanced at his wife and did not complete his sentence. He added, "It's precautionary, my dear."

She nodded and looked at Jehoiachin. "Your father is right. A rightful heir must be protected so the kingdom can endure."

Jehoiachin's stance stiffened. "I have been training ever since you made me co-regent when I turned eight. Isn't this why you did that? So I can assist you now that I'm old enough?"

Jehoiakim approached his son and placed a hand on his shoulder. "You have grown into a fine young man, Coniah, but your training also taught you to know when to go into battle and when not. This is a battle for me, but not for you." He put his index finger into Jehoiachin's chest. "You are destined to succeed me if anything goes wrong."

He turned to Nehushta. "I said *if*, mind you."

She nodded and forced a smile. "I know. I understand."

He turned back to Jehoiachin. "Do *you* understand?"

"Yes, but—"

Jehoiakim held up his hand. "There is no but." He turned to leave.

"Abba!"

Jehoiakim turned back.

"I must do *something*. I can't just sit here while every other able man is defending our city."

Jehoiakim looked at Jehoiachin for several seconds, then nodded. "All right. Agreed. You will lead a contingency army. If our enemy breaches the wall, you and your army will push them back behind the walls."

Nehushta's eyes widened.

Jehoiakim looked at her. "I don't think they will be able to breach our walls, though." He turned back to his son. "But if they do, your actions will be a crucial step in defending the city." He shook his index finger. "Very important. Do you understand?"

Jehoiachin nodded. "Yes, Father. I understand."

Both looked at Nehushta and then left. She watched until they were out of sight, fingers over her mouth and chin, eyes watering. Yet no tears came.

*****

Mikael's heart went out to her. She had no idea if, by tomorrow, she would be husbandless, childless, or both.

Mikael rose into the air and flew to Quentillious. "Place several angels around Jehoiachin and his small army. If the city walls are breached, he will be in danger."

Quentillious nodded and disappeared.

Mikael observed the scene below him. He saw Lucifer's angels intermingling within the invading army. He grimaced. They would most certainly interfere with the ensuing battle, but he was to let things progress without interference. He had to allow certain events to unfold, but not let others unfold. This was going to be trickier than he had originally envisioned.

He watched as the battle began—fast and furious. First came a barrage of arrows from skilled archers, and this killed dozens of soldiers along the wall. Many of these were flaming arrows which caused fires inside the city, so some manpower had to be diverted to take care of the fires before they would spread to other important areas of the city.

The stealthiest enemy tactic Mikael observed were the sappers who dug tunnels up to the wall to provide their troops access to the city wall without detection and without fear of retaliation. Their efforts allowed the invading army to bring materials directly to the wall to create a ramp. Because their work went unnoticed for quite some time, those on the wall did not fire on them until most of the work had been put in place. This allowed the enemy to scale the remaining distance from the top of the ramp to the top of the wall via ladders. Once a few enemy soldiers breached the wall, they defended that position to allow more and more enemy soldiers to also climb over the wall.

*****

The battle reached a higher pitch along the wall and in the outskirts of the city.

Once Jehoiachin was aware of the breach, he sent in his men to push them back. Some he sent to help his father's men, others he sent to help defend the wall at the breach, and still others he used as archers to shoot flaming arrows to burn the ladders and any part of the ramp that would burn. After setting his plan into action, he rushed to help his father defend the wall.

Before he could reach his father, several men of the invading army defeated the men around Jehoiakim and then converged to attack the king. While Jehoiakim fought bravely, he was simply outnumbered. One of the men hit him from behind. While his helmet protected his head, the force knocked him to his knees and a second then stabbed him at an angle where the sword entered just under his arm, where there was no protection, and went deep into his chest.

*****

Mikael saw Jehoiachin witness this and scream "No!" The young prince tried with all his might to get past the men he was fighting so he could assist his father, but he couldn't. In horror, he saw the attackers around his father lift the blood-stained body of Jehoiakim and throw him over the wall. This was on the Hinnom Valley side of the city, which was used as the city dump, where a fire burned almost constantly due to the refuse dumped there each day. Their actions fueled Jehoiachin's anger and propelled him to fight more furiously.

Mikael then saw one of Lucifer's angels next to one of the men who had thrown Jehoiakim from the wall. This demon practically turned the head of this man to see and focus on Jehoiachin. The man drew his bow and aimed directly for Jehoiachin. Mikael teleported near Jehoiachin and put his hands on a nearby soldier, which increased the man's strength. The man, using his foot, propelled his foe backward, right into the line of fire of the arrow aimed for Jehoiachin. The eyes of this Luciferian angel went wide; he realized his tactic had been noticed. Although this angel tried to escape, Mikael dogged him and engaged him in battle.

"I thought you were supposed to watch and not interfere," the demon called to Mikael.

"I was," Mikael replied. "Until you interfered yourself. Your interference is unacceptable."

This angel put up a good fight, but Mikael was soon able to discern his foe's fighting weaknesses. Typical of most of Lucifer's angels, their bravado was short-lived, and the angel soon realized he was outclassed. As Mikael was close to besting him, the demon quickly shot upward and disappeared.

As Mikael looked back, Quentillious and the many angels with him were now surrounding Jehoiachin and his men more closely. While they did not interfere with their fighting, they did protect them from interference by any of Lucifer's angels. Mikael flew to assist them in their effort.

*****

Jehoiachin's men were able to prevent other soldiers from breaching the wall and, after another hour of fighting, were able to best those who had come across the wall. Once the city was secured, Jehoiachin posted more men to the walls and quickly began to teach them, in groups, the tactics of their foes so they could better defend the city.

*****

Mikael then took his angels and routed all of Lucifer's angels who had been part of the battle outside the city as well. After doing so, Mikael met with Quentillious, Raphael, Gabriel, Azel, and Uriel.

"Good work, Quentillious," Mikael said. "Express my thanks to everyone."

Quentillious nodded. "I will. But what are your plans now?"

"Post your legion around the city," Mikael said. "While Jehoiachin likely has a reprieve in his battle, I fear ours has just begun." He pointed to the other angels with him. "We will go back and see how things are with Jehoiachin as you, Quentillious, keep everyone else on high alert. We've thwarted Lucifer's first attempt, but now we must turn away his second."

Quentillious gave a slight bow. "Very good, my captain." He disappeared.

Mikael looked at the other four. "Ready?"

They looked at each other and then back to Mikael. "We are ready."

In an instant, all five disappeared.

CHAPTER 7

The Battle Continues

With a lull in the battle after being on high alert for several days, Jehoiachin was back on the patio with his mother, Hananiah, and two other friends whom Mikael knew Jehoiachin used as advisors. They were as young as he was, however, so Mikael had to wonder how much wisdom these young men could actually provide him.

What Mikael feared was true: five high-ranking angels devoted to Lucifer also were present. Malphas was the first to speak upon seeing their arrival.

"Well, I expected you to show up," Malphas said to Mikael. "But you're too late. Jehoiachin is now ours to do with as we please."

"Yahweh begs to differ," Mikael said as he drew his sword. "Your confidence, Malphas, is as misplaced as is that of your master."

*****

Jehoiachin's mother, Nehushta, was speaking. "But Coniah, think about this. You have been king for only a few days. Don't be rash about this."

Jehoiachin's eyes widened, and he raised his voice slightly. "Rash?" He pointed toward the outdoors from the patio. "Did you see what they did to Father? They showed no respect. They killed him and threw him over the wall like he was some kind of dead animal." He stood and began to pace. "I won't—I can't—stand for that!"

"You have to show the mettle of your kingship," Hananiah added. "Show them no mercy as they showed your father no mercy."

Nehushta grabbed Jehoiachin's hand as he walked past her in his fury. "Coniah!"

He turned and looked at her and then glanced at Hananiah. "Mother, Hananiah is right." The other two advisors nodded. Jehoiachin looked back at his mother. "We have to be strong and send a message."

Nehushta sat more upright. "And get yourself killed in the process?" She shot a stern look to Jehoiachin. "I want revenge as much as you do." She panned all their faces. "Even more than *all* of you. After all, he was my husband." She shook her head. "Yet ensuring Judah has a king to add stability and inspire your people is more important than avenging your father's death."

"But it makes him look weak," Hananiah said.

Nehushta's eyes shot to Hananiah like black daggers. "But he will be *alive*. Plus . . . " She paused and looked back at Jehoiachin with her eyes now turning to more of a pleading look. "We must also consider the words of Jeremiah."

Jehoiachin pulled his hand from hers with a grunt and returned to his pacing. "I don't have to consider the words of someone who has paid us no respect."

"Absolutely," one of the other advisors said.

Nehushta looked from the man who spoke—shooting him an annoyed glance—back to Jehoiachin with her pleading look. "But his words came true about your father. Now . . . " She panned their faces. "We must consider his other words."

They all fell back on their pillows with a sigh. "We're getting nowhere," Hananiah said with annoyance.

*****

As the humans weighed these options, Mikael and Malphas paced around them, both now with swords raised, each looking for the exact opportunity to attack the other. Mikael glanced at Gabriel, Raphael, Uriel, and Azel, who had each also drawn their swords. Malphas's angels seemed to be rubbing the heads of Jehoiachin's advisors periodically as they kept an eye on the angels with Mikael. These other angels were evidently putting thoughts into the minds of these humans to give Jehoiachin bad advice. Mikael knew the faster they engaged the angels with Malphas the better, as that would eliminate the influence of these so-called advisors on the newly established king.

Mikael took a bold, aggressive move toward Malphas, and those with him did the same against the demons fighting alongside Malphas.

Malphas spread his large, muscular wings as wide as he could. At first, Mikael thought this just an intimidation ploy to try to convince Mikael how mighty he was and make Mikael pause in his thought of taking him on. But in another split-second, Malphas quickly rose into the air, did a somersault over

Mikael, and took a swing at him in the process. Mikael easily deflected the blow and prepared himself for countermeasures.

As soon as their blades touched, the other demons attacked Mikael's compatriots. The battle was now on, and in full force. Mikael just hoped Nehushta's logic would be heeded by her son and his advisors.

Once Malphas landed after his somersault, Mikael gave him no time to recover, but attacked immediately and aggressively. This took Malphas off guard. Yet he quickly recovered and deflected blow after blow from Mikael. Still, this gave Mikael time to search for any flaws in Malphas's battle tactics. At this early stage, he was unable to detect any. Malphas would be a strong and formidable opponent.

Mikael periodically glanced at the others fighting. It seemed all were equally matched in strength, ability, and agility. He was glad he had brought his best, here, to the patio. Apparently Malphas had done the same.

Mikael wanted to get Malphas into the air and test his ability there. So far Malphas had kept his fighting to the patio. To achieve his goal, Mikael knew he had to bring even more than his usual best. He started pushing forward with each blow, and this caused Malphas to take a step back. It seemed Malphas was initially unaware of what Mikael was doing. Once Malphas looked behind him and saw he was only inches from the edge, he fought back harder to try and push Mikael backward, but Mikael took his swordsmanship to another level, and this forced Malphas to concentrate on fighting and nothing else.

Then, in a quick motion, Malphas used his large wings and propelled himself into the air. Mikael gave the smallest of smiles; that was just what he had wanted from Malphas. Using his own majestic and powerful wings, Mikael followed close behind him, readying himself for air battle. Here he would be able to test the real mettle of Malphas's tactics. He remembered Malphas from the early days of angel battle practice, and the now-demon had definitely improved since that time, though Mikael wondered if Malphas had improved in all tactical areas.

Mikael used one powerful wing to twist himself one way and then used his opposing wing to make himself twist in the opposite direction, allowing him to deliver a second blow before Malphas had time to completely prepare for it. While Malphas was able to deflect his blows, Mikael could see Malphas's defensive techniques were not as skillful as his own, even though, Mikael had to admit, Malphas's offensive strategy had improved substantially since their last encounter. Mikael took note of every flaw he observed in Malphas's battle techniques, even though the flaws he exhibited were not many and not substantial. Yet he knew that, if fatigue settled in, these minute errors would start to become more noticeable and significant.

Mikael happened to see Azel out of the corner of his eye fighting upside down with as much ease as if he was right side up. Fighting in that position used to be one of Azel's weaknesses. Now he had turned it into one of his strengths. Apparently Lucifer had not pushed his angels as hard as Mikael had pushed his. For that, Mikael was grateful. It meant their chances, likely, were good. At least if they could hold out longer in their strength than their opponents . . .

After a long period of fighting, Mikael began to feel some of his strength starting to wane. It seemed Malphas was encountering the same kind of energy drain. Mikael noticed some loosening on the tightness of Malphas's turns and some weakening in strength in the deflections of his blows. Mikael finally found an opening to utilize against Malphas. When Malphas deflected a blow, Mikael used all his might to have his wing turn him back in the opposite direction before Malphas had time to recover, and Mikael's sword cut into Malphas's left shoulder. Although not a blow that would render him catatonic, it did take that arm out of commission for a time. Mikael mustered strength to increase the power of his blows. Malphas was able to deflect them, but no longer having the use of one arm caused his response time to slow considerably. The next thing Mikael knew, Malphas shot upward and flew away. As he looked around, the other angels with Malphas did the same.

Mikael flew back to the patio where the humans were still engaged in heated discussion. He looked at the other angels as they landed.

"Everyone all right?" he asked.

All nodded.

"Glad they retreated," Uriel said. "I was beginning to run out of strength." He glanced up. "You think they'll be back?"

"Most assuredly," Mikael replied as he sheathed his sword. "Keep vigilant."

Each nodded. Azel and Uriel went to the edge of the patio to keep watch.

Raphael pointed upward. "It looks to be quite the battle up there."

Mikael looked up and saw angel after angel falling to the ground. Then, in a matter of seconds, an angel would appear, take their sword from their hand, and disappear with the catatonic angel.

Mikael smiled. It seemed their plan was working. Yet he did notice several angels on the ground who no one was attending to. He knew those were his angels. Once recovered, they would fight again, but he knew they could only do this a few times before all their strength would be gone. Hopefully, the battle would be over before that point was reached.

Mikael turned back to the humans on the patio and listened as he felt his strength start to return.

*****

"My queen, he can't. He simply cannot do that," Hananiah said.

"He must. It is the only way." Nehushta grabbed Jehoiachin's hand once more. "My son, it is the *only* way. Jeremiah was clear. If you do so, you will be spared."

One of the other advisors replied, "That might actually be a wise choice."

Hananiah whirled and looked at this other young man. "What? A moment ago, you said that was a bad idea and agreed with us wholeheartedly."

The young man waved his hands. "I know. I know. But the more I think about it, surrender may be the best way to not only save the king but *all* of Jerusalem as well."

Hananiah gave a giant shrug, hands outstretched. "But it's a sign of weakness." He pointed toward Jehoiachin. "We can't let our king look weak."

Nehushta pulled on Jehoiachin's arm to lower him to the seat next to her. "It will not be perceived as a sign of weakness to *them*, but as a wise decision." She ran her hand through his hair around his ear and caressed his cheek. "Nebuchadnezzar will consider this restitution for your father's blatant disregard of not paying him tribute the last few years." She glanced toward the temple and sighed. "We may have to chip more gold off the temple to allay his disapproval, but you will be safe, and Jerusalem will be safe." She looked at Jehoiachin with compassion. "Sometimes, Coniah, a king has to do what is hard for the betterment of his people, even at his own sacrifice."

Jehoiachin's eyes grew wet. "I don't want to see you in prison, Mother."

She gave a slight smile. "We'll at least be alive—and together. Ready to fight another day."

"There may not be another day," Hananiah said.

"We will at least have a chance of one," Nehushta replied. "Jeremiah does not say things for no reason. Not resisting capture must be the best path."

Hananiah started to say something but Nehushta threw up her hand. "Curse or no curse, Jeremiah loves Jerusalem, even if he may no longer love us." Her eyes glistened from moisture forming. "One thing is certain: he has always spoken the words of Yahweh no matter how harsh they may have sounded." She nodded. "If not resisting capture is what he predicted, then it must be the will of Yahweh. I don't know what that will entail as yet, but that is all we have to hang onto."

Hananiah didn't relent in his position, but he did soften in it. "Let's wait and see how things go. If we hold off the mercenaries, we can perhaps judge Nebuchadnezzar's mood once he arrives."

"If we don't starve first," one of the other young men replied.

Jehoiachin seemed to ignore him as he said, "For now, we will hold but not attack." He looked at the one who had spoken last. "Go tell my army. That will allow them some needed rest for a change. If the mercenary army backs down when we do, that will be a sign they plan to follow Nebuchadnezzar's plan to surround and wait for his arrival."

The man stood, bowed, and hurried from the room to carry out his new king's command.

*****

Mikael was glad Jehoiachin had made the wise decision. Now it was a matter of keeping Malphas and his angels away from these humans so they wouldn't change their minds. Mikael was unsure how long it would be before Nebuchadnezzar arrived. He hoped sooner rather than later.

Then he remembered Ruach's words. He shook his head. They were likely in this for the long haul.

Azel spoke up. "Mikael! Get ready. Here they come again."

CHAPTER 8

Nebuchadnezzar Arrives

Mikael saw the sun come up. This was . . . what? The fifth time he had seen the sun rise during his fight with Malphas? The good thing was Malphas was starting to weaken. In the previous day, he had made several cuts to Malphas's extremities. These did not prevent him from fighting, but they did hasten Malphas's weakening. So far, Mikael had remained unscathed, so while he was tired, he was not weakening as quickly as his opponent.

In a surprise attack, even before Malphas delivered his first blow this day, Mikael went full force against him and followed that with blow after blow after blow with all his might. Then he saw it: Malphas was now just a bit weaker on his left side. He was deflecting blows from his right side more efficiently than his left. This was the window of opportunity Mikael needed. Using his right wing, he pulled his body to the right, delivering a strong blow to Malphas's right side and acting as if he was going to go all the way around. Then, in a swift motion, he used his left wing to make himself turn, swiftly, in the countering direction. Malphas had left his blade too high too long to deflect what he thought would be an upside-down attack. Mikael's blade cut deeply into Malphas's left side. Malphas's eyes went wide, his body no longer responsive as it went catatonic . . . and fell to the patio below.

No sooner had Mikael landed next to the body when one of his junior angels arrived to take the body and sword to where they were keeping Lucifer's now-captured angels.

"Wow, Kaylor, that was a fast response," Mikael said to the arriving angel.

"Thank you, Captain," Kaylor said. "Keeping my eyes peeled."

Mikael gave him a pat on his upper arm. "Very good. Who's helping to guard those captured?"

A smile crept across Kaylor's face. "Jahven."

Mikael chuckled. He knew Jahven was one of his larger angels and extremely formidable. "Very good. I've seen him take on several of Lucifer's angels at once."

Kaylor nodded. "Yes, many are reluctant to take him on, especially without a sword."

"Keep up the good work, Kaylor."

Kaylor gave a slight bow. "Thank you, my captain."

He vanished with both Malphas's catatonic body and his sword.

Now that Mikael had bested his opponent, he was free to help his comrades. The five-against-four ratio was now too much. Another was defeated, and then it was five against three . . . Before long, all four of the other angels devoted to Lucifer that his friends had been fighting these last several days were catatonic. Kaylor came and took each one away as they fell to the patio.

Mikael and his friends flew into the fray above them. They paired up with other angels on their side, giving each other slight periods of rest as they continued to attack. Mikael saw the sun rise and set for many more days before they had finally bested all of Lucifer's angels.

Mikael ordered a third of his angels to go assist Jahven in keeping all of Lucifer's captured angels at bay. The others he allowed to take a well-deserved rest, but he informed them to keep their eyes peeled. Mikael knew they had not fought all of Lucifer's angels. The dark angel could potentially send more. If that did not happen, then these would relieve those guarding the captured once they had recovered their strength, allowing their compatriots to get the rest they deserved.

Mikael settled back to the patio and sat on the railing. Raphael, Gabriel, Uriel, and Azel arrived shortly after.

Raphael sighed. "Well, that took much longer than I anticipated." He stretched his sword arm and gave a slight sigh.

"I tried to count the number of sunrises," Azel said. "But I lost count after about thirty."

Raphael's eyes widened. "Oh, it must have been at least three times that."

The others nodded.

"I'm just glad Lucifer didn't send in more of his angels," Gabriel said.

"Oh, you might as well call them what they really are," Raphael said.

Gabriel's eyebrows turned up.

"They're demons, Gabriel," Raphael replied. "I think they gave up their right to be called angels."

"They are what they originally were," Uriel said. He shrugged. "Their allegiance and desire are now just given to another."

"Exactly," Raphael said. "They're now the evil ones. They're *demons*."

Before anyone could say more, they heard the patter of fast-moving feet coming closer. Mikael, and all, turned to see who was coming.

*****

A little boy was now running as fast as his little legs would take him. He bounded up the patio railing. Mikael put his hands around him to protect him from any fall just in case. He heard a woman's voice also approaching.

"Shealtiel, come back here! Where are you going?"

As soon as she saw the child on the patio bannister, she ran with all her might toward him. "Shealtiel! Get down! Get down this instant!"

Mikael had to laugh.

The child turned with excitement on his face, totally oblivious to the danger he had placed himself in. "He's here, Savta. He's here!"

Nehushta picked up the child, held him on her hip, and looked to where Shealtiel pointed. "Who's here, child?"

Nehushta gasped and put her hand to her mouth. "Already? I thought surely we would have more time to prepare." She shook her head as her eyes grew wet. Her voice was now barely a whisper. "First Jehoahaz, then Jehoiakim, now Jehoiachin." Tears ran down her cheeks. "Royalty is not something to be envious of at all."

Shealtiel seemed oblivious to his grandmother's words. He kept trying to lift his head higher to see the approaching army. "Will Abba now fight and crush the Baby Lones?" The small boy put his fist into his other palm and twisted it as if squishing a bug.

"What?" Nehushta gave the child a questioning look. "What did you ask, Shealtiel?"

"Will Abba now fight the Baby Lones?"

She brushed away a tear and chuckled. "Baby-*lo*-ni-ans, my dear," she said, providing the child with the correct pronunciation. She ran her hands through the boy's hair with her free hand. "But, no. He will not fight. We . . . " Her voice caught in her throat. "We are going to go visit them."

Shealtiel scrunched his face. "Visit? But . . . why? Do you like them?"

Nehushta shook her head. "No, my child. No, not in the least. But one day you'll understand that we royals do things others do not so we can protect our people."

Shealtiel seemed to be in thought. "I thought the people did things for us."

She kissed the child's forehead and set him back on the patio while holding his hand. "Yes, that is true. They do things for us, but we also must do things for them. Wise kings do that."

Shealtiel looked up at her. "Like Abba?"

She gave him a smile. "Like Abba."

The child seemed satisfied with her answer, but she kept the worried look on her face.

*****

Mikael heard her add, quietly, "At least I hope he does." He noticed the child had not heard.

Gabriel turned to Mikael. "Did you hear her last words?"

Mikael nodded.

"What do you think that means?" Raphael asked as he stood and watched the woman and child enter the building. "Has Jehoiachin decided not to be taken captive without fighting?"

Mikael stood. "I don't know. Let's go find out."

CHAPTER 9

Jehoiachin's Decision

Mikael sent Azel and Uriel to find out from Jahven how things were going with the captured demons. *Raphael is right,* Mikael thought. Lucifer's angels had made their choice and had become the enemy. They were never going to return to Yahweh. The word demon now rightly defined them. He resigned that he too would now call them demons going forward.

Mikael and his fellow angels followed Nehushta into the palace. They entered the throne receiving room; Jehoiachin was pacing. Several servants and advisors were near him looking worried.

*****

Shealtiel pulled away from Nehushta's hand and ran to Jehoiachin. "Abba! Abba!"

Jehoiachin turned. At first a smile came to his face, but it was then replaced with a look of regret—likely from knowing he was surrendering not only himself but his whole family to Nebuchadnezzar.

Shealtiel stopped short and paused as if trying to remember something. The child bowed. "My king."

Jehoiachin suddenly turned official. "Yes. Do you have an announcement?"

"Are we going to visit the Baby—" He then turned and looked at his grandmother, who smiled and mouthed the syllables. He turned back to his father. "The Baby-*lo*-ni-ans?"

Jehoiachin's eyes grew wet, but he kept his regal demeanor as he spoke to his son. "We will go with them, but it will not be a friendly visit. We may be separated, but you will act like a prince and not as a child. Can you do that?"

Shealtiel nodded—but looked confused.

Jehoiachin nodded to one of the female servants. She came and took Shealtiel by his hand as she said something to him in a whisper. The child followed her out but looked back several times at his father.

As soon as Shealtiel was out of sight, Jehoiachin's demeanor changed again, and he whipped around. "I can't!" He shook his head. "I can't subject my family to this abuse."

Hananiah turned to the other advisors in the room. "See? Isn't that what I've been saying?"

Nehushta took a few steps closer and bowed. "My king."

He turned to face her as her eyes began to glisten. Jehoiachin's countenance changed from one of official capacity to a softer one meant to recognize his mother.

"Coniah, please remember what we talked about three months ago," she said.

He looked annoyed and began to pace again. "I am, Mother. But a lot has changed since then."

Her look softened still more. "Has it? Has it really? Your troops have been holding off this mercenary army all this time. We knew it was likely until Nebuchadnezzar returned. Now he's here." She took a step closer, raised her hand to put it on his shoulder, paused, and then pulled it back. "What you need to do hasn't changed. Sacrifice your family, or all of your people."

Jehoiachin continued to pace, shaking his head. "Not much of a choice."

Nehushta bolstered her stance and turned back to her Queen Mother persona. "That is true, but that doesn't change the duty of a royal."

Jehoiachin turned with a jerk. "*I* . . ." He repeatedly tapped his chest with his index finger. "*I* decide what a royal does."

Nehushta bowed. "Yes, my lord." She looked into his eyes. "Your father made bad choices, as did his ancestors." She threw her hands up with a shrug. "We've all made bad choices. Consequences have now come to our door. We must do what we must."

Jehoiachin's voice rose in intensity and came out in tones of sarcasm. "And this will appease Yahweh for our sins?"

Nehushta shook her head as a tear rolled down her cheek. "I don't know, Coniah. But it is a step in the right direction."

Her words seemed to soften him somewhat. He turned to his advisors. "What do you say?"

Hananiah now looked uncomfortable. He was being asked to put his thoughts out for a more formal judgment, not just one of advice. "Well, such an action would not be unprecedented," the brash young advisor said.

The other advisors nodded as they looked from one to another. One of them added, "It seems to be the difference between living for another day and seeing how to change your fate, or dying with much bloodshed and no hope of another outcome."

Hananiah seemed to return to his old self. "But can we be sure Nebuchadnezzar will keep his word to our king?"

"Why would he not?" one of his fellow advisors asked.

"It's a fair question," Jehoiachin said.

Nehushta shrugged. "He's an astute man. Why would he kill and destroy what he can take without effort?"

A small smile came across Jehoiachin's face. "Who needs advisors and a prophet when I have you, Mother?"

"No," she replied. "Yahweh has broken me, and I have admitted it. I place my fate now in his hands rather than in mine." She glanced at each of them. "We all must do the same." She paused, then added, "Not just for our own sake, but for those of our families and our people." Another tear ran down her cheek. "We have been judged and found wanting."

Jehoiachin sighed. "Yes, I fear you are right, Mother." He turned to Hananiah. "Go. Give word to King Nebuchadnezzar that the king of Judah will come out to him without resistance."

Hananiah bowed and quickly left the room, the other advisors leaving with him.

Jehoiachin looked at his mother and offered a slight shrug. "It is done, Mother. Your son has reigned only days and has destroyed his own son's inheritance."

She walked up to him and placed her hand on his upper arm. "What's done is done, Coniah. We can only move forward from here. Turn your heart to Yahweh, and he can turn this defeat into a victory."

Jehoiachin shook his head. "How, Mother? How?"

"I don't know," she said. "But I know he can."

Jehoiachin sighed and walked from the room as Nehushta followed.

*****

Raphael turned to Mikael. "So, our mission here was a success?"

Mikael raised his eyebrows. "It would seem so. Jehoiachin surrendering is what Ruach said should happen. It appears that will now happen."

"If Nebuchadnezzar keeps his word," Gabriel said.

Mikael rubbed his chin. "Well, he should—unless Lucifer gets to him." He stood. "I should deploy angels to the Babylonian camp to make sure Lucifer and his demons don't interfere."

Gabriel stood with him. "Let me do that for you, Mikael." A broad grin came across his face. "Then you and Raphael can go to the Baby-*lo*-nl-an camp now to view Hananiah's arrival, and I can bring a contingent of angels shortly to post around their camp."

Mikael chuckled. "I think the little boy may have started something."

Gabriel nodded, and he and his grin disappeared.

CHAPTER 10

Hananiah's Fate

Once Mikael and Raphael arrived in the Babylonian camp, a flurry of activity surrounded them. Some soldiers were sharpening swords, others were in sparring practice, and still others sat around a fire telling stories of how large their spoils of war would be from this conquest. Other men scurried around the camp getting fires ready for meals, securing tents, and corralling the horses and other livestock they brought with them. Confidence and high morale were in clear evidence within the Babylonian camp.

Raphael turned in a three-sixty. "All looks clear—so far."

Mikael nodded as he also turned. "Looks to be. Let's go to Nebuchadnezzar's tent and be sure."

It wasn't difficult to find which one was the king's tent as it was located in the center of the camp and the largest one—at least four sizes larger than any other. They didn't enter through the main tent opening, but simply walked through the tent walls. Nebuchadnezzar was sitting in a large ornate chair which had somehow been placed higher so that he tow-ered above everyone present. Another man was counting out gold pieces to two other men.

*****

"This is the price both sides agreed to," the man doling out the money said. He then told one of the men in a whisper, "I advise you not to haggle. The king is not in a haggling mood."

The other man looked from the one paying him to Nebuchadnezzar, evidently trying to gauge if the man spoke truth or not.

{ Mikael assumed the two being paid were leaders of the mercenary army Nebuchadnezzar had hired to attack and hold the city. }

Both men decided to not negotiate; they swept the gold from the table into a small sack each was carrying.

The great king lifted himself higher in his chair and spoke. "So, Nasir. Did you penetrate their defenses, or did you just hold them until I arrived?"

Nasir bowed as he stuffed the sack of gold into an inner pocket within his cloak. He grinned as he stood and made his posture more erect. "We were able to kill a good number before their reinforcements prevented the rest of us from breaching the wall."

The other man nodded and also gave a slight bow. "Yes, my soldiers were able to penetrate the farthest and throw their king over the city wall—into the refuse with all the other filth of which this city reeks."

Nebuchadnezzar now looked a bit dejected. "Oh, pity. Akeem, I did tell you to fight with patience. What was the rush? What sport is left for me?"

"Apologies, my king," Akeem said with another bow and a chuckle. "My soldiers get carried away with their work." He raised his index finger. "But I hear they have made his son king." Akeem cocked his head, still grinning. "He's a young man, so there's probably a lot you can think up for him to perform."

Nebuchadnezzar gave a dismissive gesture. "I promised his father last time I was here I would not kill his son." He drummed his fingers on the arm of his chair. "I'll have to think of another way to show my dominance." He looked back at Nasir. "Who else is left that can be made king?"

Nasir looked at Akeem and then back to Nebuchadnezzar. "Uh, I'm not completely sure, Your Majesty. I think there is at least one left of noble birth, if you can call these people noble—much less even people."

"I heard his name to be Mattaniah, I believe, my lord," Akeem said.

Nebuchadnezzar scrunched his nose. "'Gift of Yahweh'?" He shook his head. "No, I can't have him keep such a name, one with a meaning like that."

Nasir smiled. "I know my lord loves irony."

Akeem chuckled. "So, after you take away everything, you leave him with nothing and call him 'plenteous.'" He laughed harder. "What will his people think of him then?"

Nebuchadnezzar laughed with him. "I should keep you around, Akeem. You've given me a great idea."

Akeem bowed. "Glad to be of service, my lord."

Nebuchadnezzar turned to the servant who had just paid the two men. "Ghalib, another gold coin to each of them."

Nasir and Akeem looked at each other and smiled. The servant scowled but did as his master said. Each put the coin in a separate pocket from where they had placed the other money.

The meaning was obvious: they were going to keep this gold piece for themselves.

"I'll name him Zedekiah," Nebuchadnezzar said. "'Righteousness of Yahweh.'" He pointed to Akeem. "You're right. The people will spurn his name because of him now ruling over the dregs I will leave for him. Certainly, nothing righteous will be left in the city except for his name."

All three of them laughed a raucous laugh.

"You are clever, my lord," Nasir said.

"Indeed," Akeem added. "Very clever, and very wise."

Nebuchadnezzar turned to Ghalib again. "Take Nasir and Akeem to the royal cook so they can have a good meal before they leave." He raised his arm. "Pleasure doing business with you. I shall call on you again, I'm sure."

Both bowed. "Thank you, my lord," each said.

"Call any time," Akeem added.

Both followed Ghalib from the tent. Nebuchadnezzar leaned back in his chair and looked to be in deeper thought.

*****

"No Lucifer. No demons. And things seem to be going to plan," Raphael said, looking at Mikael.

Mikael nodded but said nothing.

Raphael gave him a questioning look, cocking his head slightly. "What's wrong?" He shrugged. "Isn't all going to plan?"

Mikael glanced at Raphael and back to the king. "I suppose, but he missed the blood sport he craved. I'm just not sure what he's now thinking."

Raphael suddenly got a concerned look. "You don't think he'll go back on his promise to Jehoiakim, do you?" He looked at Nebuchadnezzar and squinted. "Isn't his word supposed to be binding no matter what?"

Mikael gave slow nod. "Should be. Usually is."

*****

Another servant entered, breaking Mikael's thoughts. The man bowed to his knees, placing his head to the ground.

"Speak," the king said in an irritated tone.

The servant raised up but remained kneeling. "My lord. An emissary from King Jehoiachin has arrived."

Nebuchadnezzar sat more erect. "It's about time. Send him in."

The servant bowed again, got to his feet, and rushed from the tent.

In a matter of seconds, Hananiah entered. He looked uncomfortable being in Nebuchadnezzar's presence. He seemed to flex his nose as if he found the smell of the room nearly intolerable. He quickly bowed and looked at the king before him.

"My lord. I send greetings from my king, Jehoiachin."

A grin came across Nebuchadnezzar's face. "Oh, is that a warm greeting, or an insincere platitude?"

Hananiah eyes widened. Clearly the king's words stunned him, and he did not know how to respond. "Uh, my lord?"

Nebuchadnezzar laughed as Hananiah grew visually more uncomfortable.

*****

Raphael looked from Nebuchadnezzar to Mikael. "What's going on? The king is looking almost giddy."

Mikael sighed, shaking his head. "I think Hananiah arrived at the wrong time. Nebuchadnezzar is looking for a way to spill blood."

"What?" Raphael watched Nebuchadnezzar carefully as the king rose and walked forward to Hananiah. "But why?"

Mikael looked at him. "As we said before. He made a promise to Jehoiakim he would not kill Jehoiachin. As you stated, his word is binding, no matter to whom he made it. Akeem's men killed Jehoiakim, so there is nothing for Nebuchadnezzar to do but take captives." He shook his head. "I don't think that alone will appease him. He wants to satisfy his thirst for blood."

*****

Nebuchadnezzar walked around Hananiah, who was now visibly shaking. This seemed to please the king even more. He chuckled as he came back into Hananiah's view. "So, are you the best the king had to send to me?"

"I am one of his trusted advisors. Did . . . did you wish to receive someone else?"

The king's stance stiffened. "I expected the defeated king to come to me personally. That would have been the appropriate response." His voice grew more irritated. "Yet he sends me this . . . attempt of a man . . . to greet me like we're here to have tea." He leaned forward. "Are we having tea?"

Hananiah's eyes grew even wider. "Uh, no, my lord. But . . . but I can have that arranged."

Nebuchadnezzar threw his head back and laughed. "Yes. Yes, I am sure you could. With China cups decorated with golden filagree, no doubt." He began to pace.

Hananiah watched Nebuchadnezzar in silence as sweat formed on his temples and upper lip. He smacked his lips as if his mouth had gone dry. It was apparent Hananiah was in a state of shock and didn't understand what Nebuchadnezzar was talking about.

"I can get you . . . whatever you desire, my lord." He swallowed hard. "What is it you desire?"

Nebuchadnezzar turned in a swift motion, his eyes showing pure evil. "Blood!"

Hananiah's head jerked back, horror on his face. "Sire?"

"I desire blood. Your puny king was killed by my mercenaries. I can't kill your current king. So, who do I kill?"

Hananiah shuffled his feet. "Uh, uh, why? . . . I mean, is there a reason to?"

"Because it pleases me." In a swift motion, Nebuchadnezzar drew his sword and turned in a swift circular motion causing his robe to flare with the centripetal force created from his turn.

Hananiah held out his hands. "No, my—"

Before he could finish his statement, the king's sword sliced cleanly through Hananiah's neck. At first he looked to be in suspended animation, but then his body crumbled to the floor like a marionette whose strings had been cut. His head rolled from his body.

Nebuchadnezzar reached down and cleaned the blood from his sword with Hananiah's robe, then sheathed it. He took in a deep breath, held it a few seconds, then let it out quickly. "There," he said. "I feel better now."

Nebuchadnezzar strolled back to his chair and sat with a satisfied look on his face. He yelled. "Ghalib!"

The servant entered immediately but stopped short. He looked from the headless body to his master as his eyes grew wide. As if suddenly realizing whose presence he was in, he quickly genuflected. "Yes, my lord?"

With a dismissive hand gesture, Nebuchadnezzar replied, "Take this man's head to Jehoiachin, and tell him I will be arriving tomorrow. And that this is what will happen to all who resist."

Ghalib bowed again. "Yes, my lord. At once."

*****

As Ghalib gathered Hananiah's body, Mikael left the tent; Raphael followed.

"Well, I had not expected that," Raphael said.

"Hopefully, all will now go according to plan," Mikael said. "Let's go check on Gabriel and Jahven."

Raphael nodded. "Anything is better than being here."

CHAPTER 11

Lucifer's Deception

*T*heir arrival where Jahvan was holding the demons as prisoners was opportune. No sooner had Mikael and Raphael teleported there when another vast army of demons approached. Mikael immediately went into his captain mode, giving orders to various angels and instructions to certain leaders of legions to prepare for another wave of demons.

All responded in short order and began forming a shield around the angels guarding the demons who had been captured in the previous battle. Mikael knew Lucifer still had time to influence Nebuchadnezzar and that Lucifer's approach could mean another battle. They had been successful so far in thwarting Lucifer's plan. Mikael wasn't about to relinquish their success to this point.

Yet the demons did not attack. They arrived and remained a distance from Mikael's angels. Their number looked to be about equal to the number already taken captive.

Suddenly, Lucifer appeared next to Mikael. "We always meet under such distressing times."

Mikael turned—his sword raised.

Lucifer held up his hands. "Really, now, Mikael. Are you so eager to slay an unarmed angel?"

Mikael lowered his sword upon seeing Lucifer had his fully sheathed. "So why are you here, Lucifer?"

Lucifer pointed to the captives. "Well, I think it's obvious. I want my angels back."

"Your demons, you mean?"

"Oh, so we're going with derogatory now, are we?" He gave a shrug. "I guess, technically, you're correct. But we're all made from the same cloth, so to speak."

"We *were*. But past tense is appropriate here. We are no longer of the same will. We are bound to our Creator."

"Yes," Lucifer said in a playful tone. "Pity you do not have free will like we do."

Mikael gave a sarcastic chuckle. "Yes, I'm sure you let your demons usurp your authority like you tried to do with our Creator."

Lucifer's eyes narrowed. "Speak of what you know, Mikael. Not of what you think you know."

Mikael gave a small smile. "Yeah. Sure, Lucifer. Whatever you say."

Lucifer's stance stiffened and he said, in a commanding tone, "I want my angels back."

Mikael shook his head. "Not going to happen. We are on a mission for Yahweh, and you will not prevent it."

"You're willing to wage another war?"

Mikael did not flinch. "If I must. You lost the last one. You'll lose this one."

"Oh, Mr. Confident, are we?" Lucifer paused, then turned more serious. "The reality is your angels are tired." He looked behind him and turned with a broad smile. "Mine are fresh and eager to fight."

Mikael shrugged. "We're ready." In truth, Mikael wasn't sure how ready his angels were for another fight. But he was not about to let Lucifer see they weren't. Besides, he knew he had his Creator on his side.

"I don't believe you, but I'm done with Jehoiachin anyway." Lucifer shrugged. "Not the outcome I wanted originally, but Nebuchadnezzar likes Jehoiachin as much as I do. He'll put the Judean king in prison for the rest of his life. That's good enough for me."

Mikael gave Lucifer an icy stare. He didn't trust Lucifer and looked for any traces of deceit in his voice or mannerisms. "What are you saying?"

"If you let my angels go, we won't interfere with whatever Nebuchadnezzar has planned for Jehoiachin."

Mikael did not respond right away. He didn't trust Lucifer.

Lucifer let out a sigh. "I give you my word."

Mikael pushed out a sarcastic chuckle. "Yes, like that's worth anything."

Lucifer gave a hard stare. "Either that, or war. You decide."

Mikael always found Lucifer hard to gauge. He didn't play by any rules except for those he wanted. Anyone else's expense was never a consideration. He knew Lucifer now had something else he was scheming for. Yet he had no idea what that was. Besides, it was true his angels still needed rest. Could he trust Lucifer's word on this?

"You leave, and don't even show your faces around the Babylonian camp or Jerusalem."

Lucifer held up his hand. "You have my promise. We leave, and you won't see us."

Mikael turned to Jahven, paused for a couple of moments, and nodded.

Jahven cocked his head as if to say, "Are you sure?"

Mikael gave another nod and Jahven returned his acknowledgement with a nod of his own. He turned and ordered the demons released. They flew to where Kaylor had their swords; each picked up their weapon and then joined their compatriots.

Lucifer gave a quick smile and then vanished. Jahven gave Mikael a look that seemed to say he felt a wrong decision had been made.

Mikael hoped not, but his eyes began to widen as he saw the demons move toward aligning in attack formation.

"Stations!" Mikael yelled as he drew his sword, unfurled his broad wings, and rose into the air to take his battle position. Would he ever learn not to trust anything Lucifer promised? Yahweh had said he was a liar. This definitely proved it.

Mikael's angels rapidly got into position while gripping hard on their swords. The demons came at them fast, with determination on their faces. Yet as soon as the demons reached fighting distance, they disappeared. At the same time, Mikael heard laughter echoing all around them. His angels looked at each other with great confusion.

Lucifer suddenly appeared in front of Mikael, still laughing. "That was priceless!"

"You're despicable," Mikael said, feeling taken advantage of, which made him even more irritated.

"Spoilsport," Lucifer said as he leaned in slightly.

Mikael took a swing at him with his sword, but Lucifer disappeared before Mikael's blade could reach its mark. All that remained was an echo of Lucifer's laughter.

Raphael came alongside Mikael. "What was *that* all about?"

Mikael let out a quick breath. "Just Lucifer being Lucifer."

"You think he'll keep his promise?"

Mikael tilted his head slightly from side to side. "He'll keep the letter of his promise, but likely not the intent."

Raphael wrinkled his brow. "Like what?"

Mikael thought about that and then looked at Raphael. "No idea, Raphael. No idea at all."

Quentillious arrived. "My captain. What is your order for us now?"

Mikael shook his head. "Nothing for now. Just rest. Have everyone get the rest they deserve."

Quentillious gave a slight bow and flew to the other angels. Mikael could see all of them gather in groups, sit, and relax. He was glad he could allow them this chance to recharge, which they desperately needed and deserved.

Mikael caught Jahven's attention and motioned him over.

"Yes, my captain?"

"Have everyone return to the angel dimension after they've had a chance to rest. Raphael and I will stay longer to see how things develop here."

"Absolutely," he said with a slight bow, then turned.

"And . . . " Mikael began.

Jahven turned with eyebrows raised.

"Just be on alert in case Lucifer does something unexpected."

Jahven smiled. "Which is most of the time."

Mikael chuckled with a nod. "Yes, that is definitely true. Hopefully, it won't be for a while."

Jahven nodded and went to deliver his news.

Mikael turned to Raphael. "Ready to head back to the palace?"

"Yes," Raphael said. "The royal family has probably received word about Hananiah by now."

"I know," Mikael said. "And I hope that leads to compliance, not defiance."

CHAPTER 12

Demoralizing Defeat

The royal family, or most of them, had gathered on the large patio to take their early morning meal. After finishing his, Shealtiel asked, "May I go play, Savta?"

Nehushta nodded and motioned for one of the servants to follow Shealtiel and keep an eye on him. The child came over and kissed her on her right cheek. She smiled and gave a kiss back on his. Shealtiel bowed to his father, who gave a smile, and then skipped off into the palace followed by the servant, who had to walk in a hurried fashion to keep up with him. This made Nehushta chuckle.

"This is his last day of freedom," she said with a tone of sadness.

"Of all our freedom," Jehoiachin said. He stood, walked to the edge of the patio, and looked out. Smoke from campfires in the Babylonian encampment could be seen. He turned. "I've been a fool, Ima."

Nehushta rose and came over to him. "We all have, Coniah." She patted his chest. "We're in Yahweh's hands now."

"You mean in Nebuchadnezzar's."

"Now, Coniah," she said in a somewhat scolding tone. "And he is also in Yahweh's hands."

Before Jehoiachin could respond, another servant entered with a covered platter and set it on the table where they had been eating.

"What is this?" Jehoiachin asked.

The servant bowed. "I do not know, my lord. It arrived, and I was told to deliver it."

"Arrived?" Nehushta asked. "From whom?"

"Me." A voice, back in the shadows where they could not see, said the word clearly.

{ Mikael, watching, knew who this was, so he braced himself for what might happen next. }

"Show yourself," Jehoiachin said in a commanding voice. "You dare come into my presence unannounced?"

The man chuckled. "Oh, I sent the announcement ahead of me with your servant."

Jehoiachin looked at his servant, who clearly was as clueless as he and Nehushta.

The man laughed. "Oh, not him. The one on the table."

Nehushta wrinkled her brow. "What are you talking about? And who are you?"

The man gave a quick bow. "Oh, forgive me." He placed his hand on his chest. "I'm Ghalib, your master's servant." He pointed to the table. "I bring the servant you sent to my king back to you."

Nehushta followed Jehoiachin to the table, both still looking confused. When he lifted the cover, Nehushta gave a shrill shriek, put her hand over her mouth, and turned away. Jehoiachin jumped back, startled, then dropped the cover back over the head of Hananiah.

He turned to Ghalib, who had a huge grin on his face. "What's the meaning of this!" Jehoiachin demanded.

Ghalib's smile dissipated. "Oh, I think the meaning is quite clear. Any dissidence will be met with the same finality."

Nehushta pointed at the table and looked at Ghalib with disdain. "And this is how you have to deliver such a message?"

"A demonstration speaks volumes, don't you think?" Ghalib hardened his look and stared at Jehoiachin. "Your master will be here any moment. You will receive him and deliver yourself to him."

Ghalib turned and let himself out. Jehoiachin's servant stood there, eyes wide, seemingly not knowing what he should do next.

Jehoiachin gave the servant a dismissive wave. The man bowed and turned to leave.

"Wait!"

The man turned and gave another bow, obviously not knowing what was coming his way.

"That . . . that . . . *thing*." Jehoiachin pointed at the table. "Take it with you."

The man went to the table and quickly lifted the platter.

"And give Hananiah a decent burial," Nehushta said as the man walked away.

The servant turned, nodded, and hurried off.

Jehoiachin stood fuming. "The audacity of that man." He pointed. "Did you see him? A servant. A servant, mind you, not bowing to me and then telling me *my* master is coming." He blew breath from his nose. "I should have had him slain on the spot."

Nehushta came next to him and held his arm. "Coniah, our world has changed. It's important that you withhold your disdain."

He looked at her with cold eyes.

She patted his arm. "I said withhold your *disdain*, not your pride. You are still royal, no matter what they say or think about it. We have our dignity, and they can't take that away from us."

Jehoiachin let out a deep sigh as he patted her hand. "You are wise, Ima, as usual."

"As are you, my son. As are you."

He placed her hand on his arm. "Well, let's go meet our *master*."

*****

Mikael and Raphael followed Jehoiachin through the rest of the day and watched all he went through. Ghalib had been correct. Calling Nebuchadnezzar Jehoiachin's master was essentially true. The entire royal family, including Jehoiachin's mother, was taken captive.

His uncle, Mattaniah, was made king with the stipulation his name would now be Zedekiah.

Yet there wasn't much left for Zedekiah to rule. Nebuchadnezzar took upwards of ten thousand individuals as prisoners with the royal family: several thousand of the prominent people of Jerusalem, at least one thousand skilled workers, and nearly seven thousand of Jehoiachin's finest soldiers.

Mikael watched Nebuchadnezzar's actions take a demoralizing toll on Jehoiachin as well as on Zedekiah. He knew that was the point. Jehoiachin, now in chains, was paraded in front of everyone, and Zedekiah was left with only the poorest of the people to rule. Nebuchadnezzar had been right. His name was now irony—a sad irony.

The worse part, Mikael thought, was seeing the look on Jehoiachin's face when Shealtiel was placed in chains with Shealtiel's mother and his other wives. He couldn't imagine what was going through Jehoiachin's thoughts seeing his family suffer knowing he was the cause of the pain.

Shealtiel, being so young, looked like he was going to cry. The boy's mother whispered something to him. He nodded, looked at his father, then gave a slight nod and stood more erect, holding his head high. Even though his eyes glistened with moisture, it seemed the child was determined to not let his emotions overcome him. He was determined to keep his dignity in check—just like the other royals. It was obvious Jehoiachin was extremely proud of Shealtiel in that moment. But it was a sad thing seeing Jehoiachin realize all of this could have been avoided if he had just heeded Jeremiah's warnings. Consequences had come due, and they affected not only himself but his family and thousands of his nation's citizens.

*****

Nebuchadnezzar broke camp quickly, and the march back to Babylon began. Those who remained in Jerusalem were crying. Zedekiah tried to keep his dignity, but everyone knew it was a sham. What did he have left to be dignified about? His new name would be a constant reminder of this day: the lack of righteousness of the leaders had led to this.

Zedekiah walked back to the palace, passing the temple along the way. As he glanced at it, he shook his head. Nebuchadnezzar's men had stripped much more gold off the building's structure—both inside and out. It now looked like a dilapidated relic.

One of the men with Zedekiah said, "My lord, look at the temple. It's so sad-looking."

Zedekiah nodded. "Yes, just like us. Sad and dejected."

"What happens now?" the man asked.

Zedekiah shrugged. "We pick up the pieces and do the best we can. Yahweh has forsaken us. We need to look to ourselves now."

The man stopped and looked at the temple for several seconds. He then hurried to catch up with Zedekiah.

*****

Raphael shook his head and looked at Mikael. "Do they ever learn?"

Mikael sighed. "Apparently not. He just witnessed the consequences of disobedience and yet he is determined to be just as disobedient as his brother and nephew."

"What a disappointing day," Raphael said.

"Indeed," Michael replied. He paused as he watched Zedekiah enter the palace. "Come, Raphael, let's go. I think I've seen enough sadness for this visit."

CHAPTER 13

Mikael's Concern

Mikael turned when he heard Raphael's voice.

"There you are," Raphael said. "I should have known this is where you would be. You seem to be constantly drawn to Eden."

Mikael grinned. "I guess I do come here often." He took in a deep breath and let it out slowly. "It's just so peaceful here. Not to mention beautiful."

Raphael sat on the boulder next to him, and this caused a nearby butterfly to flit away which in turn set off a cascade of the beautiful creatures flying into the air before they resettled on other flowers nearby. Raphael chuckled. "A true butterfly effect."

Mikael chuckled with him but then shook his head. "That statement brings back the fiasco Lucifer pulled at Babylon."

"Yes," Raphael said as he leaned back with his hands behind him to stretch out his legs. "But it all worked out in the end." He smiled. "Just like the Master wanted it to."

Mikael nodded. "Yes, it always does, I guess."

After a couple of seconds of silence between them, Raphael asked, "So why are you here now?"

Mikael's eyebrows went up. "You have to ask? After our last visit to Earth, I needed something much more cheerful and tranquil. This place always provides that."

Raphael looked around and grinned. "Yes, it does that and more. I always look forward to seeing what new creation the Master has put here. He makes even the smallest of creatures so intricate and ornate."

Mikael sat up. "That's it, Raphael."

Raphael sat up as well. "What's it?"

"New creations." He shook his head. "I haven't seen any new creations this visit."

Raphael's eyes grew wide. "None?" He cocked his head. "I don't recall that happening before. I've always found something new. It could be something small, but it has always been something."

"Exactly. But no, nothing this time."

Raphael stood. "Well, where have you been?"

Mikael shrugged. "Just here. But in the past, here was all that was necessary."

"Well, let's walk around," Raphael said. "That may help us discover what new things our Creator has added to his menagerie."

Mikael stood and walked with Raphael for quite some time. Still, everything felt odd. While walking and viewing such a diverse animal and plant kingdom was most pleasurable, there was nothing they had not seen before. As they were walking under a grove of trees, they saw one squirrel chasing another on the lower limb of a tree above them. The one being chased suddenly jumped, landed on Raphael's shoulder, dashed around his neck, and scrambled down his arm to the ground below. The other squirrel remained where it was and chattered as if scolding Raphael for helping his companion escape.

Both laughed so hard they practically cried. Mikael had never seen Raphael look so startled. The ordeal, for some reason, struck him as extremely funny. After Raphael recovered, he laughed at Mikael laughing at him. For some reason, neither could stop, and both wound up sitting on the ground trying to recover.

After several blissful seconds, both regained composure.

"Well, that was certainly different," Raphael said. "Does that count?"

Mikael grinned. "That was very therapeutic, but I don't think that was necessarily created by Yahweh. You were just in the right spot at the right time for Mister Squirrel to use you as a landing pad."

Raphael leaned back with his hands again. "Well, it is curious that we don't see any new creatures or plants." He shrugged. "Maybe the Creator feels all is now complete."

Mikael tilted his head. "Maybe. Doubtful, though."

A noise from behind made them turn.

"So this is where you two got off to," Gabriel said as he held out his hands to help his fellow angels stand, grasping their forearms and helping them to their feet.

"What brings you here, Gabriel?" Mikael asked. "Needed a touch of beauty and tranquility as well?"

Gabriel smiled. "That would be nice, but we're waiting for battle practice."

"Oh," Mikael replied. "I forgot to tell everyone that practice is cancelled this time."

Gabriel displayed a surprised look. "You've never done that before."

"After the last battle with Lucifer, I felt everyone deserved a break. Besides, it's just one practice." He grinned. "Don't worry. I know how to make it up next session."

Gabriel patted Mikael on his upper arm. "Of that, my friend, I have no doubt. I think some of us are still going to do some one-on-one dueling." He looked at Raphael. "Want to come?"

Raphael looked from Gabriel to Mikael. "Well . . . "

Mikael gave a quick wave. "Go ahead, Raphael. I'll be fine." He looked back at Gabriel. "I'm going to stay here a while longer."

Gabriel displayed a worried look. "Everything all right?"

Mikael gave a weak smile. "Yes. I'm fine. Just need a recharge after my last visit to Earth."

Gabriel nodded. "Totally understand. Even Yahweh comes here often."

"Still?" Mikael asked. If so, he wondered why he wasn't finding anything newly created.

"Oh, quite often, actually. I think he's still here somewhere."

"Hmm. Maybe I'll run into him."

As his two fellow angels left, Mikael decided to walk farther and see if he could find Yahweh. It had been a long time since they had spoken. Maybe he could explain why nothing new had been created or whether, as Raphael wondered, all was now complete. He found that hard to believe, however, as creativity seemed a prominent attribute of Yahweh's character.

Mikael walked for quite some time. While he found the walk relaxing, tranquil, and beautiful, he didn't find his Lord. He decided to return to his favorite spot on the boulder next to the stream. The babbling of the water over the rocks, the light breeze, and the fragrant flowers were incredibly relaxing. He closed his eyes for a while and let the sounds and fragrances fill his senses.

Mikael wasn't sure how long he had been in this position, but he knew he had to return to the angel dimension. He looked around at the peaceful beauty one last time, but then something caught his eye. The figure wasn't there in one instant, but was there the next. *Yahweh.*

Had he teleported? If so, he teleported in stride, which seemed odd. While possible, it was not the typical way one teleported. This made his appearance even more curious. Mikael debated whether to go to Yahweh or stay put, but it looked as though Yahweh was coming his way. So he waited.

As Yahweh approached, he displayed a bright smile. "Hello, Mikael. Is all well?"

Mikael smiled back with a nod. He knew, however, that he needed to be truthful. Deep down, he knew Yahweh already had complete knowledge of what was on his mind. "Well, not completely, my Lord."

Yahweh gestured to the boulder. "May I?"

Mikael immediately moved over. "Certainly, my Lord."

As he sat, Yahweh said, "I do love it here."

"As do I."

Yahweh nodded and turned to Mikael. "But you have a question about my creative side."

Mikael chuckled, shaking his head. "One can never fool you, my Lord."

Yahweh chuckled with him. "What you do not see does not mean it does not exist."

Mikael cocked his head. He had to think about that. Yahweh was not always straightforward, but that was usually because the truth of his words was multidimensional and not limited only to the present conversation.

"So you have been creating?"

Yahweh nodded, his smile returning.

"But it is something I cannot see?"

Yahweh nodded again.

"Forgive me, my Lord. But if no one can see it, what is its purpose?"

"What cannot be seen now comes into view in its time."

Mikael nodded. He wasn't exactly sure of the meaning of his Creator's words, but he took them to mean he would see no new creation this visit to Eden.

Yahweh placed his hand on Mikael's shoulder. The warmth of his touch seeped through him. How Mikael always longed for this touch and wished it to never end. "My son, this last visit to Earth upset you, I can tell."

Mikael nodded. "I know it's likely not the case, but Jeremiah's curse, Jehoiachin and the royal family taken to Babylon, and Jehoiachin likely destined to die in prison . . . I just don't see how your promise to King David now comes true. Has Lucifer finally won?"

Yahweh smiled. "No doubt he thinks he has."

Mikael nodded with a sigh. "Yes, he told me as much."

"Don't let his bravado get to you. He knows, very well, that my plans go beyond the obvious."

Mikael sucked in a breath. "No, my Lord. Never. I . . . I wasn't trying to imply I doubted you." He sat up straighter still. "I have trouble seeing the way out of this. Yet my trust is always with you. Forever, my Lord. You asked me that once before. My answer is, and always will be, the same."

Yahweh smiled as he nodded. "Yes, Mikael. Of that I know." He stood. "But you need some bolstering." He gestured in the direction from which he had come.

Mikael stood. "My Lord?"

"I'm going to show you the truth of what is hidden."

"Something you have created?"

Yahweh smiled. "In the process, but I think it will help bolster your confidence as well."

As they walked together, Yahweh added, "After all, the stronger your confidence, the stronger my heavenly host. Their confidence comes through you."

"May I be all you wish me to be, my Lord."

Yahweh's smile broadened. "Of that I have no doubt."

The statement struck Mikael as odd coming from his Creator. "Pardon me. But do you *ever* have doubt?"

Yahweh looked at Mikael. "Never." He stopped walking and looked deeply into Mikael's eyes. "That is why I know of your loyalty and all those here with me. Yet everyone needs some helpful encouragement now and then."

As they continued their journey, Mikael considered the meaning of these last words. So . . . he was going to see something that would most likely be greater than anything he had yet seen. That was hard to fathom. He looked around as they walked.

What could possibly be more wonderful than what is already here?

"So what will I see, my Lord?"

"Something wonderful, Mikael. Something wonderful."

CHAPTER 14

Something Wonderful

As Mikael followed Yahweh . . . somewhere, he tried to figure out where they were headed. He couldn't determine anything about their destination. He saw nothing in front of them except more vegetation.

Suddenly, Mikael felt his skin prickle. He knew something had happened; he just wasn't sure what.

Yahweh stopped and turned to him with a broad smile. "Did you feel anything?"

Mikael nodded. "Yes. What *was* that?" He looked behind him but didn't see anything abnormal.

"You just passed through a time barrier," Yahweh said.

"You mean . . . like Lucifer used when he attempted his scheme at Babylon?"

"Something like that," Yahweh said with a light laugh. "Where do you think he got the idea?"

Mikael laughed along with his Creator. "Well, at the time I had no idea. I wondered how he came up with such a clever idea."

It was at that moment Mikael saw cherubim in the distance. His eyes widened. "We're at the Garden?" He glanced at Yahweh and then back to the cherubim. "I always wondered what you did with the Garden." He looked behind him again knowing he had never seen it on his frequent visits to Eden.

"As you know, one day I'll be bringing the righteous from Sheol to Eden. I want them to enjoy Eden, but this area of Eden is off limits until the right time."

"Right time?" Mikael shook his head. "I'm sorry, my Lord. I don't understand."

"Well, the reason is *inside* the Garden." He smiled with eyebrows raised. "Want to take a peek?"

Mikael's eyes grew large. "Very much, my Lord." He had not been back to the Garden since Adam and Chavvah had been banished. He was also amazed the Creator had cherubim still present. He knew they initially prevented reentry, but he assumed they were now protecting something else. He couldn't imagine what that was. His excitement grew the closer they got to the Garden.

The cherubim genuflected as soon as Yahweh approached. Mikael knew these were also angelic beings, but even to him they were awe-inspiring to behold. Each cherub had four distinct faces representing characteristics of their Creator. No other angel looked like these special angels.

Once inside, Mikael was flooded with memories of the time Adam and Chavvah lived here. They walked past the stream where Chavvah, whom Adam called Isha at that time, learned how to transplant flowers, then where they had eaten figs with Serpent, and then where Serpent had deceived Chavvah. That was such a sad memory.

It was then that Mikael noticed it. This garden looked different than the rest of Eden did when he was here previously.

While beautiful, it didn't exhibit that certain brilliance Eden itself did, as this garden was a representation of Earth. Now this place *did* possess that colorful brilliance. The Tree of Life was as he remembered: its roots growing on both sides of the river that ran through the garden and its fruit displaying the most beautiful and vibrant colors. Next to it was the Tree of Knowledge of Good and Evil—or he thought it was that special tree. Now that the whole garden had the brilliance of color, though, the tree looked like any other tree.

"My Creator, this tree is the Tree of Knowledge of Good and Evil with which Satan tempted Adam to rebel, isn't it?"

Yahweh turned, gazed at the tree, and nodded. "Yes. It was. But no longer."

Mikael cocked his head. "I'm not sure I understand."

"This tree was a test of obedience—a choice provided. The tree itself had no special power. It was Adam's disobedience that caused him to understand the difference between good and evil as well as understanding the consequences that must come from such actions." Yahweh walked over and patted the tree's trunk. "This is just another tree now." Yahweh smiled. "It will be interesting to see how long it takes Adam and Eve to eat of this tree again in the future."

"Eve? Future?" Mikael shook his head. "I'm sorry, my Creator. I am lost to the meaning."

Yahweh's smiled widened. "Yes, I can see why that would be true. We are presently standing in the future. Chavvah eventually becomes known as Eve." He leaned in and chuckled. "Easier to say for some." He turned with arms wide. "Yet this, Mikael—all of this—is the future of my people: all those who will put their eternal hope in me."

Mikael nodded but felt he was only halfway following Yahweh's words. Apparently, humans would occupy this garden again. He still wasn't sure when, but it seemed to be sometime in the humans' future.

Yahweh motioned for Mikael to join him as he sat on a boulder next to the river. He looked toward the river for several seconds and then turned to Mikael. "You see, Mikael, the Earth I created will one day be destroyed and made new."

"Why, my Lord?"

A sadness came over Yahweh's face; his eyes grew moist. "Sin has deeply polluted all that is there." He gave a brief smile. "But once all is made new again, only happiness and joy will exist." Yahweh leaned in toward Mikael. "And that is what I want to show you: a sneak peek at what is in store for all who follow me." His smile broadened. "Are you ready for that?"

Mikael's smile matched that of his Creator's. "Yes, my Lord. I'm . . . very excited to see what you have prepared."

Yahweh held up his right index finger. "Preparing. It's not yet finished."

Mikael knew how his Creator could make such unique and magnificent things. His degree of excitement surprised him. Mikael had no idea what he would see, but he knew it would be spectacular. "Understood, my Lord," Mikael said.

Yahweh tapped Mikael's knee with his palm and stood. "Wonderful. Then follow me."

Mikael followed Yahweh across the river while walking over the thick roots of the Tree of Life. They went a little farther beyond the river.

Yahweh turned and looked at Mikael. "This is it, Mikael."

Mikael looked but couldn't see anything. Before he could say something, Yahweh waved his right hand, and Mikael could only gasp. Then: "My Lord!" He stood in awe. "It . . . is . . . magnificent!"

Before Mikael stood a city, extremely wide and extremely high. He had never seen so many gemstones and so much gold utilized in such a unique way. Everything literally sparkled. Mikael searched for words, but his mind drew a blank. All he could say, and he said it over and over, was, "Magnificent! Truly, magnificent!"

"I want you to get the full effect. I chose gemstones that are even more brilliant when exposed to pure light." He smiled and held up his hands. "You stay here. I will go inside the city and expose it to my Shekinah glory, the purest light which exists and for which this city was designed."

Mikael nodded. He was still speechless. As Yahweh disappeared, he wondered how any of this could be even better. Yet, in moments . . . it was true! Yahweh's Shekinah glory yielded light that made the gemstones and gold turn to glorious colors. Mikael had no other words for what he was experiencing: glorious color. But that was only the beginning; water now flowed from the highest pinnacle of the city, and it reflected and refracted the light making the entire city literally breathtaking. It was so beautiful tears formed around Mikael's eyes. He was not one to get emotional, but this was overwhelming his senses.

When he turned, he was again taken aback with what he saw. All of the garden was now literally glowing. Flower petals looked like crystals which glowed their individual brilliant colors. Even the leaves of trees seemed to glow. Yet it wasn't luminescence. It was . . . more . . . more wonderful and glorious than that. Everything shone more glorious than he would have thought possible. He had no idea how his Creator did this; Mikael just knew he was truly the master of creation as well as imagination. Only Yahweh could have imagined something like this. Mikael felt absolutely giddy. He knew his fellow angels and humans would also be blown away with such beauty. He didn't think he would be able to describe such wonder to them. All words failed; the experience was beyond words. A totally different grouping of words would have to be created, he thought, to describe such a world.

Then, just as quickly as the overwhelming beauty appeared, it disappeared. What was left was the scene he had experienced before his Creator displayed his Shekinah glory into the city. By comparison, even these wondrous sights paled. He couldn't believe he had thought this degree of beauty could not be improved upon. He shook his head. *Only by the touch of the Master.*

Yahweh reappeared, a smile on his face. Mikael couldn't help but smile in return as he wiped his eyes.

"My Lord. It was truly more magnificent than I could have imagined. I don't think there are words to describe what I saw."

Yahweh put his hand on Mikael's shoulder. "Do you now feel encouraged?"

Mikael chuckled as he nodded. "Very much, my Lord."

"And all of this is tied to what you witnessed with Jehoiachin."

Mikael cocked his head. He was lost again.

"This is a long-term vision, Mikael. Short term can look like defeat. But rest assured, the final outcome will be what you just witnessed." He looked directly into Mikael's eyes. "Do you believe this, Mikael?"

Mikael nodded. "Yes, my Lord. I don't have doubt. I just don't have a vision like yours. But I trust you. That is enough for me."

Yahweh nodded. "That is the secret. And one we must help others find."

The only response Mikael could make was to nod as Yahweh began walking back the way they had entered the garden. The cherubim again genuflected as they exited.

"I think you should go to Babylon and observe further," Yahweh said. "I think that may give you more insight as to how things will develop and bring about the results I have designed."

"Of course, my Lord."

Mikael felt his skin prickle as they passed back into Eden: from the future into the present. He looked back and saw no evidence of a garden. It looked just like the rest of Eden in both directions.

Yahweh stopped once they had reached Mikael's favorite spot. "I think you should take Raphael with you." He displayed a warm smile. "Two is always better."

Mikael smiled in return and nodded. "Indeed, my Lord. I'll be sure and tell him."

"Very good. We'll speak again."

With those words, Yahweh disappeared.

Mikael sat back on the boulder he had spent so much time on before. He wondered if he would be able to appreciate this place to the same extent now. After seeing such indescribable beauty, he thought, that could prove to be a challenge.

CHAPTER 15

Visit to Babylon

Babylon stood bathed in morning sun as Mikael and Raphael arrived back on Earth on the bridge which crossed the Euphrates River connecting the great city to Nebuchadnezzar's glorious palace compound. Even from this distance, the palace grounds were impressive. On one side stood the palace itself with its notorious hanging gardens, arranged in several tiers to create a garden for each floor of the palace. It stood like a jewel against the backdrop of the desert all around. On the other side stood the temple of Marduk. Mikael noticed it had an uncanny resemblance to the ziggurat that had been erected when Babylon was first created so long ago. This one was not as high as the former, but it still showed evidence of who was behind its design.

As if on cue, Mikael heard a voice behind him. "Impressive, isn't it?"

Mikael turned. Lucifer had an admiring look on his face as he scanned the city.

Mikael nodded. "I'd be lying if I didn't admit the beauty of the place." He looked at Lucifer as he cocked his head slightly. "I'd almost think this was a sign of you missing your former life."

Lucifer's eyes shot to Mikael; they now looked like hot daggers. "This is *my* creation. I can make things just as impressive as my foe."

Mikael's eyes widened. *"Foe?"* He could only shake his head and let out a sigh. "Lucifer, your pride always astounds me. It shouldn't anymore, but it always does. You're not on equal footing with Yahweh. You're at the same level compared to him as we are."

Raphael leaned in. "Or maybe a little lower."

Lucifer's annoyance turned to Raphael. "Oh, please! I was never at *your* level—then nor now."

Mikael turned back toward the palace grounds. "While the palace is certainly impressive, I can't say the same about your temple. Seems like you couldn't come up with a new idea."

Lucifer gave each of them an annoyed look. "Well, aren't both of you just the complimentary ones this morning?" He pointed toward the temple. "You don't mess with perfection. I saw no reason to have it change. It served its purpose the first time and is doing so again."

"So, once deceived, always deceived?" Mikael chided.

"I don't have to stand here and be insulted," Lucifer said as his look intensified with growing hatred.

"No. No, you don't," Mikael said. He couldn't help but be pleased when he realized he had put Lucifer on the defensive for a change.

"And don't think I don't know why you're here," Lucifer said. "But your efforts will be fruitless. Jehoiachin is in prison, Jerusalem is in shambles, and Nebuchadnezzar is even now becoming dissatisfied with Zedekiah." He gave a wicked chuckle. "It won't be long before they're all just a distant memory. They'll be a people who . . . well, future archaeologists will wonder if they ever existed."

Raphael took a step forward, raising his index finger to make a point, but before he could say anything, Lucifer vanished. Raphael lowered his hand and turned it into a fist. "That angel gets to me every time."

Mikael put his hand on Raphael's shoulder. "That's what he wants to happen. He brings out the worst in everyone." He gave a couple of pats to Raphael's shoulder. "Let's go accomplish our mission."

Raphael nodded. "Yes. You're right. Yahweh's will trumps his, for sure."

As they headed into the heart of the city, Mikael could see Babylon already alive with activity: merchants setting up their shops, artisans placing their wares on display to draw in customers, people hurrying wherever they needed to go. Periodically, soldiers would come through certain streets as the citizens scurried from their paths as the soldiers advanced without the slightest slowing of their pace. They were impressive, and intimidating, a spear in one hand and round shield in the other, both glistening as brightly in the morning sun as the mail which surrounded their chests. A sword sheathed at their side swayed slightly with the cadence of their steps, occasionally hitting their shin guards and producing a thud in beat with their advance: *step, step, step-thud, step, step, step-thud.* The red plume of their helmets also bobbed in rhythm to their marching cadence.

Mikael thought the beauty of the city awe-inspiring. By Earth's standards it was truly a wonder. Yet the majestic sights here paled in comparison to the rich wonderment of Eden and the overwhelming beauty Yahweh had revealed to him of the Creator's future city. Lucifer's pride, Mikael knew, would never allow Lucifer to admit the contrast.

The farther from the palace they walked, the less pristine the city became. Not long into their journey, they were in the Jewish section of the city, where most places were kept neat, though it was clear the people had no money for much upkeep. It was evident the government was not actually interested in their well-being except for keeping them sufficiently healthy to work "for the betterment of the kingdom," as they were told.

Raphael pointed to a man, dressed much better than anyone else in this part of the city, walking between buildings. "That must be him," he said to Mikael.

Mikael nodded. "Must be. Only a Jew would be inclined to be in this part of the city." He motioned with his hand. "Come. Let's follow Daniel and see what he's up to."

As they followed Daniel they also passed several Babylonian guards who were evidently here to watch this section of the city. While the Jews were not in chains, it was clear they were not free either. Mikael noted several guard stations dispersed throughout this area of the city as they continued to follow Daniel, who seemed to know exactly where he was going.

Soon Daniel stopped at a specific house, which had a soldier standing guard at the door. Clearly this house was under more scrutiny than others in the neighborhood.

*****

The soldier stood at a more exact stance of attention. "My lord, Belteshazzar, I was not expecting you."

"Good morning, Ramin. I trust your family is well."

"Yes, my lord," the soldier replied. "Since you got me this position I've been able to take care of them more properly. I am ever grateful."

Daniel smiled. "I'm just happy Yahweh has allowed me to help you in this way."

The soldier gave a slight nod. "As am I, my lord. Did you wish to enter?"

Daniel nodded. "I do. Is that all right?"

"If it were any other," the soldier replied with a slight smile, "I would refuse."

"Bless you, my son," Daniel said as he entered the abode.

{ Mikael and Raphael walked right through the closing door to follow him inside. }

The room looked extremely modest: it had a dirt floor, but one swept so well it was quite hard, resulting in keeping the dust down; a table with a few supplies next to a small kitchen area; a goat, for milk, in a corner stall; and a few blankets on straw for sleeping. A man, woman, young lad, and toddler were at a low table eating a meager meal.

The woman's face lit up with a brilliant smile as she turned to see who had entered. "My lord, Belteshazzar." She rose and bowed. "What brings you by?"

"Oh, forgive me," Daniel said. "I did not realize you were eating."

"Nonsense," the man replied. "Come, join the feast Hadcast has prepared."

"Coniah, let's not be sarcastic. Lord Belteshazzar has been good to us."

"Call me Daniel," he said as he came alongside and sat by the youngest, tousling the boy's hair in a playful gesture. The lad giggled.

He pulled out two small treats of some kind and handed one to each of the boys. They each looked eagerly to their father for approval. Jehoiachin smiled with a nod and the boys took the treat, said their thanks, and plopped it in their mouths.

"Shealtiel. Pedaiah," Hadcast said. "Why don't you take the goat for a walk? It's time it got some exercise."

Both boys rose with a nod. "Yes, Ima," the oldest said.

"Be back within the hour," Jehoiachin added.

Both boys gave another nod and left with the goat in tow.

Daniel smiled. "They're both growing up so fast."

"Yes," Hadcast replied. "All thanks to you, Daniel."

"That is true," Jehoiachin replied. "Apologies for my earlier tone. It's not your fault I'm in this position. We are fortunate to have someone among us who has a position such as yours to help my people."

"And us," Hadcast added.

Jehoiachin nodded. "Yes, I can't tell you how wonderful it is to be able to visit my family periodically. The prison does get tiresome quickly. This small reprieve every so often is a wonderful privilege."

"That's why I'm here."

Hadcast and Jehoiachin looked at each other and then back to Daniel.

"What do you mean?" Jehoiachin asked.

"Your uncle has rebelled against Babylon, refusing to pay taxes due. Nebuchadnezzar is furious. I don't think things will go well for him."

Jehoiachin shook his head. "How could he think he's able to stand up against Nebuchadnezzar? He was left with nothing. Their strength is no match for Nebuchadnezzar's army."

A worried look came over Hadcast's face. "Will the king also retaliate against those of us already here in Babylon?"

Daniel reached over and patted her hand. "I don't think so, but . . . " He looked back to Jehoiachin. "I don't want to take any chances. I was able to get Parviz, the head of the prison, to allow you to be under permanent house arrest."

Hadcast sat up more erect. "Really?" She looked from Jehoiachin to Daniel and back. "That's . . . that's wonderful."

{ Mikael could tell Jehoiachin was pleased but also cautious. }

"But how did you manage that?" He too sat up straighter. "What does that mean? I have nothing to pay Parviz for such a favor. I know he would not do this out of the goodness of his heart."

Daniel smiled. "No payment needed. It's already taken care of." He chuckled. "Actually, when I told him the king was likely bringing more prisoners from Jerusalem, he almost jumped at the chance to free up prison space."

Jehoiachin held up his hands. "Don't get me wrong. I'm grateful." He looked to Hadcast and then back to Daniel. "Very grateful. But . . . why?"

"I need to disassociate you from your uncle. If he is placed in prison, I don't want the king to associate his displeasure of him with you."

Jehoiachin nodded. "That's actually a good plan." He was quiet for a few moments, then added, "Daniel, why do you care about me?"

"You're still my king. Plus, I don't think Yahweh is done with you."

Jehoiachin gave a sad chuckle. "Really?" He panned the room with his outstretched hand. "Look around. How can he use me when I can't even leave my own house without an armed escort? What could he possibly have for me to do?"

"Don't forget, Coniah, our God is a God of miracles. Don't let your circumstances dictate your expectations."

"Why would God perform a miracle for me?"

Daniel stood. "I must go. God will perform a miracle for you because, like it or not, you are part of prophecy."

Jehoiachin looked more directly at Daniel. "What kind of prophecy?"

Daniel smiled. "I'm still figuring that out. But I'm confident you are here for a bigger purpose than just being punished for your disobedience to Nebuchadnezzar."

"I have prayed for his forgiveness," Jehoiachin replied. "I don't know if he is willing."

"Oh, he is more than willing, my king. You have experienced his justice, but you will soon experience his mercy. I'm confident of it."

Jehoiachin rose. "I do trust you are correct."

Daniel gave a bow. "Just be patient. Yahweh doesn't work on our timeline. Just be patient."

{ As Daniel left, Mikael saw hope on the faces of both Jehoiachin and Hadcast as they sat at the table once more. }

CHAPTER 16

News from Jerusalem

Daniel weaved his way through the city as he traveled back to the palace grounds where he worked as one of the king's Wise Men, as they were called. Many thought of these men as magicians, or astrologers, or sorcerers. For the most part, Mikael knew that was true as many of the men depended upon Lucifer's demons to divine for them when the king requested a judgment on a matter for which he sought counsel. But not Daniel. He always depended on Yahweh to give him the guidance needed. Therefore, Daniel used the term Counselor to describe himself and his friends. *What irony,* Mikael thought. Daniel, a servant of Yahweh, amidst the servants of Lucifer— and thriving. He had the respect of the king, the court, and the people: Babylonian as well as Jew.

Mikael was impressed as he watched Daniel periodically stop to help someone or assist a child, ending the exchange with a treat from his cloak pocket. Seeing the child's eyes widen with delight was heartwarming. It was obvious Daniel cared about his people. He did not let his success let him forget those who had wound up less fortunate than he.

*****

No sooner had Daniel arrived at his work room when a man could be heard calling to him. His calls grew louder as he suddenly burst into the room, out of breath. "Belteshazzar! Belteshazzar!"

Daniel turned and placed his hand on the man's shoulder. "Almelon? What's wrong?"

The man bent over, putting his hands on his knees as he caught his breath. "Sorry." He held up one hand. "Just give me a minute." He gave a slight chuckle. "I need to remember I'm not as young as I used to be."

Daniel patted the man's shoulder. "You're not old, Almelon. Just a little . . . overweight."

"From too many sugared dates, most likely," said a voice from the corner of the room.

Almelon stood erect and adjusted his robe, which accentuated his portly frame, and pointed at the man who had just spoken.

"Well, Shadrach, if you would stop bringing them into the shop . . . "

Shadrach interrupted with a laugh. "You would just go buy some. You're addicted, Almelon."

Almelon grinned. "You may be right."

"And your message?" Daniel asked.

"Oh, yes. Yes. The message." His face and tone became serious. "A caravan just arrived. They say Nebuchadnezzar has besieged Jerusalem."

Shadrach came over from the table where he had been working. "Are you sure?"

The man nodded. "That's what they said. He has the city surrounded."

{ Mikael thought back to what Daniel had told Jehoiachin. It seemed he had worked out the arrangement with Parviz to bring Jehoiachin out of prison and into permanent house arrest at just the right time. }

Shadrach looked at Daniel, a worried look on his face. "What does that mean for our people?"

Daniel shook his head. "Yahweh is completing his justice. I fear for King Zedekiah. Nebuchadnezzar does not tolerate well those who withhold tribute money."

Almelon looked from one to the other. "I'm . . . I'm very sorry, Belteshazzar. I know you hoped your people would one day return."

"Oh, they will. One day."

Almelon's eyes widened. "How is that?"

Daniel put his hand to his chin and seemed to get lost in thought.

Shadrach put his hand on Daniel's shoulder. "Are you all right, my friend?"

"What? Oh, yes. Yes, I'm fine. Just thinking."

"Obviously," Almelon replied. "About what?"

Daniel went to the nearby wall and began pulling documents from various cubbyholes. "About what the prophetic scrolls say about the future of our people."

"Which is?" Almelon asked as he looked at the documents Daniel pulled and placed on the table behind him.

"I recall prophecies saying a king would sit on David's throne forever," Daniel said.

Shadrach had picked up one scroll to begin studying it. "But wasn't that conditional?" He let go of the document as each end rolled back to the center. "I mean, it seems the entire crown is now gone. How will it be forever?"

"I may have a partial answer."

A new voice had entered the room. The three of them turned to see who made the statement.

Daniel smiled. "Meshach! Once again arriving at the opportune time, I see."

Meshach laughed. "One of my many talents."

"Oh, I see humility evidently isn't one of them," Shadrach replied with a grin.

"I think you're mistaking that for confidence."

"Okay. Okay," Daniel said. "Can we get back on topic?" He glanced at each of them. "Everyone is so easily distracted today." His focus returned to Meshach. "So, what confident revelation do you have for us?"

"Well, somehow one of King Zedekiah's palace servants snuck into the caravan. He's heard of you, Daniel, and wanted you to know a prophecy Jeremiah was touting."

Daniel lowered the parchment he was holding. "Do tell."

"You were just quoting what the prophet Nathan told King David."

Daniel nodded.

"This servant said Jeremiah was saying something similar but said there would always be a king over Israel."

Daniel's eyes widened. "Are you sure? *Israel* and not Judah?"

Meshach tilted his head to one side with a slight shrug. "That's what he said. Curious, isn't it?"

Daniel rubbed his chin. "Yes. Definitely."

Almelon looked at each of them. "So what does it all mean?"

"Unsure," Daniel said as he tapped his chin with his forefinger. "David reigned from Judah, yet Jeremiah is saying someone would reign over Israel. Curious. The Israelites are now under Nebuchadnezzar's control." He shrugged. "As well as all Jews now, I guess." After several seconds in deep contemplation, Daniel came out of his thoughtful state and looked at Almelon. "Go find Abednego. We have some investigative work to do."

"Did I hear my name taken in vain?" Still another person had entered the busy room.

Daniel smiled. "Oh, quite the opposite, I assure you." He pointed to a small bag Abednego was holding. "What did you bring?"

Abednego held up the bag. "Oh, the caravan brought some fresh sugared dates. Expensive, but worth it."

Almelon's eyes widened. "Here, let me put those in a bowl for you."

"What did we just talk about, Almelon?" Shadrach asked with a chuckle while handing Almelon a bowl.

As Almelon poured the dates into the bowl, he replied, in a self-righteous tone, "You heard Belteshazzar just say we have to do investigative work."

"And what does one have to do with the other?" Shadrach asked as he crossed his arms over his chest as if challenging Almelon.

Almelon held up the bowl. "Brain food, of course."

All laughed.

Shadrach patted Almelon on his upper back. "Just remember that we all need some of that brain food. Don't want you to overstimulate your brain, you know."

Almelon looked at Shadrach with a hard stare and plopped a date in his mouth almost as an act of defiance. Shadrach laughed still harder.

Daniel held up his hands. "Okay, everyone. Gather around."

As they did, Daniel handed each of them a parchment. "Go through these meticulously and find whatever they say about the future of Israel or Judah. I feel we are to be part of something big."

"Like what?" Shadrach asked.

"Like preserving our people."

Everyone took a parchment, went to their normal work areas, and began to pour over the documents, scrutinizing each sentence and recording their insights.

*****

Mikael and Raphael walked around each man and looked at what they were writing. Mikael wasn't sure what they would uncover, but he couldn't wait to understand what Daniel was actually thinking. He knew, somehow, that Jehoiachin was undoubtedly part of all this. He was all but sure Daniel felt the same.

CHAPTER 17

Zedekiah Conquered

Several months passed, and it was clear everyone was avoiding what was really on their minds: the return of King Nebuchadnezzar. The fateful day did finally come.

A young lad entered. "Master!"

Daniel looked up from his work, startled. "Sumai! I told you that to be my apprentice you need to be here first thing in the morning. You . . . " His voice trailed off as he cocked his head listening to sounds from a loud commotion outside. "What's that?"

"Master, he's back! The king has returned!"

They all scurried out to the main thoroughfare entering the city to see the parade that Nebuchadnezzar was leading into Babylon. The street was already crowded with people. Most, seeing Daniel's fine clothes representing his status, yielded to him as he and his friends squeezed to the front of the crowd.

{ Mikael and Raphael stood with Daniel and his friends but knew they would not like what they were about to behold. }

Behind the soldiers on horseback came the Jewish royal family, now in chains, looking weary and worn from their long journey. Daniel was the first to gasp, but the others did so shortly afterward as each saw King Zedekiah. The man's eyes had been gouged out, and dark brown streaks had formed down his cheeks from the blood which had dried and not been wiped away. He looked like a freak someone would portray to scare little children. It was obvious this scene broke Daniel's heart.

Shadrach leaned over and spoke. "King Zedekiah's sons are not with him."

Daniel nodded. "I noticed. Likely killed . . . no doubt killed."

Shadrach shook his head. "Tragic on many levels."

Daniel turned. "I think I've seen enough."

The others followed him back to their workroom. Each went to their station without talking. It was obvious the only person really accomplishing anything was Sumai as he cleaned the floor and put documents into their proper cubbyholes.

After several minutes, Daniel stood. All eyes turned his way.

"I'm going to see Jehoiachin. Most Jews would not have seen what we did, but some did, and word will spread."

Each nodded, but all remained quiet except for Abednego. "Need some company?"

Daniel shook his head. "No. But thank you, Azariah." He gave a small smile. "I want to use this time to think as well."

Abednego nodded. "Thank you for using my Hebrew name. It's good to hear it occasionally."

"Yes," Daniel replied. "We need to not forget our roots. They are what bind us together." He looked at Almelon. "And our important work is what binds us together, my friend. Your devotion to us and to our cause is as binding as blood."

Almelon smiled and gave a nod but didn't say anything.

{ Mikael could tell this man respected and adored Daniel greatly. }

With those words, Daniel left his comrades and headed toward the city's Jewish Quarter.

{ Mikael and Raphael followed him as they had done before. }

Once he reached Jehoiachin's humble house, Daniel once again greeted the guard. "Peace be with you, Ramin. I trust all is well."

Ramin smiled at the man. "Indeed, my lord."

Daniel returned the smile, but as he started to enter, Ramin put his hand on Daniel's shoulder. Daniel's eyebrows turned up.

"I'm sorry about your city Jerusalem and your country-men. Truly, I am."

Daniel nodded, gave a weak smile, and entered.

Hadcast greeted him with a smile and a hug, and Jehoiachin motioned for him to sit. Shealtiel and Pedaiah looked at Daniel with anticipation, and he did not disappoint. The boys gladly took their treat and left the table so the adults could have their conversation.

"Daniel, you're going to spoil them," Jehoiachin said, though his tone lacked sincerity.

Daniel laughed. "Well, it's well deserved, at times."

"You came because of the news?" Hadcast asked as she served tea.

Daniel nodded. "Yes. And thank you." He looked at Jehoiachin. "I'm afraid your uncle has been brought in chains and is now blind."

Jehoiachin nodded while looking solemn. "That is what I heard. And that his sons were slain back in Jerusalem."

Daniel nodded and took a sip of tea. "I just wanted to check on you."

Jehoiachin gave a slight smile. "You mean, you wanted to know how I was going to react."

Daniel gave Jehoiachin a hard stare. "You must instill calmness in our people. I'm sure Nebuchadnezzar's mood is currently a foul one, and I don't want any of his attention drawn to our people here in Babylon. Let him focus on the new prisoners for now."

"Our people are upset—and rightly so," Jehoiachin said.

"Yes, Your Majesty. But you are now their king, and they need your leadership."

Jehoiachin returned Daniel's stare, then sighed. "Of course, you are correct. We are in no position to rebel. We would be squashed like bugs."

Daniel sighed as well. "Thank you for your wisdom in this. I'm not sure everyone will see this as rationally."

Jehoiachin nodded. "I will do what I can."

Daniel sat in a contemplative mood for several minutes as he sipped his tea.

"You seem preoccupied, Daniel. What is on your mind?"

Daniel came out of his trancelike state and looked at Jehoiachin. "Oh, sorry. Forgive me. A lot of things, I'm afraid. But I was thinking about what we just said."

Jehoiachin cocked his head. "And what was that?"

"You are the leader of our people here in captivity now."

"Well, technically, Zedekiah is still alive," Jehoiachin said.

"But without any further influence."

Jehoiachin nodded slowly. "True." He cocked his head. "What is it you want me to do?"

"Just stay levelheaded. We can't afford to have Nebuchadnezzar think of you as rebellious."

Jehoiachin leaned in. "Something is brewing in that mind of yours. What is it?"

"I think God still has a miracle planned for you, Jehoiachin. I'm not exactly sure what or when. But I need you to promise me you will not entice rebellion against Babylon. God put us here because of our sin. We need to be sure his timing is right for something else to happen. He brought us here. He will lead us home at the proper time." Daniel cocked his head, giving his hard stare again. "Promise me."

Jehoiachin laughed. "I promise." He shrugged. "What else can I do? I'm under guard all the time."

"You have wives."

Jehoiachin's eyes widened. "You think I'll lead a rebellion through my wives?" He laughed. "You either think me wiser than I am, or more stupid than I appear."

"I think you're quite shrewd, my king."

"Don't worry. I'll follow your lead. I can tell Yahweh is with you and leading you somewhere."

"Indeed," Daniel replied. "Somewhere. Just not sure where that is yet." After a few more seconds of silence, he added, "Elohim's timing is not our timing. It may take longer than we desire."

"Understood."

Daniel looked over at the boys playing on the floor. "It may be that Yahweh will wait until you have an heir sufficient to follow in your footsteps."

Jehoiachin looked over at the boys and then back to Daniel. "But an heir of what? I have nothing to give them but misery."

Daniel held up his index finger. "No. Don't forget the coming miracle. Remember, it happened for Joseph. It can happen for you."

Jehoiachin laughed. "Somehow, I don't see myself in the same league as Joseph."

"No," Daniel replied. "But you are in the right place, one where it will be obvious that it is Elohim who changes your circumstances—and your opportunities. But . . . "

Jehoiachin shook his head. "I knew you'd have a 'but' in there somewhere."

"Just remember, I feel strongly that your place is here and not back in Jerusalem. God has something for you here. Promise me you'll not try to regain the throne in Jerusalem. I fear that would be disastrous. Your allegiance will have to be to Babylon—at least for the near term."

"After all our city and people have been through, you want me to be supportive?"

Daniel shook his head. "Don't miss the bigger picture, my king. God has put us here. God is the one who will bring us out. We must embrace where God has placed us. That is how we protect our people. We protect our people under the umbrella of captivity."

"That is not logical."

Daniel nodded. "I agree. By human wisdom, that is not logical. But we now serve a higher power. We must accept the consequences we have brought upon ourselves and help our people do the same." He glanced at the boys again. "Elohim has a plan for our inheritors. We must help them be prepared for it—whatever it is, and whenever Yahweh has planned it."

Daniel rose. "I will stay in touch, my king. Just think on these things and seek Yahweh's will. As will I."

As Daniel stepped from the small house, he conversed with Ramin a bit more. "Just remember, Ramin. You are guarding this man: him from rebellion as well as others from him. His life is in your hands. Our king, Nebuchadnezzar, has at least come to respect Yahweh even if he doesn't necessarily honor him." He pointed to the doorway. "And this man is Yahweh's anointed. He must be protected."

Ramin nodded. "I understand, my lord. Your kindness has brought me here. I will protect both my king and yours."

Daniel nodded and headed back the way he came.

CHAPTER 18

Unexpected News

As Mikael watched Daniel and his friends at various times through the next several years, he had to be impressed. It took great fortitude to be a follower of Yahweh in such a Lucifer-influenced city. Nebuchadnezzar seemed to seek Daniel's counsel for everything, even over the advice of the other counselors. Jealousy seemed to be high against him, but with the king respecting Daniel so much, no one dared say anything against him. Yet Daniel offered only praise and respect for the other counselors when he spoke to the king. They owed Daniel a lot, and they knew that, but they still remained jealous of him. Also, Daniel was getting twice as many apprentice applications as any of the others, and that did not sit well with them.

*****

One spring day, as Daniel came into the workshop, he flagged Almelon over. "I have three more apprentices arriving tomorrow. Can you accommodate?"

Almelon put his hand on his head. "More?" He looked around and shook his head. "I don't know where to put them. You have already taken over two additional rooms." He looked back at Daniel. "Why do you need so many?"

"We are on the verge of something, Almelon. I just know it."

"I just wish I knew what that something was. Maybe I could then direct the apprentices better. You already have some searching your Scriptures, some historical astronomical reports, others tracking certain stars each night, and others scanning historical and legal documents." Almelon grimaced. "Others are talking and saying you're becoming obsessed, irrational."

"Well, they should be doing more to learn rather than relying on all their incantations and sorcery." Daniel shook his head. "I fear they use trickery and manipulation to guide the king rather than true logic and insight."

Almelon grinned and pointed at Daniel's chest with his index finger. "And that's why the king respects you more than he does them. You give him the truth no matter if it's hard to hear."

Daniel shrugged and gave a slight tilt of his head. "Well, he's appreciated that so far. Yet I feel he is growing unstable in his reactions."

Almelon's eyes widened. "Growing? He's always been that way. Remember when your God saved your friends from the furnace?"

Daniel nodded. "Yes, that was a turning point for him. He has accepted my advice better ever since then, and our people have benefitted."

"I'm amazed at how you defend him. Remember, he then rounded up all those Jews who did bow down to the image of himself, saying they should have been as resolute to their God as your friends had been. He then had them all slaughtered." Almelon shook his head. "Our king has been unstable for a long time."

Daniel sighed. "I know, Almelon. He's a friend and foe all wrapped into one."

"It is how Yahweh has worked through you that made me realize there is something to your God—and this has also brought me to you."

Daniel smiled. "And I am most grateful for that. Both that you are with me and that you now also serve Yahweh alongside me."

Sumai approached and handed Daniel a parchment. "Master, is this satisfactory?"

Daniel took the parchment and looked it over. He nodded and continued to nod as a smile came across his face. "This is remarkable, Sumai. No one else has recorded this trend in the stars." He looked up and smiled. "This likely means something. We just have to figure out what."

Sumai was no longer looking at him, so Daniel followed his gaze. A man had entered.

"Ramin!" Daniel exclaimed. He handed the parchment back to Sumai and walked over. "What brings you by?"

"I am sorry, lord Belteshazzar, but I bring you sad news. The eldest son of Jehoiachin has been killed in an accident."

Daniel's jaw dropped. "What?" He shook his head. "This is troubling news. I mean, he was only married a short time ago." He looked back at Ramin. "What happened?"

"As he was laying bricks, one of the scaffolds crumbled under their weight and an entire load fell on him." Ramin shook his head. "There was nothing anyone could do for him. He died instantly."

At that moment, a messenger arrived. "Lord Belteshazzar, the king desires to see you at once."

Daniel sighed. "Of course. Tell him I'm on my way."

The messenger nodded and dashed away.

Daniel focused on Ramin again. "Tell Jehoiachin I'll be by as soon as I can, and that I've been called to the king first. Express my condolences."

Ramin nodded and left. Daniel told Almelon he had been summoned by the king and left for the palace.

*****

Mikael and Raphael followed him. After hearing Daniel and Almelon's conversation, both were curious as to what Nebuchadnezzar was inquiring about.

Daniel seemed just as comfortable in the king's court as he was with the common people. He saw people as people and not as so many others did—those who considered others a different status based upon their wealth and influence. Daniel seemed to realize that some were more fortunate than others, but no one was more deserving of their fate than anyone else.

Mikael looked at how the throne room was decorated. By Earth's standards, it was very ornate, with the wall bricks painted a vibrant blue which made the area look almost festive. There were images of palm trees that went from floor to ceiling along with images of lions scattered in between all the way around the room. Nebuchadnezzar's throne was on a raised platform, and this made him nearly tower above everyone else present. Several of the other counselors were present and grouped together talking among themselves.

*****

Daniel looked at his comrades, then focused on the king and bowed in deference. "My king, you asked to see me?"

Nebuchadnezzar was leaning to one side as he sat on his throne, his head in his hand and his elbow propped on the arm of his golden, bejeweled throne. It was an impressive piece of furniture by anyone's standards; in fact, it was the only piece of furniture in the room, forcing everyone else to stand while in the king's presence.

"Yes, I have had a very disturbing dream."

Daniel gave another bow. "I am sorry to hear that, my lord. What do you wish of me?"

"I want to hear your interpretation. These others . . . " He swept his hand toward the other counselors in an almost a dismissive gesture. " . . . can't seem to come up with a consensus opinion."

Daniel gave a glance at them and turned back to the king. "That undoubtedly means, my lord, that the dream is rather complicated."

Nebuchadnezzar laughed. "Interesting that you still support them when they did not even include you in their earlier discussions."

"Just being respectful of my workload, I'm sure, my lord."

Nebuchadnezzar laughed harder. "Yes, I'm sure that was their intent." He looked at the other counselors, who bowed in deference. With a flick of his wrist, he announced, "Be gone! And be thankful this one"—he pointed to Daniel—"respects you even though you do not respect him."

The counselors looked at each other and whispered.

The king grew angry. "Be gone, I said!"

The men hurried from the room. Nebuchadnezzar rose and walked down the steps from his throne to stand next to Daniel.

"They are jealous of you, Belteshazzar."

Daniel again bowed. "Yes, my king. But they needn't be. I only do your bidding, as do they."

"You are a conundrum to me, Belteshazzar. They serve out of fear of me. You serve out of duty. They say they worship me but would just as soon see me dead. You do not worship me, but worship another. Yet I feel you would give your life for me, if needed."

"You are my king, my lord," Daniel said. "I wish for you to succeed. I desire even more for you to know Yahweh as I do."

"I respect him, but his demands are too great."

Daniel did not reply, but his disposition seemed to sadden. "What is it that is on the heart of my lord?"

Nebuchadnezzar paced as he talked. "I had a most disturbing dream. There was a tree, a most impressive tree: large, tall, and beautiful with succulent fruit which housed birds of the air and gave shade to all the animals. Then a messenger from heaven commanded the tree be cut down, stripped, and a bronze band placed around the trunk so it could not grow again. He declared this would be accomplished for seven years to prove that the Most High is the ultimate ruler over all." He shook his head as he raised his hands and let them fall to his side. "I have no idea what this means. But I must know."

Daniel said nothing, but his face became ashen.

Nebuchadnezzar took a step toward him. "Belteshazzar, I see your expression. I know your God has revealed the interpretation to you. Tell me. Whatever it is, I need to know."

Daniel slowly looked into the eyes of the king. "My king, I would give anything to not have to tell you this. I would rather have its meaning be for your enemies."

Nebuchadnezzar swallowed hard but nodded. "Tell me," he said in a low whisper.

Daniel's eyes glistened. "This tree you spoke of is you, my king. You have become strong and mighty, influencing the whole earth. Yet, the Most High has spoken against you. Yahweh has declared you will be driven from people and behave as a wild animal for seven years."

The king's eyes grew wide.

"Yet just as the stump remained, so will you be restored to your kingdom after this time—when you acknowledge that the Most High is truly ruler of all."

The king stared at Daniel. "Anything else?" he asked in a low whisper.

"May I give a word of advice?"

Nebuchadnezzar nodded.

"May I suggest that you confess your sins to Yahweh and be kind to those you now oppress? Maybe he will be merciful and allow your prosperity to continue."

The king did not respond, but turned, walked back to his throne, and sat.

"My king . . . "

Nebuchadnezzar held up his hand. "Thank you, Belteshazzar. And how would you suggest I prepare for this possible outcome?"

"Other than what I just said, I would suggest you prepare for who will make decisions in the interim. Preferably, those you trust."

Nebuchadnezzar nodded. "I see. That does make sense. Would you be willing to oversee this process?"

Daniel's eyes widened. "Me, my lord? But . . . "

The king held up his hand again. "Do you see any other being levelheaded enough, and unbiased enough, to oversee my kingdom?"

"Perhaps Nitocris, my king."

Nebuchadnezzar leaned forward. "My daughter? Explain. I grant you, she is a strong-willed individual. But she is, after all, a woman."

"Indeed, my lord. But she is a great strategist, a visionary, much like you, my king, and probably the least biased in your household toward power. She respects you and wants you to prosper."

The king sat in thought for several seconds. He slowly began to nod. "Yes, I can see your logic here, Belteshazzar." He looked at Daniel and smiled. "I can see your God has given you much wisdom. I put this matter in your hands."

Daniel bowed. "I will do as you ask, my lord." He paused, then continued. "Do you not want to be involved as well? After all . . . "

The king again held up his hand to cut Daniel off. "I will leave this to you so I can focus on more pressing matters."

Daniel had a stunned expression.

{ Mikael, watching, instantly understood. The king had already dismissed the seriousness of what Daniel had told him—giving this responsibility to Daniel seemed to release him of his personal responsibility. }

Daniel said no more, but simply bowed. "As you wish, my king."

Nebuchadnezzar motioned for a servant to enter. "Take Belteshazzar to visit with my daughter—in private." He looked at Daniel. "The fewer who know about this, the better."

Daniel again bowed and followed the servant from the throne room.

{ Mikael could see the disappointment on his face. }

CHAPTER 19

Curse Broken

"What was she like?" Abednego asked.

"Somebody has a crush," Meshach teased.

Daniel laughed. "Oh, she's like anyone else's daughter: concerned about her father."

Abednego pushed on Daniel's arm. "Oh, come on. You know what I mean."

Daniel chuckled. "Yes, I know what you mean. She's as you would expect. Beautiful, articulate, and kind—for a royal, anyway. She didn't act arrogant like many of her siblings." Daniel tilted his head back and forth slightly. "For the most part."

"What do you mean?" Abednego asked.

"Well, she considers servants, well, as servants. She doesn't tolerate noncompliance very well and was quite harsh to one of her servants who did something that displeased her." He cocked his head. "I still can't understand what made her so mad. Anyway, other than those few faults, I considered her very pleasant."

"Her skin always looks so soft," Abednego said in a dreamy state.

The others laughed. Meshach whacked Abednego's upper arm with the back of his hand. "Your chances are nonexistent, my friend. Best to get over it."

Abednego suddenly perked up. "Hey, next time, can I go with you?"

Daniel shook his head as he chuckled. "I don't think that is a good idea." He stood and put on his cloak.

"Aw," Abednego said. He sat up straighter. "Leaving again?"

"Yes. I need to visit Jehoiachin's family. I feel bad that I haven't yet made it there."

"He knows you're busy," Meshach said.

"But this is important. It's his son, after all." Daniel left and headed back to the Jewish quarter of the city.

{ Mikael, following him, heard Daniel talking to himself along the way. }

"I can't believe it's been so long since I visited them. . . . My, how time definitely gets away from one. . . . I hope they're ready to hear the news I need to tell them."

Ramin nodded as Daniel entered the house. He stopped as he entered. Hadcast and Shealtiel's widow sat in a corner, talking quietly. Jehoiachin and Pedaiah were at the table, looking lost.

Hadcast turned immediately upon Daniel's entrance, but Daniel held up his hand as if telling her not to bother.

"Jehoiachin. Pedaiah. Please forgive my tardiness."

Jehoiachin motioned for him to sit. "Please, my friend, sit with us."

Daniel sat next to Pedaiah. "Forgive my stating the obvious, Pedaiah, but you have grown into a fine young man."

Pedaiah smiled. "Thank you, sir."

Hadcast brought tea to the table and served each of them. "Daniel, you remember Assir?"

Daniel gave a warm smile. "Good to see you again, Assir. My deepest condolences. Shealtiel was a fine young man. His death will be a loss to us all."

Assir nodded but said nothing. Her eyes began to water, and she turned away and pretended to stir the fire.

The men sat in silence for several minutes. Finally, Daniel spoke. "So, Pedaiah, what are you doing?"

"Oh, the same as my brother. Building houses. Or whatever our foreman wants built."

Daniel nodded. "I see." He turned to Jehoiachin. "May I speak freely?" He waited for Jehoiachin to nod. "I know this time is not opportune, but there are several things I need to discuss with you." He looked at Pedaiah. "With both of you."

Jehoiachin nodded. "Say on."

"I need to talk to you about the curse and your successor."

Jehoiachin's eyes widened. "What about the curse?" He swept his arms wide. "Aren't I living it? Aren't we *all* living it?" He shook his head. "Sometimes, I feel Shealtiel is the lucky one."

"Father!" Pedaiah said. "You know that is not true."

"Do I?" He let out a breath. "I'm not so sure anymore."

Daniel reached out and put his hand on Jehoiachin's arm. "I believe your miracle is not that far away."

Jehoiachin squinted. "What makes you say that?"

"Shealtiel's death is tragic, and I'm not trying to make light of it in the slightest. He was a great young man. But his death, I think, ends the curse."

Jehoiachin sat up straighter. "What do you mean?"

"Well, think about it. You said Jeremiah stated you would be considered childless as no son of yours would sit on the throne of David or rule in Judah."

"Yes, that about sums it up," Jehoiachin replied in somewhat of a sarcastic tone.

"Sorry. I wasn't trying to chide, but to make a point."

"What point is that?" Pedaiah asked.

Daniel looked from Pedaiah to Jehoiachin. "Shealtiel was the firstborn, the heir to the throne. His death means the direct bloodline to the throne has ended."

Pedaiah glanced at his father. "Is that true, Abba?"

Jehoiachin nodded. "Well, technically, yes." He turned to Daniel. "But so what? I'm still paying the penalty for my sins." He threw his hands up and let them fall. "We all are. How does this change anything?"

"It's an inflection point, my king," Daniel said. "It's the start of a new path. Your heart has changed into one Yahweh can now use. You can now move beyond the curse. Raise an heir and wait for God's timing."

Jehoiachin let out a breath and shook his head. "How much longer, Daniel? It's already been almost twenty-five years. I've resigned myself that I'll die a prisoner."

"No!" Daniel said. "That is not God's plan!" He quickly decided to speak more softly, evidently realizing he had spoken more loudly than intended. "My apologies, my king. But I feel Yahweh's miracle is not far off."

Jehoiachin sighed. "If you say so, Daniel. My, you have a tenacity I have rarely seen, especially for someone out of their homeland." He readjusted and returned his look to Daniel. "Look, I know you are better off than me and my family. I accept that. After all, I created this. But I know you also would rather be back in Jerusalem. How can you be content in this land with its wicked customs? The other counselors who have your same position are wicked men. Even I can see that. Yet you seem content. How can you be?"

"Contentment does not come with money or status, my king, but in the knowledge that you are in the center of Yahweh's will. I don't know why I am where I am, but I seek his guidance and follow his lead. What more can I do?" He gently placed his hand on Jehoiachin's arm. "And that is what I wish for you, my king: contentment in spite of adversity."

"But what's the point? If I can't have my heir back in Jerusalem, what does it matter?"

"Do not despise the gift Yahweh has preserved in you."

Jehoiachin's expression saddened. "Forgive me. I had forgotten you had been assigned with the king's eunuchs."

Daniel shook his head. "God has still blessed me and given me other privileges. I have decided to serve him no matter my circumstances. I made sure you did not suffer the same fate."

Jehoiachin's jaw dropped slightly. "It was *you*?"

Daniel nodded. "You being placed under house arrest was the best way to take you away from the king's attention."

"I am grateful," Jehoiachin said with a whispered tone. "I'm sorry for what I said. What should I do?"

"I have been told of a prophecy Jeremiah told your uncle," Daniel said. "It changes everything."

Jehoiachin cocked his head. "What do you mean?"

"Jeremiah said King David will never fail to have a man sit on the throne of Israel."

Jehoiachin squinted. "You mean on the throne of Judah."

Daniel shook his head. "No, I think Jeremiah was specific in his statement. You are here, Jehoiachin, by God's design to rule over the Jews while in captivity until the Promised One will come." He shook his head. "I don't know how or when that day will come, but a miracle is coming. Of that I have no doubt."

Jehoiachin sat in silence for several seconds as if trying to let his words sink in. "Okay. But why can't Pedaiah be my heir?"

"Because there is a way Yahweh has provided for a legal heir that cannot be contested."

Jehoiachin stared at Daniel, giving a slight shake of his head.

"The Levirate vow," Pedaiah said, recognition coming to him.

Daniel nodded. "It is the way to have a legal heir through Shealtiel but not be a blood heir through Shealtiel."

"It will also protect Assir," Hadcast added.

"That is true," Daniel said. "Yahweh has considered both sides to provide the best for both parties." He looked at Pedaiah. "Are you willing to take your brother's widow as a wife?"

Pedaiah scanned each of their faces.

Jehoiachin put his hand on Pedaiah's arm. "I will not command it if it is not your wish."

"Well, it has crossed my mind. It is an honorable way to . . . honor my brother. Yet, I would want Assir to be in agreement."

Assir gave a weak smile and a nod. She blushed.

Pedaiah smiled. "All right, then. I'll do it. The firstborn will be attributed to Shealtiel." He looked at his father. "Your heir, Abba."

Jehoiachin nodded and smiled. "Very well, my son. You are a man now, so I respect your decision."

"Well," Hadcast said, "this calls for a celebration. Daniel, can you stay if I make some bread? And we have some goat cheese."

Daniel smiled. "It would be my honor."

*****

Mikael had to admire Daniel. Here he was going from the richest of the rich to the poorest of the poor and making every person he encountered feel honored and respected.

This prophet cared for both his people as well as the Babylonians. He was truly a man of inclusion, just like his Creator.

CHAPTER 20

Ziggurat Battle

On the way back from the Jewish quarter, Mikael had an uneasiness in his spirit. *Raphael needs help.* "Gabriel! Jahven!" Mikael said to his fellow angel-warriors. "Raphael needs you." With those words, all three teleported to Raphael's position.

Raphael was at the temple ziggurat where he was fighting at least a dozen demons. Mikael immediately drew his sword and unfurled his wings. He hoped that would elicit at least some intimidation. It did help; his actions allowed Raphael to incapacitate two of the demons he was fighting because they were distracted by Mikael's display.

Mikael flew in and relieved some of the numbers Raphael was fighting. Yet the number of demons they incapacitated seemed to be replaced, just as quickly, by the same number of new demons arriving to fight. The brawl seemed to be turning into an actual war.

Gabriel and Jahvan appeared and rushed into the fray. Jahvan was one of Mikael's largest angel-warriors, had great skill, and was able to incapacitate large numbers of the foe.

Mikael saw another group of demons flying at them from the ziggurat. He flew directly up, high into the sky, to distract them from the fight in which the others were engaged. As the arriving demons followed him, Mikael used his powerful wings to turn and hurl himself directly at the arriving demons. They were caught off guard as his massive wings turned him right, then left, then up and down, playing skillfully in three dimensions and keeping the demons from knowing how to prepare for their defense. In only a short time, Mikael had neutralized each of them. Their bodies fell to the ground in an incapacitated heap.

As Mikael headed back to the ground battle, he had to stop and admire Jahvan's technique. He was a master swordsman and could fight off twice as many foes as any of the other angels. One reason was because of his size, which allowed him to fight aggressively with a great deal of force, but the other was his technique. He was comfortable fighting with either hand as well as in all axes in the air. Because of the force of his attack, his opponents took longer to recover and try to return with counterattacks. Yet because his reflexes were so quick, he could deliver an incapacitating blow between the time he delivered his attack and his foe recovering. It was amazing to watch. Demon after demon fell like dominoes.

Mikael saw his friends had formed a triangle with their backs to each other so they could fight in each direction and not have to worry about their backsides. Yet he noticed some of the demons were trying to come at them from above. Therefore, Mikael stayed high and defended against any who attempted that tactic.

Eventually, they were fighting without new demons arriving. Apparently the other demons did not feel confident enough to attack. Most of those retreated into the ziggurat.

Others hovered near the ziggurat, watching, but did not advance.

Mikael incapacitated the last one fighting him. He turned to prepare for another, but none remained. He landed, and they each looked at each other with eyes wide. Mikael had his wings retract to their unfurled state, and this made him look as if he didn't even have wings.

He sheathed his sword and turned to Gabriel and Jahvan. "Thanks for coming on short notice." Both nodded. He looked at Raphael. "And what was that all about?"

Raphael shook his head. "Not really sure." He pointed at the demons all around him, still incapacitated. "I knew there would be many here at their temple, but I never thought they would attack like that." He shrugged. "I was just looking around and observing when, suddenly, one attacked, then two, then three. It all just escalated so quickly."

"It's obvious who's in control here," Gabriel said. "It seems they're very protective of how Lucifer is worshipped here."

"And they made it very clear they don't want us to interfere," Raphael added. "I wasn't trying to interfere, just understand. Apparently, even that is off limits."

"Well, I'm glad you're all right," Mikael said. "Since this is not our mission, I don't think we should head into further trouble if Yahweh hasn't asked us to do so."

Jahvan nodded. "It's not like he doesn't know about it." He shook his head. "Kind of sad, though. These poor people are duped into thinking they are worshipping gods—and it's only Lucifer."

"It's clear he's become a force to be reckoned with," Mikael said. "I think he feels like this is his headquarters, and he will not tolerate outsiders interfering."

Mikael looked at Gabriel. "Bring a legion and place them around the Jewish quarter. I don't want us unprepared not knowing what Lucifer has in mind."

Gabriel nodded and vanished. Jahvan followed him.

"So, what now?" Raphael asked.

"You go back and be with Daniel and his friends. I'm going to talk with Ruach and see if we can get any further insight."

Raphael nodded and vanished.

Mikael looked around. Other than the demons still incapacitated all around him, everything seemed quiet.

Still a bit saddened himself, he vanished as well.

CHAPTER 21

Conversation with Ruach

Mikael looked for Ruach everywhere within the angel dimension but could not find him. No angel he spoke with seemed to have seen him in quite some time. Determined to not give up, yet feeling a little frustrated, he went to the Eden dimension. After all, he thought to himself, doing so would provide an opportunity to rejuvenate by being in the presence of his Creator's wonderful creativity. He wondered if he would find anything new to experience this time.

As usual, Mikael headed toward his favorite spot at the boulder next to the stream. Rather than stopping, though, he remembered his trip with Yahweh through the time barrier to the Garden. He wondered if he could get there on his own. He realized it was a long shot but felt it couldn't hurt to try. He headed in that direction.

As he passed under a nearby tree, he saw the beautiful bird he had seen earlier, so he stopped and admired its color gradations: from red to orange to yellow, ending at its long-plumed tail. The creature let out its hauntingly beautiful trill. Mikael shook his head. The bird was truly magnificent.

"Hey there, Mister Bird."

The bird looked at him, cocking its head, as if trying to figure out who he was.

Mikael laughed. "We met each other a while ago. Don't you remember? Or was it a relative of yours I met that day? Anyway, I just wanted to tell you I love your singing."

The bird did its trill again and flew away. Mikael turned to watch the magnificent creature; it looked so regal gliding on the breeze with hardly any effort. He stood and watched until the bird was out of sight. As he turned to continue his journey, it was then that he saw it: a most unusual flower he had not seen before. Mikael smiled. This was what he had hoped to find on this trip. He walked over to a small grouping of flowers to investigate.

Mikael wasn't sure how long he stood there observing; watching the flowers sway in the delicate breeze proved mesmerizing. The petals looked almost like crystals, somewhat of a pastel pinkish-lavender in color. The magnificent color proved difficult to categorize as the petals seemed to morph in hue as the flowers appeared to bob with the breeze. He bent down to touch the flowers and inhaled with a slight gasp as the texture proved unexpected. The petals did not feel crystalline at all, but instead pliable and soft. He stood up and admired the cluster again. "How astonishingly beautiful," he said aloud. No one was near to hear him, but he felt as though he needed to tell this new creation how amazing it was to behold.

How a place could be so beautiful and peaceful, Mikael didn't know. All he knew was when he came here, he never really wanted to leave. He remembered Yahweh saying one day the righteous from Sheol would be brought here. Mikael smiled. *They are going to be in for such a treat.* He hoped he could be here when they arrive so he could see their faces.

Mikael couldn't help but chuckle. He knew the experience would leave them breathless.

Reluctantly, Mikael continued his journey, but he kept a lookout for other unexpected creations. Suddenly, the air around him felt thicker, slowing his pace. *Is this the barrier?* Yet his skin did not prickle as before. As he took more steps, it became more difficult to move forward, but he forced himself to do so. The air then seemed to become less dense and felt normal again. *Am I through? But why didn't my skin prickle?*

He looked ahead to see if he could view the Garden, but . . . *wait*, this was the way he had come! How was that possible? He had not turned around, but he could see his favorite boulder in the far distance. He had definitely been led in the opposite direction. He turned around to walk in the direction he desired, but he experienced the same phenomenon again: the air felt thick, it became hard to walk through, he pressed on, and . . . he was headed back in the opposite direction.

After the shock wore off, Mikael laughed. This was definitely an unexpected experience. Also, it was a clever deterrent to getting to the Garden uninvited. So, even if Ruach was in the Garden, he would not be able to find out. Apparently, he had to be with Yahweh to go through the time barrier to enter the Garden. Mikael cocked his head. That did make sense, or otherwise anyone would be able to go there. Yahweh did say the Garden was off limits until the proper time for it to be revealed.

As Mikael stood there pondering his next plan of action and contemplating whether to give up his quest to find Ruach for now, he saw a shimmering to his left.

"Ruach?"

The transparent figure turned his way. "Hello, Mikael. Looking for me?"

Mikael laughed. He didn't mean to, but the rhetorical nature of the question struck him as funny. "Yes, my Lord. I was."

"You have questions about your time on earth."

Mikael nodded. "Several, actually."

Mikael saw the outline of Ruach's arm extend in front of him. "Walk with me, and let's talk."

As they strolled back through the lushness and beauty, Mikael said, "Lucifer has such a strong sway over Babylon."

"Yes, that is true," Ruach said. "Yet, every kingdom has a capital."

"And his being there is okay with you?"

"Mikael, you were there when Adam gave the kingdom of the world over to him. Don't be surprised when he acts like it is his."

Ruach put his hand on Mikael's shoulder and, once again, this radiated warmth to his core. Mikael was always amazed how wonderful his touch felt. It made him want to stay by Ruach's side forever.

"Mikael, even in the darkest place, we can work—and succeed. Just look at how Daniel keeps everyone's hopes alive."

Mikael smiled. "Yes, he is a truly amazing human being. Without him, many would lose hope. You have made him very powerful."

Ruach shook his head—or it seemed that's what he did. "No. It is he who has opened his heart to us, which allows us to work *through* him. If only others would do the same. Then the dark would be dispelled even more. Only light can displace darkness."

"I see," Mikael said. "That is certainly true. It seems Daniel is on the verge of something, but I'm not sure what."

Ruach chuckled. Mikael wasn't sure why that surprised him, but it did. Yet it wasn't that he chuckled, but the tone of his chuckle—like the tone someone has when giving another person a present.

"Daniel will discover a Scripture mystery," Ruach said. "And it will set history down a course it is not yet on." He patted Mikael's shoulder. "And right in the midst of Lucifer's stronghold."

Mikael laughed. "You seem to enjoy the irony of that."

"Somewhat." Ruach's tone turned more serious. "Daniel is a key player to future prophecy and its fulfilment."

Mikael cocked his head. "Mind sharing a little more?"

"That's why I have you there, Mikael. I want you to discover the wonder of the prophecy that Daniel is, even now, figuring out."

Mikael nodded but couldn't help feeling a little disappointed at the same time. He had come here, hopefully, to get more clarity and insight. Yet it seemed he would only come away with more questions.

"This is an inflection point in the timeline, Mikael. I don't want you to miss it. What Daniel will discover will lead to a prophesied event and be something all mankind will look back on: some in worship, some in tradition, and some, even, in contempt. But for others, it will change their lives forever."

Mikael chuckled and shook his head. "Ruach, when I come to you for answers, you just provide me with more questions."

"That is the nature of learning, is it not?"

"I guess that is true."

"Truth *experienced* is truth learned. Truth *told* is often truth forgotten."

"Wise words," Mikael said.

"I thought so."

Mikael laughed. Ruach *was* truth, so his words definitely embodied truth. "So I guess I head back," Mikael said.

"Mikael, I appreciate your visit. I would love to hear your insights after you experience more."

With those words, Ruach disappeared.

Mikael thought about his conversation with Ruach. While he didn't necessarily get the answers he had hoped for, he was more reassured—as well as a little excited—to see what else he would discover.

With that thought, and that excitement, Mikael teleported back to Babylon.

CHAPTER 22

Nebuchadnezzar's Return

When Mikael walked into Daniel's workplace, Raphael turned, his eyes wide. "Well, you *do* exist!"

Mikael laughed. "What is that supposed to mean? I wasn't gone *that* long."

Raphael scrunched his brow. "That long? Mikael, about seven years have passed here."

Mikael's head jerked back. "What? How is that possible?"

Raphael gave a shrug. "Don't know, but that's the truth of the matter."

The only thing Mikael could think of was that he had tried to go through the time barrier back in Eden. Evidently it had an effect he wasn't aware of. "What have I missed?" he asked.

"Well, Nebuchadnezzar indeed did go insane, acting like a wild animal. Daniel has been working with Nitocris to keep it quiet, hiding him in one of the tiers of the hanging gardens. They've kept the kingdom running, making everyone think the king is away on royal business. Not an easy feat for sure. I hear some are beginning to question her tactics, but so far, she has been successful, with Daniel helping her deflect inquiries."

Mikael nodded. "And Lucifer?"

Raphael shook his head. "Quiet for the most part. We've seen demons here and there, but only observing for now. I think the legion Gabriel brought back with him has helped in that regard."

Mikael turned when he heard Sumai address Daniel.

*****

"Master, do you have to go back again? You're going to get caught in the middle of royal politics, which is dangerous."

Daniel patted Sumai's upper arm. "I'll be fine. Don't worry. I promised Nebuchadnezzar I would help Nitocris, and that is what I intend to do. Plus, it's almost over."

{ Mikael remembered Yahweh claimed the king would be afflicted for seven years, and that time had evidently nearly elapsed based on what Raphael said. }

A messenger entered the workplace. "Lord Belteshazzar?"

Daniel turned. "Yes. What is it?"

The messenger gave a slight bow. "Sir, the royal princess, Nitocris, requests your immediate audience."

"Tell her I'll be right there."

The messenger nodded and rushed out.

Daniel gave a slight smile. "Maybe today will be the last time I'm needed."

{ Mikael and Raphael followed him as he headed to the palace. }

As soon as Daniel reached the front steps, he was confronted by many of his rivals.

"You're visiting the royal family way more often that you used to. What's going on?" one of them asked.

"Yes. Why does the princess always ask for you, and none of us?" another shouted his way.

Daniel did not slow his gait but replied, "I am just doing the bidding of our princess. I can't speak for her actions or her intent."

All the counselors followed Daniel up the steps and continued to ask questions relentlessly, but Daniel said nothing more. They were detained by one of the royal guards who let only Daniel into the royal residence.

{Mikael and Raphael saw the other counselors huddle and discuss as they continued deeper into the palace to observe Daniel's meeting with Nitocris. }

A female servant met Daniel and led him to Nitocris's receiving room. The princess turned when the servant entered and bowed. "My lady, lord Belteshazzar, as you requested."

{ Mikael was impressed with the room; it was as opulent as the rest of the palace. Many fixtures were of gold, satin cushions provided accent to ornate sofas, and rugs with intricate, colorful designs tied all the colors and the flair of the room into a cohesive whole. }

The servant turned to leave, but Nitocris called to her. "Rubati, please stay. We will need your help."

The girl bowed and stepped to the side so Daniel and Nitocris could converse.

"Thank you, Belteshazzar, for coming so quickly. I think my father is coming out of his insanity."

Daniel glanced at the servant girl without responding.

Nitocris gestured to her. "Oh, it's perfectly fine to speak in front of Rubati. She has been helping me with father. In fact, he seems to respond better to her than, even, to me."

Daniel turned to the girl and smiled. "Well, you certainly are a brave young woman."

The girl beamed back at Daniel. Apparently, compliments were rare. "I treat him as just a giant cat. He seems to respond to that."

Daniel's eyebrows raised. "Well, brave and smart. Very impressive."

Rubati blushed slightly and took a step closer to Daniel. She was evidently warming up to him.

Nitocris gestured to Rubati again. "Go ahead. Tell Belteshazzar what you told me."

Daniel turned, giving her his full attention. This took the girl back for a second. Evidently, she was not used to being treated like a normal human being.

"Well," she started. "Normally, he will grunt when I give him food but will not let me groom him at all. Yet, just this morning, he looked at me when I fed him. His look was almost pleading, like he wanted me there. When I went closer, he did not move away. It was as though he wanted help."

Daniel turned to Nitocris with eyes wide. "This is definitely good news, my lady. We should go meet him."

"Do you really think he is coming back to us?" Nitocris asked, hope in her voice.

Daniel nodded. "I do, indeed." He glanced from Rubati to Nitocris. "I think it is a very good sign."

Nitocris smiled and looked at Rubati. "Very well. Rubati, lead the way."

Rubati went to the window, opened it, and climbed through.

Daniel chuckled. "Well, that was not what I thought you were going to do."

Rubati smiled at him. "This is the only way to the garden where the king is living without being seen. We are between the times of watering."

Daniel climbed through the window and helped Nitocris do the same. He gestured to Rubati. "Okay, my dear. Lead on."

Rubati went around several evergreens and passed a fountain filled with water.

Daniel stopped and turned to her. "Rubati, how do you get water this high in the palace?"

{ Mikael found himself wondering the same thing. From this vantage point, and this great height, he could see far into the city and almost make out the Jewish quarter. }

"Oh," Rubati said. "Many of the servant boys help turn a large wheel in the basement, and this brings water on a conveyer up to here. We then unload the rising buckets and fill the fountains."

"This allows the servants to water twice a day, and the servants below only have to pump water once a day," Nitocris added. "It was my father's idea. Brilliant, don't you think?"

Daniel nodded. "Brilliant indeed."

"But it was my mistress's idea to have the fountains here and the boys work only once a day."

Nitocris smiled at Rubati.

{ Mikael could tell there was a bond between them even if Nitocris would never admit it to anyone. }

Daniel looked at her and nodded. "Also a brilliant idea."

"Thank you, lord Belteshazzar," Rubati said. "I thought so."

This caused him to laugh, and she did as well.

Rubati held up her hand and slowed. "The king normally lies this time of day under that tree over there. The large lilac bush shields the sun this time of day."

Daniel nodded and walked behind Rubati with Nitocris behind him.

{ Mikael assumed they first wanted Nebuchadnezzar to see Rubati, with whom the king was more familiar. }

Daniel and Nitocris paused once they saw him. Rubati slowly approached the king, who was turned away from them.

His hair appeared thick, long, and matted. Extra hair looked to coat his entire nude body.

When Rubati got close, she called to him. "Your Majesty? Your Majesty, you have visitors."

Nebuchadnezzar stirred. Something like a low growl came from him. Rubati crept slowly closer and gently touched his shoulder. He turned with a jerk and immediately curled into a crouched position.

{ Mikael was extremely impressed with this servant girl. She did not run away. From what he could tell, the fingernails of this beast-man were several inches long. Thus, he could have killed her in one swift swipe. Yet she held her ground. }

Rubati continued to talk to him. The familiar sound of her voice apparently calmed him, and quickly. She went closer and patted his head. "That's it, Your Majesty. You have visitors." Rubati pointed to Daniel and Nitocris.

Daniel and Nitocris stepped forward slowly as Rubati continued to stroke the king's matted hair.

Daniel spoke first. "Your Highness. Do you remember me?"

"Father, it's me, Nitocris, your daughter. Do you recognize me?"

The king cocked his head one way and then another as if trying to understand what they were saying. The king's eyes slowly went from cold and uncaring to something like returning recognition.

Nebuchadnezzar slowly raised a shaking hand. "Help . . . help me." His voice was barely audible.

Nitocris looked from her father to Daniel. "Did he just ask for help?"

"I think so." Daniel looked at Rubati, and she nodded with a slight smile. Daniel took a few steps closer. "Your Highness, do you recognize us?"

Nebuchadnezzar nodded slowly as a few tears began to run down his cheeks, and he started to tremble.

Daniel took off his cloak, wrapped it around the king's body, took his arm, and helped him to his feet. The king took a few clumsy steps—then collapsed to the ground again.

"Is he all right?" Nitocris asked as she put her hand over her mouth, tears welling in her eyes.

{ Mikael bent down with Daniel, both to listen more closely, as Nebuchadnezzar seemed to be mumbling something. }

"Oh, Most High . . . I believe. Thank you. Thank you."

Nebuchadnezzar put his hand on Daniel's shoulder and Daniel helped him stand and walk.

Tears were now cascading down Nitocris's cheeks. "Father, welcome home."

A faint smile came across his face, and he gave her a nod.

Daniel helped Nebuchadnezzar through the window, back into Nitocris's receiving room, and into a chair.

Nitocris knelt next to him and held his hand.

"Take . . . take me . . . to my . . . room," Nebuchadnezzar said in a tired voice; it seemed he was struggling to remember the correct words to say.

"All right, Father. All right," Nitocris said as she patted his hand. She looked at Daniel. "We need to distract the guards so we can get him to his bedroom unnoticed."

Daniel's eyes raised. "Unnoticed?" He rubbed the back of his neck. "Is that even possible?"

"It is," Rubati said. "His chamber is at the end of the hallway just outside. The guards circle through the floor. We'll have ten minutes to get him there once the guard outside passes the large column on this side."

Daniel pointed to the door. "Tell us when to start, and we'll get him there as fast as possible."

Rubati nodded and went to the door, slowly opening it and peeking out. After a few minutes she looked back and said, in a loud whisper, "Now! You need to go now!"

Daniel wrapped the king's arm around his neck. Nitocris grabbed his other. They pulled the king forward, out the door, and down the hallway. Just then another guard appeared down the hallway across from them. Daniel shuffled the king behind the nearest column and out of sight. The eyes of both Daniel and Nitocris were wide as saucers.

"I thought you said we had ten minutes!" Daniel said in a panicked, whispered voice.

"That's what Rubati said," Nitocris replied. "They must have changed their routine." She let go of her father's arm. "Just . . . just stay here," she whispered. "Be ready to get to the door when I signal."

Nitocris walked casually but quickly down the hallway past the guard and then turned, calling to the man. "Guard! Have you seen anyone down this hallway?"

The man turned, wide-eyed.

{ Mikael chuckled. Nitocris had probably never spoken to this guard before—or any of the guards. Now, suddenly, she was conversing with him. }

The guard appeared almost infatuated with her voice and attention. "Uh, no, my lady." He bowed. "I have seen no one as yet."

Daniel, with the help of Rubati, got the king down the remaining short distance of the hallway, into the king's quarters, and into bed. The king was already nearly asleep.

Apparently, his body changing back to a fully human state was extremely draining on his energy.

"We did it!" Rubati exclaimed.

Daniel drew the covers over the king and turned back to her. "Perhaps you had better go and rescue your mistress."

Rubati's eyes widened. "Oh, yes. Of course."

Rubati went to the hallway and waved to Nitocris.

Nitocris nodded and turned her attention back to the guard. "Well, keep your eyes open!" she said to him. "I want everyone kept safe."

The guard nodded and continued his rounds. He had a sudden spring in his step he did not have before. Nitocris waited until he passed her father's room and then came back down the hallway and ducked inside.

"How is he?" She quickly walked to her father's bedside and found him sleeping. She turned to Rubati. "You think you can find two of the male servants who can keep things to themselves?"

She nodded. "I know a couple who owe me a favor or two."

"Very good. Sneak them up here to give Father a bath when he wakes up." She curled her nose. "And then change his bedclothes."

"Yes, Mistress. I can cut his hair if you wish."

"Oh, I definitely wish."

Nitocris turned to Daniel. "Lord Belteshazzar, you have been so helpful all of these years. And especially today."

"Well, I did promise your father I would assist."

"And I'm sure he will be appreciative and reward you handsomely."

Daniel shook his head. "That is unnecessary. It is not the reason I agreed."

"I know. I'm grateful all the same. Meet me back here in three days. That will give me time to get him presentable."

Daniel bowed. "Very good, my lady. I'll see you in three days. Until then."

Daniel bowed and left, but gave Rubati a wink just before he stepped out. She beamed again.

CHAPTER 23

Daniel's Advice

It amazed Mikael that Daniel treated these three days as any other day. He went through his same routine: praying in the morning, working throughout the morning, praying at midday, helping all his apprentices in the afternoon with whatever issues they encountered that morning, visiting various individuals—some wealthy, some poor, but treating each with the same degree of dedication and undivided attention—and then praying again at night before retiring for the evening. He was constantly looking over legal documents, historical parchments, astrological charts and, of course, Scripture scrolls. Mikael noticed that each night he prayed for his people, his Jewish king, his Babylonian king, and wisdom for how to be useful to his God.

Both Mikael and Raphael watched him climb into bed and drift off into a deep slumber quickly.

"He's like this daily, Mikael," Raphael said. "His dedication and drive never seem to diminish. Few are like this one."

Mikael nodded. "Yes, he seems driven to be used by Yahweh on many fronts."

*****

The next morning, as Daniel was in prayer, a commotion could be heard outside. He hurriedly finished dressing and went outside to find the source of all the activity.

"He's back! He's back!" he heard a number of people say as seemingly everyone was pushing to get a glimpse of someone coming down the thoroughfare.

Daniel pushed his way to the front for a better view. Some, upon seeing his status, gave Daniel deference, but not all. He happened to see Almelon and came up beside him.

"Almelon, what's this all about?"

Almelon shook his head. "I don't know, but apparently the king has returned from wherever he had gone."

{ Mikael saw the confused look on Daniel's face, for he knew the king had not gone anywhere. }

"Is that him in the chariot?" Daniel asked.

Almelon nodded. "I think so. Odd, though. He's usually up front on a horse."

"Indeed," Daniel replied. "I'll see you back at work after my visit to the palace."

Before Almelon could reply, he was pushed away with the crowd. Daniel hurried off to a side street where he could move about less encumbered. There was much buzz at the palace as everyone scurried around ensuring all was in meticulous order for the king. No one wanted him on their bad side.

There were many waiting to see the king. It seemed that, with his absence, not all had been given a chance to have their petitions heard. Daniel turned to one of his fellow counselors.

"Why are all these people here? I thought all of you were hearing the people's petitions and ensuring the king would not have to deal with all of this when he returned?"

"Oh, we did for a while," the man said. "But when the royal prince took over, he would not deal with us."

Daniel sighed. "But isn't that the very definition of counselor—to counsel him?"

"Don't get high and mighty with me," the man said with a tone of disdain. "After all, you're the one who had tea with the princess all the time. You should not have shirked your own responsibility. You decided to gain favoritism instead. I'm sure the king will be very happy when he hears how you and she spent your time."

Rubati approached Daniel. "Lord Belteshazzar, would you please follow me? The king wishes to speak to you."

Daniel gave her a warm smile. "Of course."

The other counselors began to follow them. Rubati turned. "Oh, I'm sorry. The king wishes to see only lord Belteshazzar."

*****

Mikael heard one of them say, as he turned to another, "Well, I hope this is about him getting the proper punishment for shirking his responsibilities while the king was away." }

Another laughed. "Yes, that was the princess's servant, so likely the king already knows about Belteshazzar and her spending so much time together. I'd love to be there to see Belteshazzar grovel."

Both men laughed.

Mikael and Raphael caught up with Rubati and Daniel.

*****

"Did you enjoy the commotion up the thoroughfare to the palace this morning?" Rubati asked, a twinkle in her eye.

Daniel smiled. "Enjoyed may not be the right word. But I assume this was the ruse so the king could appear in public again."

Rubati nodded. "It was actually the king's idea. Clever, no?"

"Oh, very much. It appeared everyone bought into it."

Rubati gave a final nod as she led Daniel into an ornate dining room where only the king and Nitocris were waiting; she then left. The king was once again adorned in his fine kingly attire, looking as regal as ever in tones of purple and crimson. Nitocris wore an elegant gown of burnt orange which contrasted well with her dark skin tone. The gown's sleeves had wide openings which formed what looked like wings when she held her arms upward.

Daniel approached and bowed. "My king. It is wonderful to see you have returned to us unharmed."

Nebuchadnezzar sat, then Nitocris, and then Daniel.

The king laughed. "Yes, nothing a good nap, a long soak, and a good manicure couldn't fix."

Daniel smiled as servants set a breakfast meal in front of each of them.

Nitocris leaned in. "Don't worry. I made sure everything for you is kosher. I know you have certain diet restrictions, and I wanted to express my thanks."

Daniel nodded. "That is very kind of you." He turned to Nebuchadnezzar. "So, Your Majesty, what can I do for you?"

"Oh, I think the question is the reverse," Nebuchadnezzar said as he cut into a large piece of meat.

Daniel held up his hand. "Oh, I desire nothing, my lord. Just seeing you here safe and well is enough."

Nebuchadnezzar laughed. He turned to Nitocris but pointed to Daniel with his knife. "If anyone else said those words, I would know they were just trying to get on my good side. Yet when Belteshazzar says them, I actually believe him."

Nitocris smiled broadly and looked at Daniel. "As do I."

"Well, it is true," Daniel said. "I do trust your experience has brought you new wisdom."

Nebuchadnezzar put his utensils down. "Definitely, a new respect for your God. I do concede he is greater than any god. Even greater than Marduk."

"Tell him about your letter, Father."

"Oh yes. I am drafting a letter to all my satraps over each of my provinces to tell them they should respect the god of the Jews."

Daniel smiled. "Good news indeed, Your Majesty. I'm glad to hear it, and I pray you allow him to guide you further."

Nebuchadnezzar took a few more bites of food, a couple of drinks, and then had a servant take his plate.

"Now, I must bring up how my kingdom was governed while I was . . . away."

Daniel nodded. "I did counsel your daughter here in how to choose wisely."

Nitocris sat up straighter. "Father, surely you are not displeased. We had someone with authority and experience rule for a year each so that the burden would not be too great." She gave a slight bow. "No one can rule with such wisdom as you, my king."

"But my receiving hall is filled beyond capacity. Why didn't the ones you chose see to all these needs? It will take months to straighten all of this out." Nebuchadnezzar frowned. "Most are usually petty things and not worth my time. I managed them so that they remained petty. Now, likely the petty things have escalated to far more major things."

Nitocris looked down. "I am sorry, Father. It started out well, and Belteshazzar's advice was very sound. Yet as time went on, the counselors he assigned backed off, and I didn't ask Belteshazzar to step in. I asked my brother instead."

Daniel shook his head. "Your Majesty, I am truly sorry. I should have paid more attention."

Nitocris shook her head. "No, this is not your fault."

"And why did Amel-Marduk, my son, not control this but allow it to escalate so far out of control?" Nebuchadnezzar shook his head. "He has to reap the consequences for this egregious neglect."

Nitocris threw a concerned look at Daniel as if pleading for help. She turned back to her father. "What does my lord consider an adequate consequence, as you put it?"

Nebuchadnezzar breathed out through his nose in a quick breath and shook his head. "Something that will teach him a lesson. I cannot have someone who will one day rule to be as irresponsible as this." After a few moments of silence, he looked up. "Prison." He nodded as if agreeing with his sudden decision. "Yes, that will definitely make him understand the seriousness of his offense against me."

Nitocris sucked in a gasp. "My lord, is the crime so great it warrants that severe a punishment?"

"It must be something that makes him learn. What else would do that? This he will not be able to control or manipulate." Nebuchadnezzar nodded as if assuring himself his actions were justified. "This . . . this is the course of action that I choose."

{ Still watching, Mikael knew Daniel would have to be careful in his response. Once the king made up his mind, it was next to treasonous to question his decree. Just appearing to be in opposition could place one in greater peril than the one being judged. }

Nitocris looked at Daniel with pleading eyes.

Daniel took a drink of water and cleared his throat. "My king, your advice and wisdom is always sound. Yet may I inquire if you could temper your displeasure with some of the experience you have also learned over these last several years?"

Nebuchadnezzar furrowed his brow. "What do you mean?"

"You are right, my king, to want your son to learn a good lesson," Daniel said. "Prison is definitely a place for reflection, but it can also be a ground for brooding and revenge sinking into one's heart. Why not also teach discipline at the same time?"

Nebuchadnezzar cocked his head. "I'm listening. What did you have in mind?"

Nitocris also tilted her head as if waiting for what Daniel was leading to.

"Many of those in the Jewish quarter have been assigned specific tasks for the betterment of your kingdom," Daniel began. "Why not have your son Amel-Marduk live with one of these families to learn how discipline and family are achieved together, not through commanding others alone, but through participation and compromise?"

Nebuchadnezzar seemed to think carefully on Daniel's words.

"He would be under house arrest with the others, so his freedom would be curtailed. Yet, I think there will be many benefits to him being there. It will keep him and his mind occupied with constructive things."

Nebuchadnezzar began to slowly nod. "You are wise, Belteshazzar. The more I think about your plan, the more I like it."

Nitocris also nodded. "Yes, it will make him a much better ruler in the end." She gave Daniel a look that said *thank you* without actually saying the words.

"I will have my son delivered to the keeper of the prison and you, Belteshazzar, can instruct him where to have him delivered and placed for house arrest."

Daniel nodded. "Yes, Your Majesty. I will see to it."

When Nebuchadnezzar stood, so did Daniel and Nitocris. "Now," he said. "I have to go attend to the mess that has been left me."

Both bowed as the king left the dining hall. Nitocris approached Daniel. "Lord Belteshazzar. Thank you again. I will not forget the assistance you have provided these last several years."

Daniel smiled. "I'm just glad all has worked out . . . " He tilted his head back and forth slightly. "At least for the most part. I know this has been a stressful time for you. I hope that stress will now be reduced."

She gave a slight chuckle. "Stress is a constant here, I'm afraid. But we have avoided a major crisis. My brother may not think so, but we definitely have."

Daniel bowed and she left. Rubati came and led Daniel out of the dining hall to the king's crowded receiving area. "Thank you again, lord Belteshazzar."

Daniel smiled. "Glad to be of service. If you ever need me, feel free to contact me."

She bowed, said "Thank you," then returned to the inner palace as Daniel left the palace itself.

*****

As Mikael and Raphael followed Daniel again, Raphael spoke up. "Why do you think he made that recommendation to the king?"

Mikael shook his head. "Unsure. But I'm confident we will find out soon."

CHAPTER 24

Daniel's Plan

Daniel wasted no time but headed directly to the Jewish quarter. When he reached the house of Jehoiachin, he stopped. "Where is Ramin?" he said out loud as he turned a three-sixty, looking confused. He knocked but received no answer.

When another man walked by, Daniel asked him, "Do you know where the family that lives here is now?"

The man shrugged. "Don't know. Likely working this time of day." The man walked on, shaking his head.

{ Mikael heard him mutter, "Rich people. Only they would think people would be home all day." }

Daniel retraced his steps and went to the nearest guard station. One of the guards, seeing him approach, slapped the other on his upper arm. The man turned and donned his helmet trying to look official. Daniel smiled at the men. "I'm looking for one of your fellow officers. His name is Ramin."

The officer looked in thought for a few seconds and then slowly shook his head. He looked at the other man, who responded, "Oh, isn't he permanently assigned to that family three blocks over?"

"Oh, right," the first officer said. "I think they're working on a project near the river." The man pointed. "Go down this road, turn left at the house with an outside corral, and you should then see them once you get close to the river."

Daniel thanked them and went in the direction specified. Once he reached the river area, he looked around. In a few moments, an officer rushed up to him. "Lord Belteshazzar! Is everything all right?"

Daniel gave a smile with a sigh. "Ramin! I'm glad I found you. Am I able to talk to Jehoiachin and his family?"

"Now?"

"Well, preferably. Is that not allowed?"

Ramin cocked his head. "Well, highly irregular. They have a quota to meet, and it must be met."

"Oh, of course. Sorry. I wasn't considering that."

"I'll tell you what." Ramin pointed at a nearby tree. "You go sit under that tree for a short while. They will be coming up for their noon break. I'll direct them over to you, and you can talk to them as they eat their midday meal."

Daniel nodded. "Thank you, Ramin. I appreciate it."

*****

As Daniel waited, Mikael and Raphael waited along with him.

"They work these people hard," Raphael said as he pointed. "Look, they have small children working as hard as the adults."

They observed several children filling brick molds with a type of mud mixture several of the adults had mixed. A small boy was struggling to carry the filled mold to the kiln. No one seemed to notice or care that the job was difficult for him except one of guards, who just yelled, "You better not drop that!" The boy's face became more determined, and he walked faster.

Mikael nodded. "Yes, this building will be beautiful once they complete it. Too bad these people will never be allowed access to enjoy it."

Several adults were on scaffolding applying a brilliant blue dye to the bricks. Others were painting some type of motif on one of the completed walls.

"Why do you think Daniel is so eager to speak to Jehoiachin?" Raphael asked Mikael.

Mikael shook his head. "Not sure. But apparently his conversation with Nebuchadnezzar gave him a plan."

"Really?" Raphael looked from Mikael to Daniel and back. "Like what?"

"Let's find out." He pointed. "Here comes Ramin with Jehoiachin's family."

✶✶✶✶✶

Jehoiachin was the first to speak. "Daniel? What are you doing here?"

"He's here to speak with all of you," Ramin said. "Now you only have half an hour before you must be back at your post. So eat as you talk. I can't show partiality." He looked around. "This is all irregular as it is." He put a clay jar in front of Daniel. "Here is an officer ration. Sorry, it's the best I can do."

"You really didn't need to do that, but it's appreciated," Daniel said. He motioned to the others. "Please, everyone, sit. We don't have much time."

They all took out their rations, which were more meager than those given to Daniel. He distributed most of his to the others.

Pedaiah laughed. "You can come around every day if you like."

Daniel chuckled. "Well, I can only help this time, I'm afraid." He turned to Jehoiachin. "I would like for you to do something. It will be a sacrifice, but I feel the deed will be worth it in the end."

Jehoiachin cocked his head. "What do you have in mind?"

"Well, I can't go into detail, but there is a man being put in prison. I want him to be placed under house arrest with your family."

Jehoiachin and Pediah looked at each other, obviously confused.

"We barely have enough rations for ourselves," Hadcast said. She put her hand on Assir's shoulder. "We also need to take care of Pedaiah's new wife."

Daniel smiled. "Oh, that's right. Congratulations, Pedaiah. Assir."

"Thank you," Pedaiah said. "But why is this so important?"

Daniel shook his head. "I wish I could tell you, but you need to trust me on this."

Jehoiachin chewed in quiet for some time. "You're asking a lot of us."

"I know," Daniel said. "I would love to tell you more, but I want both sides to know each other without the history of either getting in the way."

Jehoiachin gave a wide-eyed stare for a few seconds as if communicating Daniel was giving him a tall order.

"Please, my king. Trust me on this," Daniel said softly.

Pedaiah put his hand on his father's arm. "Abba, Daniel has always spoken truth to us. I feel we need to trust him now."

"Well . . . " Jehoiachin looked at the others. All nodded. He sighed. "All right, Daniel. We'll do it your way."

"Thank you, my king," Daniel said. "He should be coming around soon. I'll let Ramin know." Daniel looked back at Hadcast. "He will be assigned certain provisions, so he won't be a total resource burden."

She gave a weak smile and nodded.

One of the guards called for everyone to head back to work. All said their goodbyes and left Daniel to himself again.

Ramin came over and retrieved the clay jar. "I trust all was to your liking?"

Daniel nodded. "Your gesture was very appreciated."

Ramin turned to go, but Daniel called to him.

"Uh, Ramin." The guard turned.

"I'm having someone else transferred to your care. They'll be staying with Jehoiachin and his family. Can you handle that?"

Ramin nodded. "Yes, of course. But . . . why?"

"Well, I can't explain exactly. Not yet, anyway. But I must warn you, he may be difficult at first."

Ramin chuckled. "Oh, have no fear. I can handle difficult. Have no worry."

Daniel smiled. "Of that, Ramin, I have none. Come by the prison the end of the week and I'll have Parviz deliver the prisoner to you then."

Ramin gave a slight bow. "Very good, lord Belteshazzar. Now I must get back to my post."

As Ramin returned to his duties, Daniel headed back to the main city.

CHAPTER 25

Amel-Marduk's Choice

Before heading home, Daniel stopped by the royal prison.
{ Mikael realized this wasn't a prison for the common criminal, but one mainly for people in whom the king had found displeasure. Therefore, most here were not hardened criminals. Some were there only for a short time until the king's anger against that person subsided. Others, however, were held for a long time. Evidently, Mikael surmised, Daniel was going to be speaking to the head of the prison about Amel-Marduk. }

When Daniel arrived, he flagged down a guard.

The man walked over with raised eyebrows. "Yes?"

"Would you please retrieve Parviz, the head of the prison?"

"About?"

Daniel gave a forced smile. "Just say lord Belteshazzar is here to speak with him."

"He's very busy, you know."

"Oh, I'm sure he is, as I know you are as well. All of you perform a vital function for the king."

The guard's demeanor softened slightly. "Wait here."

Daniel nodded. "I will. Thank you."

In a short while, a stout, somewhat pudgy man appeared. A smile came across his face. "Lord Belteshazzar! What brings you by this ratty old place?"

"The king is sending you a new prisoner."

The man's grin faded, and he nodded. "Yes, Amel-Marduk was delivered just a short time ago." Parviz shook his head. "It's too bad. Maybe he won't have to stay too long." The man sucked in a breath and stood more erect. "We're here to serve the king, though."

Daniel nodded. "And you do it admirably, Parviz."

This drew a smile from the prison warden. "Is there a 'but' coming?"

Daniel chuckled. "No, absolutely not. Yet the king has agreed that his son be assigned to Ramin."

Parviz's eyes widened. "Ramin? You mean send him to the Jewish quarter?"

Daniel nodded. "Is that a problem?"

Parviz laughed. "Problem? Not for me. But the king's son will be livid knowing he'll have to live there. Ramin will have his hands full."

"Can I talk to him?"

Parviz cocked his head. "Sure, but he's pretty belligerent right now. I'm not sure if now is a good time for him to listen to anything."

"Please."

Parviz shrugged. "Certainly." He motioned for one of the guards to come over. "Go retrieve the new prisoner, the one just delivered."

The guard's eyes widened as he looked from Daniel to Parviz, but he did not question the order. He gave a slight bow. "Yes, sir. Right away."

Daniel watched the man walk away and turned to Parviz. "Keep him here until the end of the week. I have asked Ramin to come by then and retrieve him. Is that satisfactory?"

"This is no problem." Parviz chuckled. "One less worry off of me." He looked back and saw the guard approaching with his prisoner. Parviz looked back at Daniel. "Well, here he is. Good luck." With those words, Parviz went back inside the prison.

{ Mikael noticed that Amel-Marduk had chains around his wrists as well as his ankles. They were also linked together, and this allowed only a restricted range of motion. He could not lift his hands above his head, and there was just enough leeway in the chains for him to walk but not run. This prevented a prisoner from being able to raise their arms enough to get them around someone's neck or attempt to run away. }

"Lord Belteshazzar," Amel-Marduk said in a somewhat sarcastic tone as they approached. "Were you just in the neighborhood and decided to visit?"

"I'm truly sorry, my prince." Daniel motioned to some nearby boulders under a large palm. "Can we sit and talk?"

"Oh, by all means," Amel-Marduk said, his tone dripping with sarcasm. "My schedule seems to be totally free this afternoon."

Daniel looked at the guard, who gave a nod, so Daniel led Amel-Marduk to the boulders.

As he sat, Amel-Marduk replied, "Thanks, by the way. I do what you and my beloved sister say to do, and this is the reward I get."

"I am sorry, my prince, but are you sure you did what was requested?"

"I did what I thought was necessary. The kingdom didn't fall apart, did it?"

Daniel shook his head. "No, my prince. Yet it seems many administrative duties did go neglected."

"Well, that's all your fault, really. I tried to tell Father that, but he's so enamored with you that he wouldn't listen."

Daniel's eyebrows raised. "Oh, and how did I fail you?"

"Those idiot counselors of yours. They're incompetent."

"You should have come to me, then," Daniel said. "Or you could have appointed someone else to fulfill their obligations rather than just ignoring the duties that went unfulfilled."

Amel-Marduk still held his air of indignation. "I don't have to take up the slack for others any more than did my father." He leaned in toward Daniel, eyes narrowing. "If my father had replaced me with another, your head would be on a pole already."

Daniel shook his head and looked at Amel-Marduk with a saddened expression. "I am sorry that you are here, my prince. I cannot reverse the king's decision. But I have come to provide an alternative."

"What do you mean?" Amel-Marduk gave Daniel a distrusting look. "What's the catch?"

"No catch. I want you to be under house arrest—"

Amel-Marduk's laughter interrupted Daniel. "Yes, I'm sure me under house arrest would look good to all of Father's visitors."

"In the Jewish quarter."

Amel-Markuk's laughter immediately stopped. "What?" He sat up straighter, wrinkling his nose. "I'm not going there. That's like . . . like . . . being cast into a leper colony."

Daniel sighed. "It's not that bad. They're just poor. Besides, you'll be with a family, so you'll be able to have people to talk with, work with, and have some rapport." He grabbed the man's chains. "And be free of these."

"No!" Amel-Marduk said harshly. "I will not do your bidding to ease your conscience."

Daniel's eyes widened. He had not expected this reaction. "My prince—"

Amel-Marduk ignored him and cut him off. "Guard!"

Daniel let out a quick breath though his nose as the guard walked over hastily.

"Take me back. I'm done here."

"My prince," Daniel pleaded. "I don't think you're safe here. My plan is really a better option."

Amel-Marduk stood, shaking his head. "I will not be a part of whatever scheme you're cooking up." His face turned red. "You don't care about me. You only care about your own plan."

Daniel's voice softened. "Not true, my prince. Both are important. I do care."

Amel-Marduk gave Daniel a blank look and then said, "You do you, Belteshazzar." He pointed to his own chest. "And let me do me." Not waiting for a response, he turned to the guard. "Take me back."

The guard looked at Daniel, who gave another sigh and nodded. Placing his hand on Amel-Marduk's upper back, the guard pushed him toward the prison.

It looked as if Daniel wanted to do something but didn't know what. He called to Amel-Marduk: "I'll check in on you sometime later, then."

Without turning, Amel-Marduk called back, in a deadpan tone, "Oh, good. I can't wait."

With sadness on his face, Daniel stood for a short time and watched the two of them walk back to the prison. He turned and headed home.

*****

As they walked with Daniel, Raphael looked at Mikael. "What do you think he will do now?"

Mikael shrugged. "What *can* he do but give Amel-Marduk time to cool off and turn more reasonable?"

Raphael nodded and they walked with Daniel to his home, all three in silence.

*****

The next day, when Daniel arrived at his workplace, one of the prison guards was waiting.

Daniel stopped and looked at the man. "Are you looking for me?"

The man gave a slight bow. "Yes, my lord Belteshazzar. Warden Parviz wishes you to come to the prison."

Daniel's eyes widened. "Is something wrong?"

The man shook his head. "I do not know, my lord. I was only told to come and retrieve you."

Daniel nodded and gestured. "By all means. Lead the way."

*****

"Do you think something happened to Amel-Marduk?" Raphael asked, shooting a concerned look Mikael's way.

Mikael raised his eyebrows. "Well, it must be something important for Daniel to be summoned when he was going to go back to the prison in a day or so anyway."

Raphael rubbed his chin. "I wonder if Amel-Marduk has changed his mind already." He shrugged. "But what would make him change it so quickly?"

Mikael motioned with his head. "We'll see. The prison is just up ahead."

*****

Once they reached the prison outskirts, the guard turned to Daniel. "Wait here, my lord. I'll retrieve Warden Parviz."

Daniel nodded and sat on the boulder he had sat on the day before. In minutes, Parviz and the guard approached with Amel-Marduk still in chains.

Once they neared him, Daniel stood, shock on his face. "What on earth happened?"

Parviz laughed and patted Amel-Marduk on his back. "Oh, he just felt the love of the people for his father."

Amel-Marduk's face was slightly swollen on one side where a bruise had already formed on his upper cheek under his right eye. Several cuts were on the side of his face, shoulders, and arms.

Daniel's gaze turned to Amel-Marduk. "Are . . . are you all right?"

Amel-Marduk gave a slight nod. "It probably looks worse than it is."

Parviz laughed again. "Don't worry. The others look just as lovely." He turned somber. "I think he wants to reconsider your offer."

Daniel turned to Amel-Marduk. "Is that true?"

Amel-Marduk didn't look at Daniel but nodded.

Parviz gave Daniel a smile. "I'll leave you to it." He spoke to the guard. "Bring him back when lord Belteshazzar is done."

The guard nodded and Parviz left.

Amel-Marduk sat on the boulder with a sigh. "You win."

Daniel sat next him. "My prince. I'm not trying to win anything. I'm trying to find a better outcome for you without disobeying your father's decree. I think being with a Jewish family will be a better place for you than here."

Amel-Marduk let out a long sigh. "And for how long?"

"That, I'm afraid, I have no control over. Yet I can promise I'll inquire about you to your father periodically to see if, and when, his anger softens."

Amel-Marduk's shoulders dropped. "Well, my father can hold a grudge a long time."

"I'll tell you what," Daniel said. "You stay with this family for three months. If you are dissatisfied with being there, you can come back here."

"Oh, what wonderful options." Amel-Marduk's sarcastic tone had returned. He shook his head and sighed. "I didn't mean to say it that way." After a short pause, he gave a slight smile. "What about the option of a house at an oasis?"

Daniel smiled. "Sorry. I just work within the options I can control."

Amel-Marduk sighed again. "Okay. Fine. Either place is terrible. But at least there I'll be able to scratch my back when it itches."

Daniel gave a light chuckle. "Good. I think it a wise decision. There's just one more thing."

"Aha. A catch after all."

"No, no. Not really. It's only this: I don't want you to tell them who you are."

Amel-Marduk wrinkled his brow. "Why? Afraid they'll collude with me, or that they'll kill me because of who I am?"

"I just want you to connect based upon you both being people in a bad situation," Daniel said. "Two people who are trying to deal with it as best they can."

Amel-Marduk stared at Daniel for several seconds. He shrugged. "Sure. Why not? I reject my oasis and accept your stinky Jewish quarter."

Daniel smiled. "Good. And for the record, you will wind up stinking whether here or there."

Amel-Marduk stared at Daniel for a few seconds and then broke into laughter. "You have me there, lord Belteshazzar. You really do."

Daniel stood. "An officer by the name of Ramin will come for you by the end of the week." Daniel paused; one more thing had come to mind. "Oh, and your name."

Amel-Marduk's eyes widened. "I have to change my name?"

Daniel shook his head. "Not completely. Perhaps just go by Amel instead of your full name. 'Marduk,' in the Jewish quarter, will not go over too well."

"Amel," he said as if mulling the shortened version of his name in his mind. He gave a slight shrug. "I kind of like it." He nodded. "Amel it is."

Daniel smiled. "Good. I will be able to check in with you every now and then, hopefully. Goodbye for now, Amel."

Daniel motioned for the guard to head over. As he left, Daniel looked back once, as did Amel-Marduk. They gave a quick nod to one another.

Daniel left the prison compound and headed back to his workplace.

CHAPTER 26

The Integration of Amel

"Look at him, Mikael," Raphael said. "He just intertwined two people's fates a few days ago, and here he is working as usual—as if he has done nothing unusual."

Mikael nodded. "That just seems to be the man Daniel is. Whatever Yahweh wishes is his desire."

"It's just hard to get over the irony of a man like him being so successful in the seat of Lucifer's headquarters."

Mikael laughed. "I think this proves our Creator has a sense of humor for sure."

Raphael nodded with a grin. "That is certainly true. Why don't we go see what he has put in motion?"

Both angels disappeared . . . and reappeared at the prison where Amel-Marduk was being transferred into Ramin's care.

*****

"Here you go, Ramin," Parviz said. "You just made my life a lot easier."

"Well, good riddance to you too," Amel-Marduk said with clear indignation.

Parviz held up his hand. "No offense, my prince. But having a royal prisoner always leads to conflicts since your father has sent many people here over the years, and many are still here. The grudges only increase over time." He touched Amel-Marduk's cheek. "I think you can attest to that."

Amel-Marduk winced. Evidently, his bruise was still sore. "True," he said, then turned to Ramin, giving him a forced, exaggerated grin. "Great to be with you, Ramin."

Ramin rolled his eyes. "You just behave and don't get on my bad side." He nudged him toward the road and gave Parviz a type of salute. "Wish me luck."

Parviz laughed as he turned and headed back to his prison. He called over his shoulder. "Something tells me you'll need it." His laughter continued but got softer as the distance between them increased.

Amel-Marduk raised his hands. "And what of these chains? I thought I was supposed to lose them."

"You will once we get to the worksite," Ramin said.

He turned to Ramin. "I thought I was going to this family's house."

"The workday has started. I'll introduce you after."

{ Once they reached the riverbank, Mikael realized this was the same place Daniel had been a few days earlier to talk with Jehoiachin. }

Ramin undid Amel-Marduk's chains.

"Remember," Ramin said. "Lord Belteshazzar said you should only use the name Amel."

"I remember. My brain hasn't been compromised, you know."

Ramin's eyebrows raised. "Respect is a virtue needed here. These chains will be in reserve for use at any time."

Amel-Marduk gave another forced grin and a slight shake of his head.

"Parviz's words are wise, my prince. You should heed them. Most of the people here were also placed here by your father. The more incognito you can be, the better."

"Understood," he replied.

Ramin called to a prisoner. "You there with the paint jar!"

The young man turned, somewhat shocked, and hurried over.

"Name?"

"Gahal, sir."

"This is Amel. Show him how to paint the wall you're working on."

Gahal bowed. "Certainly, sir." He motioned for Amel-Marduk to follow him.

{ Mikael watched them both for a time. It seemed Amel-Marduk did his work half-heartedly even though Gahal chided him. Another officer walked up to both of them. Mikael went closer to hear the conversation. }

"Whose work is this?" the officer demanded.

Amel-Marduk displayed a wicked grin. "Mine. But I'm just doing what my teacher here told me to do."

Gahal's eyes widened, but he said nothing.

The guard's eyes narrowed with fury. "You take the king's wishes so lightly, you teach such disregard?"

Gahal shook his head vigorously. "No, my lord. Never."

The officer grabbed Gahal's arm and motioned for another guard to come over. Amel-Marduk continued to grin while watching all this.

"Tie him to that pole," the officer told the other. "I think we have a lesson to teach."

Amel-Marduk's expression suddenly turned serious. "Wait. What do you plan to do?"

"Pay close attention. This is what happens when you fail to take your work seriously, like this man."

"But—"

"Silence!" the guard commanded. "Another word and I'll let you join him."

"Twenty lashes," the guard said to the second one.

Gahal shot a look to Amel-Marduk, who looked away even though he knew he was the cause of this.

All turned when they heard Gahal scream in pain with each lash. Each lash made Amel-Marduk appear more uncomfortable.

The guard then dragged Gahal over to the tree where Daniel had sat the other day, leaving him there to recover. Everyone could hear Gahal whimpering. No one dared help him without being given permission.

The guard walked over to the scaffolding and pointed. "You there!" he called to another worker. "Come teach this idiot how to paint!"

*****

Mikael recognized the man pointed out by the guard as Pedaiah. Perhaps this would forge a bond between these two, Mikael thought. Yet seeing what happened with Gahal, that was not guaranteed. Amel-Marduk most definitely needed to change his attitude, or everyone here would be against him. Hopefully, he was smart enough to learn that lesson quickly.

It seemed Amel-Marduk listened more closely to what Pedaiah told him.

Mikael was somewhat surprised Amel-Marduk was able to pick up the technique rather quickly, but that only made his previous act that much more purposeful.

*****

Not long after, Pedaiah left him to his work and climbed back up the scaffolding to complete his work higher up the wall. When their work finally met, it truly looked like one person had done both. The work blended completely. The expression on Amel-Marduk's face was one of pride and accomplishment.

The guard called for the noon break. Pedaiah led Amel-Marduk over to the tree to meet his family. Assir had arrived first and was attending to Gahal's wounds.

Seeing Amel-Marduk, Gahal burst into angry words. "Get that man away from me! I don't want to even look at him."

"Gahal, I apologize to you," Amel-Marduk said. "I had no idea the guards would do that."

Gahal's mouth dropped open. "Oh, so you thought they'd come by and we'd all have a laugh together? Where did you come from, anyway?"

Pedaiah went over and tried to calm the wounded man. "He's new, Gahal. Just give him a chance. He's very sorry."

"Yeah. Well, I'm sorry too. Sorry I ever laid eyes on him."

Pedaiah positioned Gahal on the other side of the tree so he would be facing away from everyone, retrieved his rations, and gave them to Gahal. A few other men came and sat with Gahal.

Pedaiah went back to his family. "Abba, this is Amel."

"He came in with Ramin," Hadcast said.

Jehoiachin looked at her and then back to Amel-Marduk. "You know lord Belteshazzar?"

Amel-Marduk nodded. "He had me transferred here to live with a family."

Jehoiachin smiled. "That would be us."

Amel's eyes widened. "Really?" He looked at each of them and laughed. "That's . . . just a little weird."

Jehoiachin laughed with him. "You can call me Coniah." Everyone else looked at Jehoiachin but didn't say anything.

{ Mikael knew this was a name reserved for those close to him, and Jehoiachin had just met Amel-Marduk, a total stranger. Apparently he was following Daniel's lead in this regard as well. }

Jehoiachin then introduced his wife as well as Pedaiah's.

Jehoiachin opened his rations, as did the others. "You said your name is Amel?"

Amel-Marduk nodded. "Yes, this is my first day. I guess I . . . started off wrong."

Jehoiachin nodded. "One of the rules here is that we support each other. Otherwise, what you just saw happens way too often."

"Yes," Pedaiah said. "It happens often enough on its own. Some of these guards are extremely sensitive to anything you might say to them. Best to obey and keep your head down."

Amel-Marduk nodded. "Good advice."

"So why are you here?" Pedaiah asked. "You're clearly not Jewish."

"Oh, let's just say the king and I did not see eye to eye on something."

"Well, that explains why you're in prison," Pedaiah said. "But not why you're here in the Jewish quarter."

Amel-Marduk shrugged. "Well, it seems the prison is over-loaded, and this was a chance to not be in chains. Seemed like a good idea at the time." He looked back at them. "And why did you agree to accept me?"

Jehoiachin responded with his own shrug. "Belteshazzar asked, and we agreed." He grinned. "And we heard you came with good rations."

Amel-Marduk laughed. "Ah, I see. I came with an incentive."

"No," Pedaiah said. "You came on the request of Belteshazzar. That, Amel, carries more weight than anything else."

Amel-Marduk nodded slowly. "He does have a way about him, I grant you that."

"That he does, Amel. He rises above any of us. He is more Babylonian than even the prince, and more Jewish than the most respected prophet."

Amel-Marduk's eyes widened; he appeared to be in deeper thought. "You know, Pedaiah. You may be right."

CHAPTER 27

A Lesson for Amel-Marduk

The guard announced everyone should return to work.

Jehoiachin stood. "Come on, Amel. We'll make a good bricklayer and painter out of you yet."

Amel-Marduk laughed, "Well now, Coniah, that remains to be seen."

*****

Raphael looked at Mikael. "Well, it seems a good camaraderie has already developed."

Mikael nodded. "Seems to be." He laughed. "I guess Daniel knows what he's doing."

*****

Amel-Marduk helped Jehoiachin and Pedaiah disassemble the scaffolding and then reassemble it farther down the wall that had not yet been painted.

Jehoiachin handed Amel-Marduk a clay jar filled with paint. "Want to go up on the scaffolding and paint with Pedaiah?"

Amel-Marduk looked up and gave a hard swallow. "Uh, let me paint down here. That's what I did earlier." He gave a grin, although it looked forced. "Break me in slowly."

Jehoiachin slapped Amel-Marduk's upper arm. "All right, Amel. Since this is your first day, I'll go easy on you."

Amel-Marduk gave a playful salute and began his work.

*****

After an hour or so, Mikael heard a creaking sound. "Do you hear that, Raphael?"

Raphael nodded. "Yes. What is it?" Suddenly, he pointed. "Look, the sound is coming from the scaffolding. I think there are too many bricks stacked on top."

The sound from the scaffolding opposite where Jehoiachin and Pedaiah were working began to get louder. It wasn't that noticeable at first.

The reason became clear, though, as Mikael continued to watch.

He noticed Gahal kneeling next to a pile of bricks on top of the scaffolding and loosening the ropes securing them. He then proceeded to stack more bricks.

*****

The creaking noise began to get louder. More and more workers began looking around to determine where the noise was coming from.

A shout suddenly came from Pedaiah. "Watch out! Amel, look out!"

With Amel-Marduk working between the two scaffolds, he was in jeopardy of the bricks falling on him. Amel-Marduk stared at Pedaiah, not understanding what he was shouting about. Once he did, he looked up at the scaffolding holding the bricks, saw the boards begin to buckle—and yet seemed frozen in place.

Pedaiah continued to yell, but seeing no response from Amel-Marduk, he quickly grabbed a rag, tied it along the rope securing the poles of the scaffolding to the ground, and jumped. At the same time, the boards under the bricks gave way. Pedaiah used his legs to grab Amel-Marduk around his waist, gathered his momentum to propel him sideways, and then let go of the rag. Both rolled away from the middle of the two scaffolds as the bricks fell precisely where Amel-Marduk had been standing.

Workers nearby quickly came over to see if anyone was hurt. Jehoiachin, like a monkey, scurried down the scaffolding as quickly as possible to check on Pedaiah and Amel-Marduk.

{ Mikael knew Jehoiachin had lost one son in a similar manner and certainly wanted to ensure that had not happened again. }

When Jehoiachin arrived, others had already helped Pedaiah and Amel-Marduk to their feet.

"Are you hurt, Pedaiah?" Jehoiachin asked as he grabbed Pedaiah's shoulders and scanned him up and down for injuries.

Pedaiah smiled. "I'm fine. I'm fine. Really."

Jehoiachin then turned his attention to Amel-Marduk. "And you, Amel?"

He nodded. "I'm fine. Thanks to Pedaiah." He glanced back at the pile of bricks and shook his head. "What happened?"

"The boards under the bricks gave way," one of the nearby workers said. "Not a rare occurrence, unfortunately." The man glanced at Jehoiachin, then averted his gaze.

"All right. All right," one of the guards said as he came over. "Break it up. Anyone injured?"

Everyone shook their heads.

"All right, then. Everyone back to work." He pointed to a couple of workers. "Hey, you two. Pick up all the bricks." He pointed to those on the scaffolding. "Lay more boards. And don't stack so many bricks this time. As you can clearly see, that is not saving you any time. I still expect your quota to be met come quitting time. If not, you'll each experience my whip. Now get back to work!" He turned, looking at everyone. "All of you!"

Jehoiachin directed many in what to do. He turned to Pedaiah. "Go help Gahal with the bricklaying on the other scaffold. We can't have him face the whip twice in one day."

Pedaiah nodded, ran quickly, and climbed the scaffold.

Jehoiachin turned to Amel-Marduk. "Amel, you come help me in Pedaiah's place."

Amel-Marduk looked up the scaffold. "I, uh, well . . . maybe I should finish where I was."

Jehoiachin shook his head. "You'd just be in the way until all those bricks are removed. Come on. We have to get this wall completed before the day is over."

Seeing Amel-Marduk's hesitation, he cocked his head. "Are you afraid of heights?"

Amel-Marduk grimaced. "Maybe . . . a little."

Jehoiachin laughed. "Just climb, don't look down, and work like you're on the ground."

Amel-Marduk forced a smile with a slight nod and followed Jehoiachin.

No more incidents occurred the rest of the day. The guards seemed satisfied with the progress, so no further punishments were given.

As everyone headed home, Pedaiah pulled Jehoiachin aside and whispered something to him. After Jehoiachin responded, Pedaiah nodded and ran, seemingly looking for someone.

"Anything wrong?" Amel-Marduk asked.

Jehoiachin smiled. "I don't think so. We'll find out shortly."

As Jehoiachin provided no more explanation, Amel-Marduk shrugged and followed Jehoiachin back to the house.

When they arrived, Amel-Marduk stopped short as he stepped in. "Hey, what's going on?"

Inside were Pedaiah and Gahal.

Gahal pointed. "And what is he doing here?"

"He's staying with us," Jehoiachin said.

Gahal's eyes widened, and he turned to Pedaiah. "You didn't tell me that! Is this a setup of some kind?"

"I don't know, Gahal. Is it?" Jehoiachin asked.

Gahal scrunched his face. "*What* are you talking about?"

"You're an experienced worker, Gahal. One who knows when they've stacked too many bricks for the weight of the scaffolding to hold."

Amel-Marduk's eyes widened. "What?" He glared at Gahal. "You . . . you did that on purpose? You almost killed me!"

"Oh, and what were you trying to do to me?"

"I told you I was sorry," Amel-Marduk said. "I didn't know the guard would do that."

Gahal let out a *hmmph*. "And what did you think would happen? We'd all have a big laugh about it?"

Amel-Marduk gave a slight shrug as his head tilted back and forth. "Well, sort of."

Gahal balled his fist and took a step forward, but Pedaiah held him back.

Amel-Marduk held up his hands. "Look. I've never been in prison before. I didn't know the guards would react that way."

"Well, you do now!" Gahal shouted.

"Yes. And I promise I will never do that again."

Jehoiachin held up his hands. "All right! Let's all calm down."

Both Gahal and Amel-Marduk glared at each other, but seeing Jehoiachin's stare, both eventually nodded and assumed a more relaxed posture.

"Good," Jehoiachin said. "If we are going to survive here in prison, we must support each other. We're all brothers here."

Gahal gave a quick point. "He's *not* one of us."

Jehoiachin put his hand on Gahal's arm and forced it to lower. "If he's here, he's one of us. Understand?"

Gahal at first gave a distrustful stare at Jehoiachin, then recanted with a nod.

"Gahal, you have enacted your revenge, so it's over." He forced the man to look into his eyes. "Do you understand? It's *over.*"

Gahal glanced at Amel-Marduk, looked down, and then back at Jehoiachin. He nodded. "I understand."

"Some of our guards are just looking for ways to beat us," Jehoiachin said. "We are their entertainment. Let's not give them any."

Everyone nodded.

"Good. Now, can I count on both of you to respect each other?" Jehoiachin shook his head. "I don't expect you to necessarily *like* each other, but you must at least respect each other." He glanced back and forth between the two. "Got it?"

Both nodded.

"Good. Gahal, you may go."

Gahal nodded. As he walked by Amel-Marduk, he stopped and, after a brief pause, held out his hand. "Truce?"

Amel-Marduk looked at the man for several seconds, then shook his hand. "Truce."

Gahal gave a nod, glanced at Jehoiachin, and left.

Jehoiachin let out a long breath and then gave a quick smile. "Hopefully, that's all settled." He continued to look at Amel-Marduk.

Amel-Markuk held up his hands. "Settled. You have no more worries from me."

Jehoiachin smiled. "Good. Then let's eat."

They all settled around the small, low table as Hadcast and Assir served some type of porridge.

"Who are you, really, Coniah?" Amel-Marduk asked.

Jehoiachin paused his eating and looked at him. "What do you mean?"

"All the prisoners seem to obey you."

"Well, we're all Jewish. All practically related."

Amel-Marduk shook his head. "No, there's more to it than that. They not only obey you, they respect you. You have an air about you."

A smile came across Jehoiachin's face, and he leaned in. "Well, it has been a few days since I've had a proper bath."

Amel-Marduk stared for a few seconds as the words processed in his mind. He laughed. "Well, of *that* I can tell."

Jehoiachin laughed with him.

Amel-Marduk started eating again, as did everyone else. "I'll figure you out, Coniah. But I can see why Belteshazzar put me here."

"Oh really? Why is that?"

"I think he wanted me to see what respect really looks like."

Jehoiachin raised his cup of water. "Here's to lord Belteshazzar." After taking a gulp of water, he said, "And I can see why lord Belteshazzar put you with us."

Amel-Marduk's eyebrows went up. "Oh? And why is that?"

"So we can see how *not* to work."

Amel-Marduk looked stunned for a few seconds. Jehoiachin grinned, and everyone broke out in laughter.

CHAPTER 28

Spiritual Unrest

Quentillious arrived as Jehoiachin, his family, and Amel-Marduk were preparing for bed.

Mikael turned. "Quentillious! What brings you here?"

"Gabriel asks that you come join him."

"Is there a problem?"

"We think Lucifer's demons are planning something."

"Like what?" Mikael asked.

"I'm unsure. Gabriel can explain his suspicions."

Mikael looked at Raphael, who held up his hand.

"Go ahead, Mikael. I'll stay with these here."

"So will I," Quentillious said, then added, "just until you get back."

Mikael nodded and willed himself to where Gabriel was. He reappeared far above the Jewish quarter next to Gabriel. He saw his other angels lower than they were—in positions all around the Jewish quarter.

Gabriel smiled. "Good. You're here." He pointed toward the temple ziggurat. "There seems to be a lot more activity going on at the temple lately."

Mikael looked in the temple's direction. The demons did seem to be more active than he had previously observed. They were constantly entering and leaving the temple itself. "Seems like there is some type of ceremony going on," Mikael said.

Gabriel nodded. "I've noticed the priest of Marduk visiting Nebuchadnezzar quite frequently in the last few days."

Mikael's gaze shot to Gabriel. That was not good news. "His mental state is very suggestive right now," Mikael said. "While Yahweh got through to him, his mind needs time to recover."

"Well, he's always been a little unstable," Gabriel said. "This influence will only make him more so." He motioned with his head. "Let's see how close we can get to the palace to see what may be going on."

They flew over the palace and saw demons going between the palace and temple, entering and leaving a specific window.

Mikael turned to Gabriel. "That's Nebuchadnezzar's bed-chamber. They must be influencing his dreams."

"Well, that can't be good. I wonder what Lucifer is up to."

"I don't know," Mikael said. "But two can play his game."

Gabriel cocked his head. "What are you thinking?"

"You go to Daniel's house and link his dream to that of Nebuchadnezzar's. I don't think Lucifer will expect that."

Gabriel smiled. "Very clever. But won't Lucifer find out?"

"These things only come about through a human conduit. My guess is the priest of Marduk is facilitating this through his worship of Lucifer."

Gabriel nodded. "Yes, but how do you plan to ensure he doesn't know of the link I'll make with Daniel?"

"I'm going to enter the temple. The priest will sense my presence, and that will break his concentration. Lucifer will think my presence is the issue and not that you are linking Daniel's dream to that of Nebuchadnezzar's."

Gabriel's eyes widened. "That's pretty risky, Mikael. Remember the instance when all the demons attacked Raphael? What if they attack you?"

Mikael cocked his head and gave a slight shrug. "I'll have to take that chance. My hope is that I'll have a heated debate with Lucifer rather than a fight. I won't have to stay—just be there long enough to distract from the link you'll make with Daniel."

Gabriel nodded his understanding but looked wary. "I'll have our angels on alert, just in case."

"Good. Once I see you enter Daniel's bedchamber, I'll teleport inside the temple."

Gabriel disappeared. In a matter of minutes, Mikael saw the angels below refocus their attention toward the temple. They didn't move closer but arranged themselves in more of an active line of defense.

Once he saw Gabriel teleport, Mikael did the same.

The inside of the temple looked far more beautiful than he had imagined. Several torches placed around the room provided adequate but subdued lighting. The walls were of the same brilliant blue color as many of the walls around Babylon. There were many columns with their capitals of gold and, again, reliefs of palm trees and lions. The priest stood before an altar, also made of gold, or possibly gold overlay. Some type of small animal had been flayed, halved, and was now burning atop a smoldering fire. It smelled as if incense had been mingled in as well.

The priest looked to be in a trance of some kind and was mumbling. Mikael did not have time to hear the words; his presence immediately made the priest go silent as his body stiffened. "Who's there?" he whispered, his voice nearly in a panic.

Several of the demons turned and glared at Mikael. His body also stiffened, and he prepared himself, ready to draw his sword if necessary.

Lucifer, standing behind the priest, also turned. His eyebrows raised. "Well, aren't we audacious?" He laughed. "Very brazen to go into the lion's den, so to speak."

"Yes," Mikael said. "But necessary to see what you're up to."

"Oh, I don't think that is any concern of yours," Lucifer said, his words dripping in an anger that seemed laced with mocking tones.

Mikael chuckled under his breath. "Lucifer, everything you do is a concern of mine."

"Well, aren't I special?" Lucifer said, now with total sarcasm. "Very clever for Daniel to get Nebuchadnezzar to alter his plans. So other measures have to be put in place."

"Like what?"

"None of your concern," Lucifer said as he turned back to the priest, who was now visibly shaking, apparently able to sense the spiritual conflict occurring in his presence.

The priest began to mumble his chant once more. Lucifer's attention turned back to Mikael.

"I suggest you leave. You're quite the swordsman, Mikael, I give you that. But I don't think you can hold off a whole legion of my angels by yourself. And if you want a full-fledged war, I'll give it to you."

Mikael hoped this had been enough time for Gabriel to accomplish his task. "Now who's being so sensitive?" Mikael chided.

Lucifer's eyes glared hatred.

"I'll leave—for now," Mikael said. "But be warned. You are being watched. You will not succeed."

Lucifer took a step closer. "Oh, I'm very patient. My time will come. Trust me, Mikael. My time will come."

Mikael forced a smile. "But not this time."

He disappeared as he saw Lucifer's eyes narrow with still more hatred.

Mikael reappeared in his original spot. Gabriel was already there.

"Did it work?" Mikael asked.

Gabriel nodded. "I'm pretty sure it did. Poor Daniel. He seemed to be in a very restful sleep when I arrived. Not so much when I left." He raised his eyebrows. "And on your end?"

"I think I was distracting enough. I think Lucifer also was not very restful by the time I left."

Gabriel laughed. "Sounds like you were definitely successful." He turned serious. "You know, this will just make him all the more determined."

Mikael nodded. "Likely. But we do what Ruach and Yahweh have declared for us to do. Daniel's efforts must prove successful."

"Too bad we don't know what Daniel is dreaming," Gabriel said.

Mikael cocked his head. "We'll likely find out come morning."

CHAPTER 29

Confronting Nebuchadnezzar

Daniel seemed to go about his day as usual. While he did seem more pensive, he did not convey concern about his dream the previous night. Mikael wondered if the dream did not stick in his mind for him to remember, if it simply did not concern him, or if he was mulling it all over in his mind.

Yet Mikael was concerned, for he knew Lucifer could prove unpredictable. Therefore, he had Quentillious stay with Jehoiachin and his family when he or Raphael were not with them.

*****

About midmorning another messenger came for Daniel requesting him to come to the palace. Daniel had the messenger return with his reply to Princess Nitocris that he would come immediately.

"What now?" Meshach asked.

As Daniel prepared to leave, he said, "I had a disturbing dream last night. I fear this visit will be about that."

Everyone in hearing distance looked at each other in bewilderment.

"What did you dream, Daniel?" Shadrach asked, leaning forward waiting for a response.

Daniel waved his hand. "It's a long story. I'll tell you when I return."

Shadrach sighed. "You know, you shouldn't set someone up and then let them down like that."

Daniel turned; he clearly had other things on his mind. "What? . . . Oh, yes. Sorry. I'll certainly fill you in when I return."

Shadrach looked at the others and shook his head. Most returned to their duties.

Upon his arrival at the palace, Rubati met Daniel and led him to Nitocris's receiving room.

"What's going on?" Daniel asked in a whisper.

Rubati shook her head. "I'll let the princess fill you in. She's very concerned about her father."

Daniel bowed when they entered the room. Nitocris sat looking at a large parchment of some kind. As she stood, the sun through the window made her royal blue gown almost glow, and its rays did make her diamond and ruby earrings and necklace sparkle.

{ Mikael noticed the parchment to be some type of architectural plans. }

Daniel smiled when he saw them. "My lady, you certainly have your father's engineering mind."

Nitocris smiled. "That's kind of you to say. I was just trying to keep my mind occupied until you arrived. I've been so concerned about Father."

Daniel cocked his head. "I thought he was recovering quite nicely."

Nitocris nodded. "As did I. He seemed to be." She began to pace and wring her hands together. "But yesterday, and especially today, he has acted so irrationally. He's already thrown several people out of his throne room this morning. He's in a very ill mood." She turned, her eyes moist. "He almost had the cook thrown in prison at breakfast this morning because he thought the eggs were too runny." She shook her head. "I just don't know what to do." She looked at Daniel. "I was hoping you could talk to him."

Daniel gave a slight shrug. "I can try."

Relief seemed to flood through her. "Thank you, lord Belteshazzar. If anyone can reach him, I know it will be you."

"Well, let's pray to that end."

She smiled and headed for the doorway. "Follow me."

When they arrived at the throne room, Nitocris spoke to one of the guards, who retrieved one of the king's servants. Before she had a chance to tell of their desire for an audience with the king, however, Nebuchadnezzar spoke.

"What's going on over there. Why all the whispering?"

Nitocris swallowed hard but quickly donned a bright smile. "My king, someone is here who wishes to talk with you."

Nebuchadnezzar cocked his head and motioned for her to approach. "Who do you have, my daughter, that comes at this hour to talk?"

"It is lord Belteshazzar, my lord."

"Lord Belteshazzar?" Nebuchadnezzar said as if he had not heard that name in a very long time. "He's here?"

Nitocris nodded. "Yes, my king." She gestured to where Daniel stood next to the guard she had just spoken to.

The king suddenly clapped his hands. "Everyone! Out!"

Everyone in the room stiffened as if in shock at this sudden change of events, but they began to shuffle out of the room. Nebuchadnezzar motioned for Daniel to approach. Nitocris gave Daniel a smile as she left the room as well.

"Ghalib, get this man a chair."

Daniel held up his hand. "No need, my king. I can stand in your presence."

The king gave a dismissive wave. "Nonsense. You will sit."

Daniel bowed. "As my king wishes."

Ghalib brought a chair, faced it toward the king, and then left with a bow to the king.

"And what brings you to me this morning?" Nebuchadnezzar asked.

"You, my king. You are disturbed. I only wish to lighten your load."

Nebuchadnezzar sat quiet for several seconds. He smiled. "That is what always amazes me about you, Belteshazzar." He threw his hand wide. "I have dozens of so-called wise men who use divination, sorcery, and even pray to Marduk to give them answers to my inquiries, and not one of them knew I was disturbed in spirit today." He chuckled as he tilted his head back and forth slightly. "Likely knew I was irritated, though."

Daniel smiled. "No, my king, I don't think that was a secret today."

Nebuchadnezzar laughed, then turned serious. "But you, Belteshazzar, not even being here until now, knew of my troubled spirit. Did your God tell you this?"

Daniel nodded. "Yes, my king. He can be your God as well, you know."

"I do respect him."

"Yes, my king. That I know, and I am grateful. He can be more for you, though."

"And what did he tell you?"

{ Mikael sighed. The conversation had gone so well up to this point, but the king deflected—again. }

"You are still upset with your son. You don't believe you can trust him and even have thoughts about doing away with him or leaving him in prison the rest of his life."

The king nodded. "Remarkable. I have told no one this."

"Yahweh knows all, my king. Even your very thoughts." Daniel shifted in his seat. "My king, do you really harbor such ill for him? I do feel he will benefit from the arrangement for his shorter-term sentence."

Nebuchadnezzar stiffened. "You doubt my reasoning?"

Daniel's voice became low. "My king, I believe there is a struggle between Marduk and Yahweh in your heart. Only one can win. And the victor is your decision."

Nebuchadnezzar looked away in thought, chin in palm with elbow propped on the arm of his throne chair. He turned back to Daniel. "Maybe you are correct. Yet I have a kingdom to consider. What Amel-Marduk has done is almost unforgiveable."

"Perhaps your perception of his actions are not that different from Yahweh's perception of your own actions."

The king furrowed his brow. "Explain."

"What did Yahweh think of your actions?"

Nebuchadnezzar blew a quick breath through his nose. "He made me go insane for seven years. I'd say he wasn't too happy with me."

Daniel gestured toward him. "And what is your status now?"

The king raised his arms. "Well, I'm back on my throne."

"So, in some ways he has forgiven you."

Nebuchadnezzar nodded. "I guess you could say that."

"And your son displeased you. You have punished him—in a way less harsh than yours, I grant you—but still, seemingly very hard on him."

Nebuchadnezzar continued to nod.

"Now, the question is whether you will forgive him as Yahweh has seemingly forgiven you."

Nebuchadnezzar gave a brief smile. "You seem to like analogies."

Daniel smiled back. "Those are sometimes the easiest to understand, my king."

After thinking for several seconds, the king sat back. "So, if we are going to stick with the analogy, I should keep him in prison for seven years."

"If that is what my king feels is right."

Nebuchadnezzar nodded. "I do. That is what I feel should be done."

"Would my king be willing to put that in writing to the head of the royal prison?"

"Why?"

"As you have seen, my king. Life is uncertain and takes unusual turns. In case some at a later date would want to go against your wishes for whatever purpose, this would ensure those wishes would be carried out just as you have decreed."

The king looked at Daniel for several seconds without saying anything.

{ Watching, Mikael was impressed that Daniel appeared calm even though he was likely unsure what Nebuchadnezzar was thinking. The king had acted so irrationally that morning; he could do almost anything. Yet it seemed Nebuchadnezzar was always much calmer in Daniel's presence than when Daniel was not around. }

"Ghalib!" the king suddenly shouted.

The servant rushed in and bowed. "Yes, Your Highness?"

"Bring a scribe immediately."

Ghalib looked from the king to Daniel and back, his eyebrows raising. He did not question. He bowed again and rushed from the room.

Daniel gave the king a nod. "Thank you, my king. You are most gracious."

Nebuchadnezzar laughed lightly. "I'm not sure why, but you seem to bring out the best in me when others only bring out the worst."

"Yahweh always brings clarity, my king."

Ghalib reentered, nearly dragging a man by the arm who, in turn, dragged a portable desk with his free arm. "Here he is, my king."

The scribe bowed. "You wish to declare, my king?"

Nebuchadnezzar looked at Daniel. "Yes." He looked at the scribe. "Write this, record it in the archives, and deliver a copy to Parviz, head of the royal prison."

The scribe nodded. "Yes, my king."

"Amel-Marduk will be under the care of the head of the royal prison for a total of seven years. At that time, he will be released and regain his full royal status and all of its benefits."

The scribe wrote quickly. "Yes, my king. Anything else?"

The king looked at Daniel with a slight grin. "Yes. He is to be told that when counsel is needed, he should receive it from lord Belteshazzar even if other counsel is also sought."

The scribe looked at Daniel, then refocused on his parchment. He took a candle and heated the royal wax, then presented the document to the king. Nebuchadnezzar impressed his signet ring into the soft wax.

The scribe bowed. "Very good, my king. The decree is now official."

Daniel stood and bowed. "My king, I am honored you think of me in this way."

"You have quelled the restlessness of my spirit, Belteshazzar. No other counselor of mine has ever done that. Go in peace."

Daniel bowed. "As well as you, my king."

Daniel left the room.

*****

Mikael was quite pleased with this outcome. He wasn't sure why Daniel was so ready to agree to Amel-Marduk being in prison for seven years, but perhaps he considered a definite time, no matter the length, a better outcome than what he had observed in his dream.

CHAPTER 30

Planning for the future

Time marched on, as it always does. Mikael and Raphael kept informed but did not spend as much direct time in Babylon as they had to this point. They assigned Quentillious that task and directed him to call them immediately if anything important developed. He kept them abreast as Daniel continued with his normal routines: directing the work of his office, counseling his apprentices in the areas of their studies, countering many of the harmful insights the other counselors attempted to give the king, meeting with the king periodically and with Nitocris occasionally, and meeting with Jehoiachin and Amel-Marduk.

As Mikael returned from battle practice one afternoon, he saw Quentillious approach.

"Quentillious! How is everything?"

"Everything is fine. Most things are pretty routine, even mundane."

Mikael cocked his head. "So what brings you here?" He chuckled. "Need some time off?"

Quentillious shook his head as he also laughed. "No, I just wanted to let you know that Daniel is having an important meeting with all his apprentices. I think he may lay out the plans he has been having all of them work on. I thought you may want to be present."

"Oh, absolutely. I have wondered what was going on in that head of his."

As Gabriel and Raphael came by, Mikael waved them over. "Want to hear what Daniel's plans are going forward?"

They both raised their eyebrows. "Sure. That could prove interesting," Gabriel said.

"How much time has passed on Earth, Quentillious?" Raphael asked.

"About five years. I think he's trying to get something in place for when Amel-Marduk is released. Or, at least, I hope to hear what he has planned for that."

"Well, that would be interesting," Gabriel said.

"Let's head to Babylon," Mikael replied.

All nodded and teleported together.

Upon their arrival, Daniel had all his apprentices packed into the main room.

Mikael looked around. "There are almost two dozen people here. He's been busy."

Quentillious nodded. "Yes, he keeps bringing in more. Many of his peers think he is either crazy or power hungry."

*****

Daniel turned as he talked, standing in the center of all of them. "Let's go over all we know to date. I've had each of you work on specific areas, so it's time we brought each other up to date. Let's go over the Hebrew Scriptures first." He pointed to

Meshach. "Give everyone an update on what your group has been doing."

Meshach stood. "Well, as most of you know, Jews believe a Promised One will restore the earth in peace, and will somehow deal with our sinful condition." He waved his hands. "We didn't really dwell on how all of that would be done, but focused on when the identified One should be coming."

Most nodded their heads.

"Go on," Daniel said, intrigued.

"When our ancestor Jacob prophesied on his deathbed to his sons who became the head of each of our clans, he told Judah that the scepter would remain between his feet until the Promised One would come."

"That makes sense," Sumai said. "That sounds like he's talking about the constellations."

Daniel turned to him. "I'm impressed, Sumai, with your devotion to the astrological charts. Tell us what you found."

"Well, from what I've read about your tribe of Judah, its emblem is a lion."

Daniel nodded.

"And the king constellation is also a lion, and in that constellation is the king star. That would seem to fit what Meshach said. This Promised One would be a kingly descendant from the Jewish tribe of Judah. So, something must happen in the constellation of the lion to predict this One arriving."

"So," Meshach continued, "we should focus on what we see in the feet of the lion constellation. That will tell us when the Promised One is to come."

Daniel rubbed his chin in thought, then nodded. "That seems to be true."

"But that could happen well after we are all dead," Almelon said. He looked at Daniel. "No offense, lord Belteshazzar, but we don't know when that prophesy will be fulfilled."

Daniel nodded. "That is true. But I do know that the prophet Jeremiah has said there will be a king over his people until that day." He pointed to Almelon. "Tell us how we can maintain that legacy from generation to generation."

Almelon cleared his throat. "Well, I've . . . " He looked at those next to him. "We . . . have been investigating that." He gestured to Daniel. "Based upon the parameters you gave us."

Daniel nodded.

Almelon continued. "Normally succession passes from firstborn to firstborn."

Everyone nodded.

"However, a firstborn may or may not be the best candidate for a strong leader. In order for this to be sustainable over a long period of time, the best descendant, whether firstborn or not, should be chosen."

Daniel nodded. "That makes sense."

Abednego interrupted. "But how do you prevent sibling rivalry from taking place—which could lead to civil war?"

Daniel cocked his head and gestured back to Almelon. "Any answers?"

Sumai raised his hand slightly, a bit hesitantly. "Excuse me, sir."

Daniel, and everyone else, turned his way. "Almelon's group, and mine, collaborated on that idea. It's kind of like what I noticed with the stars. Some seem unpredictable until you look at them long term. In almost every case, there is a pattern to them. Some have patterns that repeat over a short term and some over a longer term. But there seems to always be a pattern—a predictable pattern."

Daniel nodded. "Can you explain the correlation to what Almelon was saying?"

Sumai nodded. "I think so. If we set up the pattern from the very beginning, it will be known by everyone, and everyone will know what to expect. There won't be any need or reason for sibling rivalry because even if one did murder the other, there would be no guarantee that they would be selected for the throne since succession cannot be achieved by that means."

"What pattern did you come up with?" Shadrach asked.

Almelon took over again. "We thought having two houses, if you will, is a solution. One royal, meaning made up of all those with at least a potential of being selected ruler, and the other a type of Senate, if you will, which will help select and find the best candidates for selection. Both houses will vote so no one has power to influence the other. The Royal House can vote, but not select. The Senate can select and vote, but never be ruler. Somewhat of a check and balance, if you will."

Daniel's eyes widened. "Well, I see you've thought this through very well."

Everyone in their group looked pleased.

"And I suppose only those of the Senate can select who will be part of the Senate?" Daniel asked.

Almelon nodded. "Anyone can nominate, but only those already a member of the Senate can vote for who becomes a member of the Senate."

"Does anyone have anything else to add?" Daniel asked.

Everyone looked at each other, but nothing more was said.

Daniel smiled. "Great work, everyone. I think we have the making of a plan. So I think this group, here, will form the first Senate, and Jehoiachin and his family will be the first part of the Royal House." He paused. "Yet I think we will need a spiritual element to this. I will speak to Seraiah and Zephaniah, the leaders of the Levites, and get them involved. I think they will be supportive. Their insight will prove helpful. We'll have the Senate be a combination of counselors and priests. I think we'll call ourselves Megistanes, or noble advisers, since we would be a combination of wise men and priests who support succession of Jehoiachin's descendants."

"What if word of this gets out to others, or to king Nebuchadnezzar?" Abednego asked. "Won't this seem like we're trying to establish a coup?"

Daniel held up his hands. "First and foremost, whoever is part of the Royal House must be devoted to the Babylonian crown. We are not here to depose anyone, but to plan for the one Yahweh has chosen to bring peace not only to the Jews but to everyone."

"So, you plan to bring this before Nebuchadnezzar?" Meshach asked. "Somehow, I don't see him bringing a prisoner and promoting him to a position of authority knowing that person could be a potential threat." He held up his hands. "Not that he would be, but he could be perceived as one."

Daniel nodded. "I understand your point. But I think Nebuchadnezzar's son, once out of prison, will have a different view of that. Plus, those brought here from Judah and those in the north who came from Israel will have a respect for Jehoiachin as a leader. If he follows Babylonian rule, they will as well if he is made a satrap over them."

"Ah," Meshach said. "They follow a ruler they respect, and Jehoiachin follows a ruler he respects. A kind of win-win scenario."

Daniel smiled. "Exactly." He clapped his hands. "All right, then, we have legal documents to draft to ensure all of this is on the up and up, and so that we get official buy-in for this entire plan. I want all of this in place by the time the prince is released from prison."

"You think it will take that long?" Almelon asked.

Daniel shook his head. "Not the first draft. But we must test every contingency and then rewrite it to ensure all loopholes are covered so we have the best plan moving forward."

"All right, everyone," Almelon said. "Let's get to work."

*****

Gabriel looked at the others as Daniel's team returned to work. "This is quite ingenious, don't you think?"

Mikael nodded. "Who would have thought up such an elaborate plan for how to move forward to fulfill all of Scripture?" He chuckled. "Quite remarkable."

"It fulfills both of Jeremiah's prophesies," Raphael said. "The kingship is preserved, and the priesthood is preserved."

CHAPTER 31

Mikael's Lesson

Gabriel suddenly bowed. Mikael and Raphael turned to see who he was bowing toward, and then also quickly bowed.

"Ruach," Mikael said. "Do you wish something of us?"

Ruach laughed lightly, his shimmering, transparent frame looking like heat waves distorting one's vision. "Does my presence always mean something is wrong?"

Mikael smiled. "No, not necessarily." He cocked his head. "But often."

"True. This time I bring you a message. Yahweh is calling for all angels to meet at the Sacred Altar of Stones."

Ruach disappeared.

Mikael laughed. "He certainly knows how to end a conversation."

The others smiled and nodded.

Mikael looked at Daniel and his friends and then back to his two companions. "All does seem under control here. Let's head to the Altar."

All three disappeared and reappeared near the Sacred Altar of Stones. Many of the other angels had already congregated.

Jahven, Azel, and Uriel went to the altar, turned with their backs to it, and raised their swords above their heads. Their swords began to resonate with each other as the blades emanated a rainbow of colors from hilt to tip and then extended upward, far above their swords.

Mikael knew this served as a beacon for all angels to attend. As the triple beam continued, more and more angels appeared. The beam then began to lessen in height. As all looked up, Yahweh descended with the beam and touched down on the Sacred Altar.

He displayed the warmest of smiles. "My sons, I am very pleased with each of you. Your devotion to me is exemplary and sincerely appreciated."

He stepped from the altar and walked among them, periodically placing a hand on an angel's shoulder, smiling at each.

"We have accomplished much. You have helped keep the human world on course through all the deception Lucifer and his forces have instituted in his domain. Rest assured: we will prevail. Despite all his bravado and seemingly the strides made in his own plan, we will achieve the ultimate plan."

He walked back to the altar and turned. "Gabriel, please step forward."

Gabriel's eyes widened, but he did as requested.

"As most of you know, ever since we dispersed the humans at the Tower of Babel into many languages, which have now formed other nations, Lucifer has put certain demons in charge of those territories and has been trying to reunite them into another one-world empire. He is attempting that even now, and he feels he is succeeding."

Yahweh turned to Gabriel. "In a similar manner, I am placing Gabriel over the nation of Israel to watch over them and guide them." Yahweh looked directly at Gabriel. "You will be my messenger to certain individuals going forward, and you will be their protector."

Gabriel nodded. "It will be my honor to serve in this manner, my Lord."

Yahweh smiled, nodded, and faced the other angels. "Whatever help Gabriel needs to accomplish his missions, you will assist."

Mikael could see many nods among the angels. They were as devoted to Yahweh as he was.

"Gabriel and Mikael will be working in close harmony so that, as captain of my host, Mikael can guide what needs to be done."

Again, there were nods throughout the angel congregation.

"As Mikael, Gabriel, and Raphael have just discovered, Daniel is preparing for how my prophecy will be fulfilled going forward until my visit to Earth. You will be assisting to ensure this prophecy will be fulfilled as prophesied." He stood back, now on the altar. "Lucifer has the kingdoms of Earth, for now. But I am the Creator, and my will cannot be thwarted."

All bowed deeply as Yahweh turned into his Shekinah glory and disappeared as an ascending beam of light.

Mikael approached Gabriel. "Was that announcement a surprise to you?"

"Not exactly. He and I have talked about this for quite some time, and I have been overseeing Israel for a while." He smiled. "Yet, I guess this makes it official."

Mikael chuckled. "I guess it does." He turned more serious. "And speaking of that, I think you should return with a legion of angels to again protect the Jewish quarter in Babylon. Once Lucifer hears of Daniel's plan, Jehoiachin may be in more danger."

Raphael had walked closer upon hearing the last part of their conversation. "As well as Amel-Marduk, most likely," he said.

Mikael turned to him. "Good point, Raphael. Since they are currently together, protecting the Jewish quarter will protect them both."

Gabriel nodded. "I'll get on that immediately." He disappeared.

Raphael turned to Mikael. "Heading back also?"

"Soon. I want to spend just a little time in Eden." He smiled. "I need a little energy boost before heading back into the fray."

Raphael nodded. "Understood. I'm going to visit with Azel and Uriel. I'll meet you back on Earth."

Mikael nodded and watched Raphael walk away. He was grateful for Raphael's company through all his time on Earth. Yahweh was correct. Two is always better than one.

Mikael teleported himself into the dimension of paradise . . .

The beauty here never ceased to amaze him as well as rejuvenate his spirit. He stopped at his favorite boulder and simply soaked in the scenery. He wasn't sure how long he had been there when he began to sense a presence next to him. He turned, immediately stood, and bowed.

"Yahweh, my Lord. Apologies. I did not see you."

Yahweh chuckled. "No apologies needed, Mikael. May I join you?"

Mikael gestured. "Of course. What do you wish to discuss?"

"You."

Mikael's brow furrowed. "Me? I'm not sure I understand."

"You've been in deep thought for some time. I thought I'd try and clear up some of your confusing thoughts." Yahweh looked into his eyes. "What are your doubts and concerns?"

Mikael always found Yahweh's eyes so mesmerizing. They were like looking into eternity—and yet not into an emptiness. It was as though the deepest wells of love emanated from them. He tried to make sense of that thought, but couldn't exactly. Yet he knew no other way to describe his Creator as he gazed into his mesmerizing eyes.

Mikael shook his head. "It's not really doubt. Or at least I don't think that is what it is."

"But you wish for clarity."

Mikael's eyes widened. "Clarity. Yes, my Lord. I think that is a much better word for my thoughts."

Yahweh gave a nod and sat quietly, waiting.

Mikael shifted his position on the boulder. "Yes, well . . . I was thinking about Jehoiachin, and the curse Jeremiah gave."

Yahweh nodded. "Yes, and you want to know why I allowed such a curse when it seems to inhibit other prophecy."

Mikael nodded. "I know you always have a plan, but . . . " He glanced at his Creator with a sheepish look. "Forgive how this sounds, but it is not always clear."

Yahweh smiled. "I think it will be clear once you understand what is at stake."

This time Mikael sat quietly, waiting for more explanation from his Creator.

"The curse was needed to demonstrate the gravity of the sinful state the Jewish monarchy has sunken to."

"And the captivity," Mikael said, "was the consequence."

Yahweh nodded. "And what else did it accomplish?"

Mikael thought about that, and about Jehoiachin. "It seems it helped him understand he does not really control his fate, but you do."

"Exactly. Thankfully, he has repented of his unfaithfulness."

"Yet the curse remains," Mikael said. "How do you now overcome it?"

"Who is his heir?"

"Pedaiah's firstborn will be his heir."

Yahweh smiled. "Yes, a son of Shealtiel, but not of Shealtiel."

Mikael nodded slowly. "I see. A curse effected, but a curse avoided."

Yahweh continued to smile. "Some may see it that way. But it is a foreshadowing of what is to come."

Mikael cocked his head. "Sorry, my Lord. I'm lost again."

"Some will view Pedaiah's firstborn as sidestepping the curse, but not all."

"And why is that, my Lord?"

"Well," Yahweh said, "a legitimate king can arise through a non-firstborn. There are many examples. The most notable being Solomon. He was not David's firstborn, but he still received the blessing of the promise of the Coming One being through his descendants."

Mikael let that sink in. "So the death of Shealtiel did not necessarily solve the curse, but the act of Pedaiah was a foreshadowing of what will occur in the future?"

Yahweh nodded. "Soon I will go to Earth and become the Promised One of Scripture. As you know, this has been ordained even before the time of Adam."

Mikael nodded. He remembered a similar conversation he had with Yahweh after Adam rebelled and was banished from the Garden. Suddenly, realization hit him. "My Creator, you will be born . . . but not through the normal union of man and woman."

Yahweh nodded, a deep smile broadening.

"As Pedaiah's firstborn will technically be his, it will legally belong to his brother Shealtiel," Mikael said, understanding growing. "At your birth on Earth, you will be divine, but legally belong to a legal, human heir to David's throne."

Yahweh nodded. "Yes, Mikael. The curse has limited who can claim themselves as the Promised One. There is only one who can fulfill all the prophecy—and that one is myself."

Mikael smiled. "Very clever, my Lord."

Yahweh's eyebrows raised. "I thought so."

Mikael laughed. "So the Megistanes Daniel is now creating will fulfill the other prophecy of Jeremiah by helping to preserve both the crown through Jehoiachin's descendants and the priesthood through Seraiah and Zephaniah's descendants—until your arrival on Earth."

Yahweh nodded. "Exactly. I will come as a prophet, become a high priest for all believers in me, and return one day as King. Through me will all prophecy be fulfilled."

Mikael shook his head. "My Creator, you are truly the most creative designer ever known."

Yahweh leaned toward Mikael and said, in a low tone, "That's my specialty."

Mikael stared at Yahweh for a few seconds. A grin came across Yahweh's face and Mikael laughed. "Indeed, my Lord. Very true."

Mikael suddenly turned somber. "But my Lord. There's such a sad side to this. I recall what you said before when we talked about you going to Earth. You must atone for the humans."

Yahweh nodded. "Yes, that too was decided even before Adam was created."

"But, why, my Lord? Why go through all of that for those who cause you harm?"

"Love, Mikael. Love. They are my creation." He shrugged. "I love them too much to allow Lucifer to claim them." He placed his hand on Mikael's shoulder. "I gave you choice." He smiled. "And you chose wisely. I am giving the humans choice. Those who choose wisely, I will ensure will be able to be here in this wonderful place just as you are here now and enjoy it. So will they. Only if I atone for them can that ever come true."

Mikael nodded slowly. "I think I understand that. Yet . . . " He shook his head. "The sadness is still very great."

"Love is sacrificial, Mikael. That's what makes it love."

Mikael looked back in Yahweh's eyes. Yes, his Creator was pure love. He could see that. Yet love did not shrink back from consequences. He thought back to Jehoiachin. His consequences brought him back to accepting Yahweh as his Lord. Through the pain and suffering, love was still the dominating theme.

Yahweh returned his hand to Mikael's shoulder. Mikael could feel the warmth of his Creator's love emanating through his very being.

"Are you now ready to go back and complete the mission?"

Mikael smiled. "Yes, my Lord. I'm ready."

CHAPTER 32

Nitocris's Concern

Mikael arrived at Daniel's workshop and found Raphael already there.

"It seems we have returned a few years later than we left," Raphael said.

"Oh, how much later? What's going on?" Mikael asked. He saw Daniel again talking to all his apprentices, who were gathered for a meeting . . .

*****

"First, some good news," Daniel said. "Sumai, come up here with me."

Daniel motioned with both hands for Sumai to step forward. Everyone in the room clapped.

Daniel smiled as he stood behind Sumai, placing one hand on each of his shoulders. "In case anyone has not heard, Sumai is graduating from being an apprentice to being a Counselor, a Wise Man for Nebuchadnezzar. He will be specializing in astronomy."

"Big surprise there," Almelon said, grinning, his words carrying over the clapping of the others. "He practically has the entire sky memorized."

Everyone laughed as Sumai developed a red tinge in his cheeks.

"All right, son," Daniel said. "You can sit back down."

Sumai seemed eager to return to his seat.

Daniel held up his hands and motioned for everyone to quiet. "One other excellent thing to report is that Almelon has drafted the document for how the Megistanes will operate moving forward." He gestured to everyone in the room. "And thanks to you all for running through various scenarios to be sure it holds up to the scrutiny in the various situations each of you were able to submit."

All clapped. Almelon stood and gave a slight bow.

"Now," Daniel said. "I only have to get this endorsed by both kings: Jewish and Babylonian."

"When is that?" someone in the room asked.

{ Mikael didn't see who asked the question. }

"Well, timing is critical," Daniel said. "Unfortunately, that brings us to the bad news. I just heard that King Nebuchadnezzar is very sick. The princess informed me she is worried about whether he is going to pull through."

Everyone looked at each other and whispered; mumblings could be heard around the room. Daniel motioned for everyone to quiet once more.

"I plan to go see him as soon as her messenger arrives to tell me he is strong enough to see me. The other good news, though, is that the prison sentence of his son Amel-Marduk is up this week. Therefore, I hope to be able to speak to him about our plan. I don't think I'll trouble Nebuchadnezzar with this plan due to his condition."

Everyone nodded. At that moment, Nitocris's messenger arrived. "My lord Belteshazzar, the princess is requesting your attendance."

Daniel nodded. "Tell her I will arrive very shortly."

The man nodded and dashed off.

Daniel started to don his cloak as he began wrapping up his talk. "Again, I just want to thank all of you for your hard work on this. Now the king may want to know what his counselors say about his condition. Therefore, I urge you to pray for guidance. The other counselors will likely have a lot of other ideas, but I want ours to be the right one."

Almelon approached Daniel as the others nodded and the meeting broke up. "Don't worry. I'll be sure all of us do as you ask."

Daniel nodded, then shot an intense look at Almelon. "What is it, Almelon? Something is on your mind."

Almelon gave a brief smile. "Just gratitude, my lord. I did not grow up with the knowledge of Yahweh as you did. Yet you have shared him with me . . . " He gestured to those behind him. "And to others of us." His eyes grew moist, but no tears came. "I . . . we . . . just want to express our thanks."

Daniel smiled. "Almelon, you were once a brash and vocal young man."

Almelon smiled and gave a slight chuckle. "That's putting a positive spin on it. I opposed you at every turn."

Daniel nodded as he smiled back. "Yes you did. But I knew Yahweh could use someone like you." He waited until Almelon looked at him. "And he has. You are a great Counselor. A Wise Man who Yahweh has, and will, use greatly."

"Thank you, Belteshazzar. We will not let you down."

Daniel patted him on his upper arm, turned, and left for the palace.

{ Mikael and Raphael followed. }

Rubati again met Daniel and led him to Nitocris's receiving room. "The princess wants to talk with you before you see the king," she said as she walked.

Daniel nodded. "And how are you, Rubati?"

Rubati stopped and looked at him, somewhat shocked. "Me? Oh, I'm fine."

Daniel smiled at her. "My offer still stands. If you ever need to talk, I'm willing to listen."

There was a visible change in Rubati's disposition. "I know why the king likes having you around."

Daniel's eyebrows went up. "Oh? And why is that?"

"You make each person you talk with feel special. As though they are important."

"Well, you are important."

Rubati shook her head. "No, lord Belteshazzar. I am a servant, and always will be."

Daniel gave her a big smile. "Yes, Rubati, you are. But we are all servants of Yahweh."

She cocked her head.

"Plus," he added in a whisper, "how would anything get done around here without you?"

Rubati giggled. She looked at him with admiration. "Maybe I will come and talk to you."

"Good," he said. "I'd like that."

Rubati then announced Daniel to Nitocris. Rubati smiled at him and left the room.

{ Mikael realized Nitocris rarely wore the same dress twice. This time it was a pale yellow with flecks of black throughout. The large black onyx beads of her necklace provided a stunning accent to her gown. }

Daniel undoubtedly thought her beautiful. He paused before he bowed, as if he had to remember to do so. "Your Grace, my condolences regarding your father."

"I wanted to talk to you about him before you see him."

Daniel cocked his head. "Is he in a foul mood again, in addition to his sickness?"

Nitocris sighed. "I'm afraid so." She began to pace. "As you know, my brother is supposed to be released from prison this week."

Daniel nodded. "Is that a problem?"

She turned to him and shook her head. "Not for me. But . . ."

Daniel pressed his lips together. "But it is for your father."

Nitocris returned to pacing. "It shouldn't be." She stopped and gestured to Daniel. "You had him sign the decree." She started walking again. "But he has either forgotten it or is ignoring it."

"Ignoring it? How—"

She cut him off. "He wants his stay in prison to be extended."

Daniel's eyes widened. "Why?"

Nitocris turned to Daniel and shrugged. "I don't know. He won't say, but he gets so angry when I bring up the decree he signed about Amel-Marduk's release." She walked over to Daniel and grabbed both of his hands with hers. "You always seem to bring a calming demeanor to him. See if you can again."

Daniel nodded. "I can certainly try."

She let go and turned. "Follow me."

Nitocris led Daniel out the door and down the hallway to her father's bedchamber.

{ Mikael knew this was likely a déjà vu moment for Daniel as these were the same steps he had taken with the king when he had to sneak him into his bedchamber just after he had recovered from his insanity as a beast. }

Nitocris softly opened the door. Another servant girl was putting cool compresses on the king's forehead as he sat halfway up on a mound of ornately decorated pillows. The king looked extremely pale. When the girl saw who had entered, she curtsied and stepped back from the bedside to allow Nitocris and Daniel access.

Nitocris acted as if the girl did not exist. Daniel gave the girl a smile and a small nod. Her eyes widened slightly for a brief second, and then she gave a small smile with a nod in return.

"Father," Nitocris said as she approached the bed. "I've brought someone I think you want to see."

"I don't want to see anyone!" the king said with a hateful tone. He then went into a coughing fit. "Just . . . just let me be."

"But Father," Nitocris said. "You don't even know who it is yet. I think you'll be happy to see him."

"No one!" The king coughed again. "I said no one!"

*****

Mikael stopped in his tracks when he saw the king. It wasn't his pale complexion that drew his attention.

It was a demon next to the king, stroking Nebuchadnezzar's head.

CHAPTER 33

Daniel's Powerful Prayer

Nebuchadnezzar's foul mood was now understandable to Mikael. He knew the demon by the king's bedside was the culprit.

The demon gave Mikael and Raphael a hateful stare. "What are you doing here? You have no right to be here!"

"I have every right to be here," Mikael said. "I have Yahweh's permission. And he does not want you here."

The demon smiled a wickedly evil grin. "My instructions come from a higher source."

Mikael let out a *hmmph* with his breath. "There is no higher source than Yahweh."

"My lord rules the earth," the demon snarled.

"And mine *owns* the earth," Mikael said. "That's a big difference."

The demon bolstered himself. "Even if both of you fight me, you can't defeat me. Marduk's high priest is right now praying for my success."

"Oh, so you think his prayer is powerful enough to save you?"

"Yes. His prayers are extremely powerful. I can feel them flood strength into my being."

"Well, two can play your game," Mikael said as he walked up to Daniel, placed his hand on his shoulder, and whispered something into his ear.

The demon looked at Mikael and then Daniel. "What are you doing?"

Mikael didn't answer but stood back and waited.

*****

Daniel approached the king's bedside. "My king, may I pray for you?"

{ "No!" the demon shouted. }

"No!" the king said.

Daniel sat on the bed next to the king so the king could look into his eyes. "My king, this is lord Belteshazzar. You remember me, don't you?"

{ Nebuchadnezzar looked at Daniel, but the demon stroked the king's head and Nebuchadnezzar looked away. }

Still, Daniel was not deterred. He gently turned the king's head back toward him and gave a smile. "My king. This is Belteshazzar, your friend. You recognize me, don't you?"

Nebuchadnezzar nodded.

{ The demon hissed. "Don't look at him," the demon said. }

Daniel did not let go of the king's chin but held it in place. "May I pray for you?"

Nebuchadnezzar again nodded.

{ "Tell him no!" the demon demanded. "Tell him no!" }

Daniel held Nebuchadnezzar's gaze and the king did not say what the demon had shouted. A couple of tears formed and ran down Nebuchadnezzar's cheeks.

Daniel began to pray . . .

*****

The demon put his hands over his ears. "No! I don't want to hear that!"

Mikael stepped forward, ready to draw his sword at any moment if needed. He pointed to Daniel. "Do you still feel your high priest is more powerful than this man's prayer? His prayer is going to Yahweh himself. Your high priest's prayer can only go to Lucifer. Your lord is not greater than Yahweh. Your lord is a created being, just like you. Just like me."

The demon put up his hand in a way that told Mikael to halt. "Stay back. Stay back!"

Mikael kept moving forward. "This man's prayer is powerful. More powerful than that of your priest of Marduk. You know it. You can feel it, and so can I." He pointed at Daniel again. "With this man's prayer, I won't even need to rely on my companion. Daniel's prayer will give me enough power to defeat you easily."

Mikael took another step forward. "Want to try me?"

Fear was now in the demon's eyes. He looked at Daniel and then at Mikael.

The demon took a step back. Mikael took a step forward. The demon looked more and more nervous. Mikael could feel the strength of Daniel's prayer. He glanced at Daniel. Just from seeing his face, it was clear he wasn't just saying words; he was truly communicating with Yahweh. Daniel had a *relationship* with Yahweh. Mikael could feel it, and he knew the demon could feel it also.

Mikael looked back at the demon and drew his sword. The demon's eyes widened; he knew he was defeated before he even started. Mikael took one more step toward the demon and the demon disappeared. Mikael sheathed his sword.

Raphael laughed. "That was awesome, Mikael."

Mikael smiled but then shook his head. "No. This man is the one who is awesome. I have heard many pray before, but few have prayed like this man. He is a prayer warrior—an elite prayer warrior."

When Daniel finished praying, Mikael could see the change in Nebuchadnezzar's disposition. It was visibly obvious. Both Daniel and Nitocris could see it as well . . .

*****

Nebuchadnezzar put his hand on Daniel's. "Thank you, my friend. I was in a dark place and you brought me back."

Nitocris wiped away her tears. "Welcome back, Father."

Nebuchadnezzar looked at her and smiled. "Thank you for bringing him here."

Nitocris nodded. "Are you hungry? You haven't eaten in quite some time."

Nebuchadnezzar nodded.

She turned to the servant girl. "Get some soup from the cook and bring it here."

The girl curtsied and rushed from the room.

"When you get your strength back, my king, we have a lot to talk about," Daniel said.

Nebuchadnezzar nodded. "I know." He tried to sit up. Daniel helped him do so, and Nitocris put more pillows behind him to prop him up.

"I think we should talk now," the king said.

Daniel looked from the king to Nitocris, who nodded, and then back to the king. Daniel smiled. "Of course, my king. You go first."

"Amel-Marduk."

Daniel nodded. "Yes, my king?"

"It is time, is it not?"

Daniel cocked his head, apparently unsure which direction the king was going.

"For him to be released," Nebuchadnezzar said.

Daniel nodded. "Indeed, my king. It has been seven years."

Nebuchadnezzar gave a slight nod. "Then have him released."

Daniel smiled. "I will see to it as soon as I leave the palace."

"Good. Good," the king said. "Now your turn."

The servant girl arrived with the soup. Nitocris took it and Daniel traded places with her. Nitocris began to feed her father. Daniel stepped aside, paused all conversation, and waited.

Once fed, Nebuchadnezzar became sleepy. He tried to keep his eyes open but couldn't. The servant girl stepped forward and removed some of the pillows so the king could sleep better.

Daniel returned to the bedside and bent down. "We'll talk again later, my king."

Nebuchadnezzar gave a slight nod and then was fast asleep. Daniel smiled and stood. "It's nice to see him resting peacefully."

"Yes, it is," Nitocris said. "Thanks to you, Belteshazzar." She shook her head. "We have all of these others who supposedly know how to heal, but none of them produce the desired effect like you do."

Daniel smiled. "I have to give that credit to Yahweh, My Princess."

"Well, thank your God for me."

"I will." Daniel paused, then added, "You could also, if you wanted."

Nitocris smiled. "Maybe sometime later."

Daniel bowed. "Of course, Your Grace."

"Now, about my brother."

Daniel's eyebrows raised. "Yes. I will have Parviz release him today if possible. It may be tomorrow, but it shouldn't be any later than that."

"Again, I can't thank you enough."

"I will need an audience with him as well, as soon as possible," Daniel added.

Nitocris looked at Daniel with a slight smile. "You have something going on, don't you? You're always thinking, Belteshazzar."

Daniel smiled. "As are you. I see you looking at architectural plans every time I visit."

She laughed. "It keeps me occupied. So what are you planning?"

"I've heard of some unrest up north."

Nitocris nodded. "Nothing major. But some of those absorbed from Assyria seem to be not easily pacified."

"I have found that many of those came from the Northern Kingdom of Israel."

Her eyes widened. "Oh, so they are from your country?"

"In a way, yes. But my nation was divided many years ago. Yet we have a common belief in Yahweh, even if it has become somewhat distorted. I think I have a way to help decrease the dissidence from these people and even of the Jews here in Babylon."

Nitocris shook her head. "Sometimes, I forget that you are from somewhere else. You are more Babylonian even than some of us."

Daniel nodded. "Thank you, Your Grace. That is very kind of you. I am certainly supportive of my people, but I admire your father as well. I want the best for both our countries."

"Well, if I can help in any way, do let me know."

"I will. Thank you."

Rubati met Daniel as he exited Nebuchadnezzar's bedchamber. "I'll see you out, my lord."

Daniel smiled and gestured. "Lead on."

"I heard what you did for the king," Rubati said as she began walking.

Daniel's eyes widened. "Well, news certainly travels fast."

Rubati nodded. "The king's servant told the cook. Once the cook knows, everyone knows."

Daniel laughed. "Well, now I know who to talk with when I want the world to know."

As they came to the main part of the palace where others were conducting business, Rubati said, "I would like to better understand your God."

Daniel smiled and paused. "Perhaps you could come to the synagogue this Sabbath," he said. "I can introduce you to other women who can befriend you better than myself. It's in the Jewish quarter, though."

Rubati smiled. "That's all right. No one notices servants around here—except for you."

Daniel grinned. "And Yahweh, my dear."

Rubati turned. "Maybe I'll see you there."

Daniel nodded and headed to the royal prison.

{ Mikael, pleased at having seen all this, noticed Daniel had just a little more spring in his step. }

CHAPTER 34

Amel-Marduk Released

Parviz met Daniel at the prison entrance after one of the guards retrieved him.

"Well, lord Belteshazzar. It has been quite some time. What do I owe the pleasure?"

Daniel bowed. "Hello, Parviz. Yes, it has been a while. Good news this time."

His eyebrows raised. "Oh, really? Well, I always like to hear that. What is it?"

"The time of Amel-Marduk's sentence is up. He can now be released."

"Really now? How about that?" He motioned for Daniel to follow him. "Let me find the paperwork, and we can begin to get him released."

Daniel followed Parviz to the front of the prison where Parviz kept his office—if one could call it that. It was just another hewn-out space into the rock face housing the prison.

{ Mikael could see the look on Daniel's face, even though he tried to hide it, as they entered. The pungent odor of sweat and urine was strong even this close to the entrance. Apparently

Parviz had smelled it long enough that he didn't notice it any-more. }

"Interesting place, Parviz."

He looked back at Daniel briefly as he rummaged through the parchments looking for the one he needed. This area was quite the contrast to the neat and orderly way Daniel and his friends kept their work area. Again, Daniel was quiet, but his expression told volumes.

"Oh, yes, isn't it?" Parviz replied as he continued to hunt. "To keep the prisoners busy, we have them chip out more and more rooms into the rock. Over time we've built a siz-able prison that can house quite a few." He shrugged. "Still gets overcrowded once in a while—depending upon the king's mood, typically."

Parviz suddenly held up a parchment. "Aha. Here it is." He spread it out, read through it, and nodded. "Yes. It is official. I can release him." He looked at Daniel. "Do you want to tell Ramin, or do you want me to do so?"

Daniel smiled. "I'd like to, if you don't mind."

Parviz raised his hand. "By all means. Go right ahead."

Parviz walked him outside. Once there, Daniel took in a deep breath.

Parviz laughed. "Sorry about that. I forget that outsiders aren't used to all the prison smells."

Daniel nodded. "That's all right. It helps one gain an appre-ciation for not being in prison."

Parviz slapped Daniel's upper arm. "Good one. I think I'll use that on the new arrivals: keep your nose clean and you won't have to smell the prison."

Daniel stared briefly at Parviz, then smiled. "Interesting paraphrase." He turned. "Thank you for your help, Parviz."

Parviz waved as he headed back to the prison. "Anytime, lord Belteshazzar."

Daniel quickened his step and headed to the waterfront in the Jewish quarter. Yet when he arrived, no one was there. As he surveyed the worksite, he noticed everything looked to be completed. The walls facing the interior of the Jewish quarter were simply natural adobe brick. Yet when he went outside, facing the waterfront side, the wall was beautiful with its blue hue and colorful palms and lions.

*****

"It's a shame," Raphael said.

Mikael looked at him with raised eyebrows.

"That those who create the beauty aren't allowed to enjoy it," Raphael added.

Mikael nodded. "Seems like morale would be better if the prisoners were allowed to have beauty inside their part of the city as well."

They followed Daniel as he walked down the riverbank toward a bridge that was under reconstruction. Mikael saw Ramin in the distance. Evidently the workers had been moved to this location since they had finished the previous job.

*****

When Ramin saw Daniel approach, he walked over to meet him. "Lord Belteshazzar, how are you? Anything wrong?"

Daniel smiled. "I am fine, Ramin. I actually have good news."

"Oh? What is that?"

"Amel-Marduk can finally be released."

"Has it really been seven years?"

Daniel nodded. "Why? It doesn't feel like seven years?"

Ramin shrugged. "One day blurs into the next. It's hard to keep track of how long I've watched over these people."

"And how are they?"

"They are fine."

Daniel scanned those working on the bridge. "So, where are they?"

"I let them leave early."

Daniel's eyes widened. "What? That seems very unusual. Not like you, a guard, to do that."

"Oh, one of the other guards walked them home. I'll replace him once the prisoners here are done with their work." He pointed at some workers on the bridge. "These are not very trustworthy, so I'll be sending them back to the prison. They are almost done here."

Daniel gave Ramin a blank stare. "I still don't understand."

Ramin held up his hand. "Give me a minute. I'll let the other guard know he can take these prisoners back to Parviz. I'll explain as I accompany you to Jehoiachin's house."

Ramin approached one of the other two guards on duty and said something. The guard nodded and Ramin returned. "All right," he said. "I'm free to relieve the guard at Jehoiachin's."

Neither man spoke for several seconds as they walked. Daniel broke the silence. "So, Ramin, why were they allowed to leave early?"

"It's Assir. She's pregnant."

Daniel's eyes widened. "Well, that's wonderful." He narrowed his eyes. "But you let the entire family go home because of one?"

"When you're short-staffed, you do what you need to do. I don't have the manpower to provide an escort several times."

Daniel nodded. "I see. Speaking of family, how is yours?"

Ramin smiled. "I have a little boy. He's almost two years old now."

"Ramin! That's wonderful."

"Thank you, lord Belteshazzar. I really can't thank you enough for getting me this job all those years ago. It allowed me to support my family." He shook his head. "I probably would have wound up in prison myself if it wasn't for you."

"Well, I'm glad I could help."

The guard on duty stiffened to attention when Ramin arrived. After Ramin explained to him to help the other guards take the prisoners to Parviz, Ramin looked at Daniel. "I'll let you explain things to Amel. I'll take him to the palace first thing in the morning."

Daniel nodded and stepped through the entrance.

Pedaiah was hovering over Assir. Evidently their relationship had developed into deeper love for each other. Hadcast was preparing dinner as Jehoiachin and Amel-Marduk were engrossed in conversation.

Hadcast turned; a smile lit up her face. "Lord Belteshazzar!"

Jehoiachin turned. "Come in. Come in. What brings you by?"

Daniel smiled. "I apologize it has been such a long time. Yet I bring some good tidings."

"Then sit down and eat with us," Hadcast said as she put another plate on the table.

"Yes, yes," Jehoiachin said. "Please sit."

Daniel nodded. "Thank you for your hospitality."

They all sat as Hadcast served each plate.

Pedaiah looked at Daniel. "Lord Belteshazzar, since you are here, would you lead us in a prayer over our food?"

"I would be honored." Daniel bowed his head. "Yahweh, our Lord, I thank you for this family and how you have blessed them, and Amel, who has joined them over the last several years. I pray that you continue your blessings to them, help their friendship continue, and bless this food as we partake. Amen."

As they began to eat, Jehoiachin looked at Daniel. "So, what are these good tidings you spoke of?"

Daniel smiled. "They are actually for Amel."

Amel-Marduk stopped eating. "Really?"

Daniel nodded. "It has been seven years. Your time in prison is over."

Amel-Marduk looked at Jehoiachin and then back to Daniel. "I go . . . free?"

Daniel nodded again. "Ramin will take you back first thing in the morning."

Jehoiachin slapped Amel-Marduk on his upper back. "Congratulations, Amel. I'm happy for you."

Amel-Marduk grinned. "Thank you." He shook his head. "I really can't believe it." He turned solemn. "I'm sorry, Coniah. I'm rejoicing, but you're still here."

Jehoiachin shook his head. "No, this is time to celebrate. Our God will visit us one day. But today is your day."

"We'll miss you, Amel," Pedaiah said. Hadcast and Assir nodded.

"I'll miss all of you too." He looked at Assir. "And I'll miss the birth of your baby."

"Congratulations, by the way," Daniel said to Assir. "I'm very happy for both of you."

Pedaiah shook his head. "Be happy for Shealtiel."

Amel-Markuk cocked his head. "Pedaiah, I don't really understand your custom, but I'm impressed you would honor your deceased brother this way." He laughed. "I can't imagine doing that."

"Yahweh is far wiser than we," Pedaiah said.

Amel-Marduk held up his hand. "I'm not going against you, Pedaiah. I'm just saying your heart is far bigger than anyone in Babylon."

Once their meal was done, Daniel stood. "Thank you, Hadcast, for the meal, and all of you for including me." He turned to Amel-Marduk. "Ramin will retrieve you before work starts tomorrow, so be up before first light."

Amel-Marduk nodded. "I'll be ready."

After wishing them all well, Daniel left. He stopped and talked with Ramin on his way out.

"I'll be here first thing in the morning. I'll take him to the palace so you can take Jehoiachin and his family to their work," Daniel said.

Ramin nodded. "Very good, lord Belteshazzar. Thank you again."

Daniel waved and headed home.

CHAPTER 35

Amel-Marduk Reinstated

Daniel was back on the road to the Jewish quarter just as the sun began to make the clouds glow but had not itself yet peaked over the horizon. He had a bundle under his arm.

Ramin chuckled when he saw Daniel approach. "Well, lord Belteshazzar, when you said first thing, you really meant it."

Daniel smiled. "I want to get him back to the palace before anyone recognizes him."

Ramin turned and knocked on the door. Hadcast answered. Her eyes widened. "So early?"

Ramin nodded. "Lord Belteshazzar is here for Amel."

She turned and called Amel. A groggy Amel-Marduk came to the door wiping his eyes. "Wow! When you said first light, I didn't know you meant it so literally."

"I'm afraid we have a lot to do," Daniel said.

Amel-Marduk nodded. "Let me say a final goodbye."

Daniel waited outside with Ramin. In only a few minutes Amel-Marduk stepped outside. He looked at Ramin, who gestured to Daniel. "Lord Belteshazzar will accompany you to the palace."

Amel-Marduk nodded, then looked down at himself. "Like this?"

Daniel smiled. "I have a contingency plan. Follow me."

Daniel thanked Ramin and left him at the doorway.

Amel-Marduk walked with Daniel. "So what is your plan?"

"I came this early so you can wash in the river and then wear the clothes I brought with me." Daniel held up the package he had been carrying.

Amel-Marduk nodded. "Oh, getting all this grime off me will be wonderful."

Once at the riverbank, the sun was just slightly peering over the horizon. Amel-Marduk quickly stripped and waded into the water. He dunked himself several times, rinsing his hair and scrubbing his skin with his hands.

After a few minutes, Daniel said, "I don't mean to rush you, My Prince, but people may come by soon."

Amel-Marduk waded to shore and put on the clothes Daniel gave him.

"How do you feel?" Daniel asked.

Amel-Marduk smiled. "So much better. I could still use a proper soak, but this will do until I can accomplish that. At least noses won't be upturned as I walk by."

Daniel chuckled. "I'm sure everyone will be excited to see you."

"Everyone?" Amel-Markuk asked.

Daniel nodded. "Oh, I'm sure of it. Your father is the one who requested I come retrieve you."

"Really?" Amel-Markuk seemed to have doubt on his face. "He was so fixated to put me in prison. I'm surprised he's as eager to get me out."

Daniel was quiet for several minutes. Amel-Marduk looked at him several times before speaking. "What's wrong, lord Belteshazzar?"

"I fear your father is dying."

"What's wrong with him?"

Daniel shook his head. "Nothing in particular, I don't think. Partly old age. While many others have lived longer, luxurious living sometimes yields to a faster demise, unfortunately."

Amel-Marduk nodded. "It seems consequences come with all decisions."

Daniel looked at him and nodded. "It seems wisdom has come to my lord after all."

Amel-Marduk laughed. "Yes, I guess even a stubborn mule can be taught once broken."

Daniel smiled. "I had multiple reasons for putting you in the Jewish quarter with this particular family. Learning a few lessons was one of them, for sure. Yet breaking you was never my intent."

Amel-Marduk nodded. "What other reason did you have?"

"I fear I need more time to explain than this stroll to the palace will provide. I trust you will give me audience once you are king. The attention of your father should come first."

Amel-Marduk nodded. "Yes, lord Belteshazzar. You can have an audience with me whenever you wish. I am in your debt."

Daniel shook his head. "Never a debt, my lord. Hopefully, a friendship. I only want to see you prosper."

"You are also a Jew, are you not?"

Daniel nodded. "I am, my lord."

"Yet you don't wish me harm even though your kinfolk are slaves in my kingdom?"

Daniel shook his head. "No, my lord."

"Why?"

"Yahweh has put us here because of our transgressions. He will take us away from here when he deems the timing is right."

"Consequences?"

Daniel nodded. "Yes, my lord. Consequences. We can blame only ourselves. Don't get me wrong. I care for my people. But Yahweh has put me here, and I serve my Babylonian king with as much passion as I do Yahweh. I don't consider one contradictory to the other."

"You are a unique man, Belteshazzar."

Daniel smiled but did not say anything more until they reached the palace.

Daniel walked with him to the royal residence where Nitocris was waiting. She bowed. It was obvious she wanted to throw her arms around her brother's neck and hug him, but she maintained her royal decorum.

"It is wonderful to have you back, Amel-Marduk. Father is eagerly waiting to see you."

Amel-Marduk took his sister's hand and kissed the back of it. "It is my honor to be back, Nitocris. I trust all is well."

She smiled. "All is well now that you are back. I trust your time away yields no ill will."

Amel-Marduk laughed lightly. "For the first few years, yes." He shook his head. "No more, though." He glanced at Daniel. "This one ensured that humility and wisdom would be part of my training."

Nitocris glanced at Daniel with a thankful expression and then turned back to Amel-Marduk. "Yes, lord Belteshazzar has proven many things to many of us, and we are all better for it."

Daniel bowed. "I leave you, Amel-Marduk, in very capable hands." He smiled at Nitocris. "Now I must leave while my head still fits through the door."

Both Amel-Markuk and Nitocris laughed. "Thank you again," both said.

"Remember," Daniel said. "Save me an audience. I have some important information to share with you."

Amel-Marduk nodded. "I'll remember."

With that, Amel-Marduk followed Nitocris into the inner palace while Daniel turned the opposite way and left.

CHAPTER 36

funeral Procession

Again, Mikael found Daniel faithfully adhering to his normal routine. Mikael was impressed that nothing seemed to shake Daniel's dedication to Yahweh, Babylon, or his position.

*****

Only a couple of weeks after Amel-Marduk's return, an announcement was made that King Nebuchadnezzar had died. The city quickly became a mixture of sadness and happiness.

Daniel stood, impatiently waiting for his friends. When all had arrived, he said, "Let's hurry. We can't be late for the funeral."

"I hate that my first act as a counselor is to attend a funeral," Sumai said.

"It is unfortunate," Daniel said. "But all the king's counselors are expected to be part of the procession and attend the funeral."

"I just hate we have to go to Marduk's temple for this," Shadrach said. "Plus, the dancers are so licentious."

"Once the official funeral is over," Daniel said, "we can pay our respects and then come back."

Daniel, his three friends who had been with him since their capture from Jerusalem so many years ago, and his two newest converts and counselors, Almelon and Sumai, headed to the thoroughfare and waited for the procession.

{ Mikael and Raphael followed them. It looked as though the entire city had come out to see the king's corpse paraded through the city. }

Daniel and his friends moved to the front of the crowd and waited.

In only a few minutes, a voice could be heard even before the procession arrived. "King Nebuchadnezzar has passed! His royal son, Amel-Marduk, is his choice for succession!" This message was continually repeated by an orator who walked at the front of the procession.

Almelon leaned toward Daniel. "It seems the prince wanted no one to be in doubt of the legitimacy of his claim to the throne."

Daniel nodded. "Probably important considering the animosity that initially existed between he and his father."

"They reconciled?" Almelon asked.

Daniel nodded again. "As far as I could tell, they did."

Immediately behind him rode Amel-Marduk dressed in his finest on a black horse whose coat glistened with the rays of the late afternoon sun.

When he saw Daniel, Amel-Marduk gave a nod. Daniel returned the gesture. Everyone else, of course, bowed simply because of their respect for the crown.

Behind the prince were other members of the royal family. All onlookers continued to bow until the entire royal family had passed.

Nebuchadnezzar's corpse, on an ornately decorated bier, was behind the royal family pulled by seven beautiful horses whose coats also had a striking sheen. The lead horse was pure white, the next two were slightly speckled, the next two even more so—with very little white showing—and the final two were black as midnight, similar to the horse the prince was riding.

"Beautiful horses," Meshach said.

"Absolutely gorgeous," Sumai replied. "It's as if they're demonstrating the king going from life to death."

"I think that's the imagery they're designed to convey," Abednego said. "Someone coordinated this very well."

Once the king's corpse had passed, Daniel and his friends walked behind other counselors who had joined the procession.

*****

Mikael did not go with them. Raphael gave him a questioning look.

Mikael shook his head. "I'm not going to act like I approve of this ritual which Lucifer has created for these people. We'll go to the temple and wait for their arrival. The funeral parade will make a circular path through the city and end at the temple ziggurat across from the palace."

*****

When the funeral arrived at the temple, the sun had almost set. The priests lit many torches and placed them throughout the complex to provide ample light for those attending the ceremony the priests and priestesses of Marduk would be performing.

*****

"I must admit," Raphael said. "The light does make everything look somewhat ethereal."

Mikael nodded. "Yes, but look how many demons are here. It's almost like looking at bees around a beehive."

Both Mikael and Raphael watched as the priests of Marduk took the king's body and carried it just beyond the temple altar, which lay in front of the temple entrance.

They watched, as did all the guests, who stood while the priests and priestesses performed the various rituals. The royal family stood near the temple altar while everyone else stood behind them.

*****

Musicians on both sides of the altar began to play, producing a melody that was both ethereal and haunting. Priestesses, on both sides of the temple, paraded to the altar, turned, and stepped in time to the music's beat as they entered the temple to place various food items in the king's tomb.

Other priests took clay jars to the Euphrates River and brought them back filled with water. They also stepped in time to the music's beat. The high priest uncovered the king's body, which was kept hidden from those standing, and washed it with the water brought from the river. He rewrapped the body.

The priest turned to the people. "The king has been cleansed for his approach to the afterlife. We will now prepare for his spirit to accompany him."

Two goats were brought before the high priest of Marduk. He laid his hands on their foreheads, one hand on each. He said some type of incantation; he seemed to enter a trance-like state. The man's body quivered and his eyes rolled upward revealing only the whites of his eyes. He came out of the trance suddenly as his right hand lifted off the animal with his left hand still on the other animal.

The priest turned. "Marduk has chosen the scapegoat."

The other priests then led the goat that had been chosen to the river and put it on a raft, releasing it to flow down the river. The volume of the goat's bleating became fainter and fainter as the raft carried the animal down the river.

The high priest spoke. "The goat is like the king's spirit. Both are on a journey. The king is on the journey to the afterlife. I will now atone for his spirit by making offerings to Marduk. Pray that Marduk accepts these offerings and that the king is found pure to enter the abode of Marduk."

The other goat was then slain and offered on the altar. Following the goat, several other animals of various types were sacrificed as well. Some type of incense was added, and this caused smoke to rise. The scent filled the area with its fragrance.

*****

Raphael turned to Mikael. "It's uncanny how similar Lucifer kept this ceremony to what Yahweh required of his people."

"Yes, *similar*," Mikael said. "But their purposes are completely different. The sacrifice should be while the person is alive to show their belief in an ultimate sacrifice to come, one which Yahweh will send. Not done when a person is dead and their fate already sealed." He shook his head. "This is a useless sacrifice. I'm afraid Lucifer has them all so deceived."

"So unfortunate," Raphael said. He pointed. "Look, you can see the sadness on Daniel's face."

Mikael nodded. "He knows the real meaning of sacrifice and knows this is not the way. The ritual is corrupted from what Yahweh originally intended."

*****

Once the sacrifices were complete, the music took on a different tone. The drums became more prominent as the priests took the king's body, bier and all, and transported it into the temple where the king would be sealed in his tomb. The steps of the priests were in time with the beat of the drums. When they returned, the lead priest was carrying the king's crown, and he handed it to the high priest of Marduk. Amel-Marduk stepped forward, knelt, and the priest placed the crown on Amel-Marduk's head.

The priest faced the temple and raised his hands. He offered some type of incantation, but because he was facing the opposite direction, his words were not clear. Next, he turned to face the crowd. "The transfer of power is complete!"

Amel-Marduk stood and all bowed or genuflected. He returned to where the royal family stood.

The music now became more festive. Many of the priests and priestesses removed their robes, turned into dancers, and began to perform. Both the women and men wore sheer fabric that did not leave much to the imagination. Food tables were uncovered, and guests sat at low tables so they could eat and watch the dancers perform.

*****

Mikael watched as Daniel led his friends to pay their respects to the royal family.

Most knew each of them, except for Sumai, who looked totally enamored with meeting them.

*****

As they were all in conversation, Daniel spoke to Nitocris. "My deepest sympathy for losing your father."

"Thank you, Belteshazzar. He was in a much better frame of mind during his last days." She placed her hand on his arm. "And that was all due to you."

Daniel shook his head. "All due to Yahweh, my lady."

She smiled. "Who responded to your prayers."

Daniel smiled in return. "I guess we're both correct."

Nitocris chuckled. "You're always so humble, and diplomatic, Belteshazzar."

"I also wanted to compliment you on your organization of the processional horses," Daniel said.

Nitocris cocked her head. "And what makes you think I was responsible?"

"Am I wrong?"

She shook her head. "No. But what made you think it was me?"

"It just had the touch of a designer."

Nitocris chuckled. "I see nothing gets past you."

"I had wanted to see your brother before I left, but I see he is barraged with attention."

Nitocris looked over at him and frowned. "Well, I'm sure he'd rather talk with you than those fawning all over him." Her eyebrows raised. "I could go interrupt."

Daniel held up his hands. "Oh no, no. Don't bother. The other counselors are irritated at me enough. I'll give them their time."

Nitocris smiled. "I'll add sly to your list of attributes."

Daniel chuckled. "If you could work out an audience with your brother for me, I would be appreciative."

Nitocris nodded. "I'll do that first thing tomorrow. It may be a week or so before it happens, though."

"I understand. But you might mention this: I think I have a way to help cut down on potential uprisings that may occur in the north. Certain territories may try now that your father is no longer king."

"I'm sure he'll benefit from your wise counsel," Nitocris said.

"I wish you a good night, then."

Nitocris's eyes widened. "You're not staying for the feast?"

"I need to get up early, so I'll make this an early night."

"Good night, Belteshazzar. Thank you again."

As soon as Nitocris turned, she was surrounded by others vying for her attention.

Daniel chuckled and went over to where his friends were gathered. Just before he got there, Rubati met him.

His eyes widened. "Rubati! I didn't expect to see you here."

She handed him a bundle.

"What's this? It smells like food."

Rubati nodded. "Yes, this is all kosher, so you and your friends can have a meal tonight."

"Well, how thoughtful."

She smiled. "I went to the synagogue and met several women. We are meeting periodically."

Daniel grinned. "I'm so happy for you, Rubati."

"All thanks to you, Belteshazzar."

He patted her hand. "All thanks to Yahweh."

She smiled. "Agreed." She looked around, somewhat nervous. "I need to go before I'm seen here."

Daniel nodded. "Well, congratulations. And many thanks for the food."

He watched her head back to the palace. Daniel's friends approached him.

"Who was that?" Sumai asked. "She's cute."

Daniel laughed. "The princess's servant." He held up the bundle. "She gave us food—kosher."

Abednego grabbed the bundle. "Good. I'm starved."

Daniel gently but firmly pulled the bundle back. "Patience, Azariah. Let's get back first."

As they headed back to the main part of the city, Sumai asked, "Lord Belteshazzar, do you think you can introduce me to that woman?"

Almelon pushed his upper arm. "Forget about her, Sumai. I doubt your paths will ever cross."

"I don't know," Daniel said with a smile. "She may be at synagogue this Sabbath."

Sumai's eyes widened. "Really?" Sumai suddenly seemed lost in thought. "Hmm."

Daniel laughed as Almelon rolled his eyes and pushed Sumai onward. "Now you're going to be impossible to live with."

Sumai's cheeks turned bright red. Everyone had a good laugh.

CHAPTER 37

Daniel's Plan in Jeopardy

The next few days returned to a semblance of normalcy for Daniel and his friends.

"I'm surprised Amel-Marduk hasn't asked Daniel to come yet," Raphael said. "I thought he said Daniel could meet with him anytime."

"I'm sure he meant it at the time," Mikael said. "But he is likely distracted with many things now."

*****

At that moment, Sumai rushed into the room. "Lord Belteshazzar!"

Daniel turned. "Sumai? What's wrong?"

"And why are you so late?" Almelon asked. He shook his index finger at him. "You've been with Rubati again, haven't you?"

Sumai looked at Almelon. "Well, yes." He looked at Daniel. "But she told me something that affects you, Belteshazzar."

Almelon started to say something, but he stopped and looked from Sumai to Daniel and back. "What do you mean?"

"She said several counselors are spreading rumors about you," Sumai said. "She said they are saying you are plotting treason against the king."

"What?" Almelon said. "That's preposterous."

Daniel sat with a sigh.

Almelon came over and put his hand on Daniel's shoulder. "The king knows you, Belteshazzar. He won't believe them."

Sumai shook his head. "Rubati says the king is furious."

"Against whom?" Abednego asked. "Against these counselors or against Daniel?"

Sumai grimaced. "Apparently, he has asked that the so-called king of Judah be arrested and brought to him."

Daniel's eyes widened. "Oh no. That is not good. This is not the way I wanted this to work out."

"But why would the king believe anything these counselors tell him?" Abednego asked. "He knows they are jealous of you. And he *knows* you."

Meshach stepped forward. "We should pray."

Daniel nodded. "Very wise, Meshach."

Shadrach also came forward as they held hands and Daniel led them in prayer.

*****

Raphael looked at Mikael. "Lucifer is certainly behind this."

Mikael nodded. "Most assuredly. Yet prayer is the best defense."

*****

Just as Daniel finished his prayer, a knock was heard. Ramin stepped into the room.

"I'm sorry, lord Belteshazzar, but the king has asked me to bring you to him."

Daniel nodded and gave a weak smile. "I was somewhat expecting you, or someone, to be arriving. I've heard the king is upset."

Ramin's eyes widened. "That's an understatement, I'm afraid. He's absolutely livid. I'm not exactly sure why."

"I'm afraid I do," Daniel said.

"We'll continue to pray," Amelon said as Daniel left with Ramin.

Daniel stopped when he stepped outside his work building. "Jehoiachin!" He put his hands to his temples. "This is all going wrong."

"What's going on, Daniel?" Jehoiachin asked.

Daniel shook his head. "I don't know how to even start."

The other two soldiers with Ramin pushed Daniel and Jehoiachin forward.

"And how does this new king even know about me?" Jehoiachin asked.

Daniel glanced at Ramin, who shook his head. "I haven't said anything to anyone."

Daniel sighed. "How did the other counselors even find out about this?"

Jehoiachin's eyes widened. "You're saying the accusations are true?" he asked.

Daniel shook his head. "No. Just misconstrued."

"I don't understand," Jehoiachin said.

Daniel tapped the air with his hands, signaling for the two men to slow down and listen. "Just give me some time and I'll straighten all of this out," he said.

Jehoiachin cocked his head as if expecting an explanation.

Daniel put his hands to his temples once more. "Just give me this time to think."

Jehoiachin's lips pursed, but he kept his thoughts to himself.

Everyone remained quiet until they reached the palace.

{ Mikael could see Daniel close his eyes periodically. He knew Daniel was praying. }

As they neared the king's receiving room, the other counselors were huddled and snickering, some even laughing. Daniel glanced at them. Some diverted their gaze, but others gave him a hardened stare. It seemed their jealousy had reached an all-time high.

As soon as they entered, Amel-Marduk stood, his eyes wide. He held up his hand to the one counselor talking to him. The man paused and then looked in the direction the king was looking. The man looked from the soldiers with the two prisoners to his king and back, a bewildered look on his face.

"Everyone out!" Amel-Marduk said.

The counselor started to say something, but then apparently thought better of it and backed away. He turned and left. All the others also turned and left but kept looking back as they did so.

{ Mikael knew most of these knew Daniel and likely wondered what was going on. }

As the king approached, the guards bowed. Amel-Marduk glanced at Ramin. "You may go."

Ramin bowed. He motioned for the other two soldiers to join him.

{ Mikael heard one of the soldiers protest. }

"Ramin, this is highly irregular: to leave a prisoner with the king unguarded."

Ramin, in a strong whisper, replied. "Then you go tell the king that! I'm obeying. You decide what you're going to do."

The other soldier paused, but when he saw the look on the king's face, he relented and followed Ramin from the room.

*****

Raphael grabbed Mikael's arm. "Mikael! Behind the king's throne."

Mikael turned and saw a glimpse of someone peering from behind the throne. He walked closer and to the side to get a better view. "Who is there? Come out!" he ordered.

A demon stepped into the open. Mikael recognized him as the one who had been at Nebuchadnezzar's bedside. Apparently, mistrust was this demon's specialty.

"Why are you here?" Mikael demanded from the demon.

The demon puffed out his chest. "My lord desires me to be here."

"And mine desires you to leave."

"You have no jurisdiction here," the demon said. "I am at my lord's bidding."

Mikael unfurled his wings and drew his sword. "And I am here at the bidding of Yahweh, our Creator."

The demon's eyes went wide. Mikael's mighty, wide, and fully unfurled wings seemed to be giving off the intimidation effect he desired.

"You . . . you can't intimidate me."

Mikael smiled. "And you cannot stay here."

The demon drew his sword but looked wary.

Mikael rose with his wings spread as wide as possible, held his sword high, and rushed the demon.

The demon's eyes almost bulged from his head before he disappeared just as Mikael arrived.

Raphael laughed. "That was awesome, Mikael."

Mikael smiled as his wings retracted to their dormant state in which it appeared he had no wings at all. He motioned with his head. "Let's see if the king's mood changes without Lucifer's demon here to influence him."

*****

Amel-Marduk's gaze went from Daniel to Jehoiachin and back several times. "You must have taken me a fool."

Jehoiachin's eyes were also wide. "Amel?" He shook his head slightly as if in shocked disbelief. "You're . . . you're the new king?"

Amel-Marduk huffed. "As if you didn't know."

Jehoiachin shook his head. "No. No, I had no idea."

Amel-Marduk did not back down. He pointed between them. "You wanted to get on my good side so you could establish a coup and stab me in the back."

Jehoiachin shook his head but said nothing.

"No, my king. No, that is not how it is. Allow me to explain," Daniel said.

"Do I need to hear an explanation when it all seems clear now?" Amel-Marduk said.

"What is clear?" Jehoiachin asked. "Nothing is clear to me." He looked from the king to Daniel. "I have no idea what either of you are talking about."

"What has been told to you, my king, is a lie," Daniel calmly said.

Amel-Marduk's gaze shot to Daniel. "My counselors fabricated all of this?"

Daniel shook his head. "Half-truths, my king, are more deadly than lies."

Amel-Marduk narrowed his eyes. "I used to admire your adages, Belteshazzar. Now, they just anger me."

"Truth will add clarity, my lord."

The king crossed his arms in front of his chest. "All right, Belteshazzar. Speak truth." He pointed his index finger in Daniel's face. "But if I discern treachery, it will be your last."

Daniel nodded. "You are wise, my king. I trust you to distinguish between the truth and the lie."

Amel-Marduk's expression softened somewhat. "Your words can be patronizing, but when you say them, I feel they are sincere."

Daniel bowed. "They are indeed, my king."

Amel-Markuk gestured for him to continue. Jehoiachin also was looking at Daniel intently.

*****

Mikael looked at Raphael. "Keep your eyes peeled for any other demon appearing. I think the king's shell is melting. Let's ensure that is not interrupted."

Raphael nodded and continued scanning in all directions.

*****

Daniel took a deep breath and let it out slowly. "My king, when your father sentenced you to prison, at first he wanted you in chains for an indefinite period of time. I persuaded him to send you to the Jewish quarter."

Amel-Marduk's eyebrows raised, but he did not comment.

"He thought that almost comical because he believed that would irritate you even more than being in chains would."

The king nodded. "And he was right." He glanced at Jehoiachin. "For a time."

"I put you with Coniah's family in hopes that the two of you would form a bond with each other."

"You put me with the captured king of Judah? For what purpose?" He turned to Jehoiachin. "You didn't know I was heir to the throne?"

Jehoiachin simply shook his head, saying nothing.

Amel-Marduk turned back to Daniel. "Explain."

"If the two of you would develop a positive relationship, I wanted it built on your character—not your status."

"For what purpose?" Amel-Marduk asked.

"To try and save both of you."

Amel-Marduk turned his head. "I don't understand."

"I don't either," Jehoiachin said.

Daniel sighed. "I'm afraid it sounded much simpler in my mind than trying to explain it out loud."

"But you must," the king said.

Daniel nodded. "Do you have unrest in the north, my king?"

Amel-Marduk's head jerked back. "Yes. Some. But what does that have to do with this?"

"Everything, Your Majesty. What did you notice about your time with Coniah?"

"Well . . . " He glanced at Jehoiachin and then back to Daniel. "The most impressive was how all the Jews respected him. Yet I had no idea he was their king." Amel-Marduk folded his arms in front of his chest once more. "Sounds like he could start a rebellion if he so chose."

Daniel shook his head. "Just the opposite, I assure you. The unrest in the north is from those captured from Israel by Assyria, which you inherited when you captured Assyria."

Amel-Marduk's eyes widened. "This is sounding more like potential rebellion the more I hear."

Daniel sighed. "No, my king. Think larger. What is needed to ensure rest in these trouble spots that are composed of Israelis or Jews?"

Amel-Marduk thought for a few seconds. "Honestly, a trustworthy satrap who could lead them."

Daniel smiled. "Exactly, my lord. Someone they respect and someone who respects you."

Amel-Marduk stared at Daniel, without words, for several seconds. "You're saying . . . "

"Do you not both respect each other?"

Both Jehoiachin and Amel-Marduk looked at each other; neither man said anything.

"You lived with each other for seven years," Daniel said. "Surely one misunderstanding will not destroy the bond you shared."

Jehoiachin shook his head. "No, I still think of you as Amel, the one I have learned to depend on. The one who has my back. The one my family can depend on."

Amel-Marduk nodded slowly. "Coniah, I've missed you—and your family."

Daniel pulled out a document and handed it to Amel-Marduk. "Here is what your counselors were talking about. This is the treasonous document of which they spoke."

Amel-Marduk squinted, slowly took the document, and began to read it. The more he read, the more engrossed he became. Periodically, he looked up at Daniel, but then became further engrossed in it.

After he had finished reading, he looked at Jehoiachin. "Coniah, are you in agreement with this?"

Jehoiachin shrugged. "I don't know. I have no idea what it says."

Amel-Marduk turned to Daniel. "He doesn't know about this?"

Daniel shook his head. "My original intent was to meet with you, my king, and get your buy-in, and then go to Coniah and get his buy-in."

Amel-Marduk looked at Jehoiachin. "Coniah, this says you will pledge your allegiance to me as you lead your people here in Babylonia. You will not make your allegiance back to your homeland, but to me alone. Can you—will you—do that?"

Jehoiachin looked at Daniel. "This is what Yahweh wants?"

Daniel nodded. "It is. It is the best for our people—and for Babylon's."

Jehoiachin looked back at Amel-Marduk. "Then the answer is yes."

A broad smile swept across Amel-Marduk's face. "Wonderful." He looked around and motioned for a servant to approach. The servant ran to him and bowed low.

"Get me a scribe. Right away."

The servant bowed again and rushed from the room.

Amel-Marduk locked forearms with Jehoiachin. "Coniah, you will sit at my table from this time forward. You and your family will be provided for, as well as any other wives you have had or will have."

Jehoiachin bowed. "Thank you, Amel . . . I mean, my king."

Amel-Marduk laughed. "When it's just us, you can call me Amel."

A scribe hurried into the room with his portable desk and bowed. "Yes, my king?"

Amel-Marduk handed him the document. "Make this document official."

The scribe quickly read through it. His eyes widened but he didn't comment. "If you and . . . " He looked back at the document. " . . . uh, Jehoiachin, sign, then I'll enter it into the archives, and it will be official from this day."

Both men signed. The scribe bowed to each of them and scurried away.

Amel-Marduk looked at Daniel. "Forgive me, Belteshazzar. I should have known you would not have done what the other counselors said. That is just not your character."

Daniel shook his head. "I'm just glad all is now worked out."

"Don't worry," Amel-Marduk said. "These counselors will receive their just reward."

Daniel bowed. "I will leave that to your wise judgment."

"All I can say is, you may need to find some replacements for some of the counselors."

Daniel smiled. "I think I can accommodate that."

CHAPTER 38

Zerubbabel

Daniel knocked. A young girl opened the door.

"Hello, Sarah."

The girl bowed. "Lord Belteshazzar. Welcome. I'll tell my mistress you are here."

Daniel entered and waited for an official invitation to enter.

Hadcast came around the corner. "Daniel! Come in, come in. You of all people need no official invitation to enter."

Daniel smiled. "That is very kind of you."

She grabbed his arm and led him in. "Oh, kindness has nothing to do with it. You are our miracle worker."

Daniel laughed. "I think you have me confused with someone higher."

Hadcast laughed with him. "We are indebted to both of you."

"Daniel!"

As Daniel turned, Jehoiachin approached and kissed him on both cheeks. "Thank you for coming to the brit milah."

"Wouldn't miss it, Your Majesty." Daniel looked around. "And where is the little one?"

Jehoiachin led him through paneled doors to an internal courtyard. In the middle was a tiered fountain with several benches around. Flowering shrubberies were present with some ivy growing over an archway leading to a type of gazebo where the ceremony would be held.

Pedaiah and Assir were already present.

Daniel approached the couple. "Congratulations to both of you."

Assir held the infant toward Daniel. "Do you wish to hold him?"

Daniel's eyes widened with pleasure. "Oh, may I?"

"Certainly, lord Belteshazzar. We owe you much."

"Oh, no. Only Yahweh deserves anything. I'm just happy to be part of all this."

Daniel took the child and held him gently. He moved his free hand and used his index finger to rub the infant's cheek. "Oh, his skin is so soft. He's precious, Assir."

Daniel looked at the infant. "Hello there. It's nice to meet you, my prince."

The infant yawned and stretched while making a grunting sound. Daniel laughed. "You sound like your grandfather coming back from a day of work at the waterfront."

"Hey, I heard that," came a voice from behind Daniel. Jehoiachin put his hands on Daniel's shoulders. "Thankfully, those days are behind us."

Daniel nodded and smiled as the infant's fingers wrapped around his index finger. "Yahweh is good, my lord."

"Indeed," Jehoiachin said.

"My lord," Sarah said with a bow. "The priest is here."

Jehoiachin turned and raised his hands. "Seraiah, welcome."

Seraiah bowed. "My pleasure, my lord. I also brought Zephaniah. I trust that is fine."

"Oh, absolutely," Jehoiachin said. "A double blessing."

Zephaniah bowed. "That's kind of you, my lord."

"I think everyone is here," Pedaiah said. "Shall we get started?"

Everyone gathered inside the gazebo. Pedaiah pointed to a chair. "Lord Belteshazzar, you have agreed to be the sandek, the one who will hold my son for the ceremony?"

Daniel nodded. "It is my pleasure, Pedaiah." He sat in the chair and laid the infant in his lap.

Pedaiah and Seraiah stood in front of Daniel.

Seraiah poured wine into Daniel's hands. "You are required to sit very still and keep the infant from squirming during the procedure."

Daniel nodded as Seraiah poured wine into his own hands and Pedaiah did the same on the knife.

Pedaiah then handed the double-edged knife to Seraiah. "I choose you, Priest Seraiah, as my mohel to perform the brit milah."

Seraiah lifted one hand and held the knife in the other. "Blessed are you, Yahweh Elohim, who has sanctified us with your commandment of circumcision."

He began the procedure as Daniel quieted the infant as best he could.

Pedaiah continued. "Blessed are you, Yahweh Elohim, who has sanctified us with your commandment to enter my son into the covenant of Abraham our father."

The infant cried an intense cry.

Everyone then said, in unison, "Just as this one has entered into the covenant, so may he enter into the Law of Moses, into marriage, and into good deeds."

Daniel stood, holding the infant, and did his best to comfort him. Seraiah continued with the ceremony. "Blessed are you, Yahweh Elohim, who sanctified this beloved one from the womb and provided this seal of the sign of the holy covenant. Blessed are you, Yahweh, who makes this covenant."

Jehoiachin poured wine into a cup on a nearby table. Seraiah dipped his little finger in the wine and then placed it to the infant's lips. The baby sucked on his finger for a few seconds. Seraiah prayed again.

"Yahweh Elohim, preserve this child for his father and mother. His name in Israel shall be called Zerubbabel the son of Shealtiel under the care of Pedaiah. May Pedaiah rejoice in him and may Assir be glad about this fruit of her womb. We follow the pattern set by Abraham, who circumcised his son Isaac when he was eight days old as Yahweh commanded him. Give thanks to Yahweh, for he is good; his kindness is everlasting. May this little Zerubbabel become great. Just as he has entered the covenant, so may he enter into the Law of Moses, into marriage, and into good deeds."

Seraiah dipped his little finger in the wine and let little Zerubbabel suck on his finger again. Both Pedaiah and Assir drank the remainder of the wine from the cup.

Pedaiah prayed, "Yahweh, may Zerubbabel's circumcision be regarded and accepted by you. May his heart be open to your holy Law to learn, teach, observe, and practice its teachings. Please grant him long life, a life imbued with the fear of sin, a life of wealth and honor, and fulfill the desires of his heart for good. Amen."

Afterward, Seriah prayed once more. "May you, Yahweh, who blessed our fathers—Abraham, Isaac, and Jacob, Moses and Aaron, David and Solomon—bless this tender infant Zerubbabel, the son of Pedaiah, because Pedaiah, the son of Jehoiachin, has pledged himself to you and has promised to raise him in your Law, to marriage, and to good deeds. And let us say, Amen."

Everyone repeated, "Amen."

Daniel then yielded Zerubbabel, still somewhat crying, to Assir, who comforted him as only a mother can do.

Everyone clapped and there were hugs all around.

"Come, everyone," Jehoiachin said. "A celebration feast has been prepared."

As everyone sat, there was much levity around the table. Assir had Zerubbabel near her and comforted him until he finally fell asleep. She was then able to concentrate on the conversation and was soon laughing as well.

*****

Mikael leaned against the side of the gazebo. "Raphael, this is so satisfying, to see how this has turned out. I know it will not remain happy, but it's good to see that even in the heart of Lucifer's lair, Yahweh can achieve something so wonderful."

Raphael nodded. "It is wonderful to see."

"Oh, you're so smug, aren't you?"

Mikael turned to see Lucifer behind him, a smirk on his face.

"Admit it, Lucifer," Mikael said. "You have failed again."

A smile swept Lucifer's face. "I don't count this as failure, but a step for my next plan."

Mikael's stance stiffened. "What do you mean?"

Raphael gave a dismissive wave. "Oh, he's just boasting. Trying to save face."

Lucifer's eyebrows went up. "Maybe." He cocked his head. "Or maybe not."

Mikael shook his head. "Lucifer, I've never met anyone with so much pride, so much that it blinds them to reality."

Lucifer shot him a glaring look, then displayed a smile, even though it looked somewhat forced. "What you call pride, I call confidence."

Mikael shook his head. "You can never give up, can you?"

Lucifer got a determined look. "No. Never. I will never give up until I win. And win, I will. Maybe not today. But there's always tomorrow."

"But you keep forgetting," Raphael said.

Lucifer shot his gaze to Raphael. "Forget what? I don't forget."

"Yahweh is also in your tomorrow."

"It's more than that, Raphael," Mikael said. "He's already there."

Lucifer displayed a scowl and said, in a sarcastic tone, "What do you know, anyway?"

Mikael's thoughts turned to what Yahweh had shown him about the new city he was building and would be provided for so many in the future. It was glorious—more glorious than anything yet revealed in history. Mikael laughed. "Oh, more than you know, Lucifer. Oh, so much more than you can ever know."

"You're no fun," Lucifer said.

He disappeared.

Raphael laughed. "I just love it when you get him so flustered he can't think of a comeback."

Mikael looked at the laughter around the dining table and then back to Raphael. "I love it when we can be assured of a future that will be absolutely wonderful."

I hope you've enjoyed *The Defining Curse*. Letting others know of your enjoyment of this book is a way to help them share your experience. Please consider posting an honest review. You can post a review at Amazon, Barnes & Noble, Goodreads, or other places you choose. Reviews can also be posted at more than one site! This author, and other readers, appreciate your engagement. Also, check out my next book, *The Luciferian Plague*, coming soon!

Also, check out my website: www.RandyDockens.com.

—Randy Dockens

COME EXPLORE THE NEXT BOOK OF
THE ADVERSARY CHRONICLES

The Luciferian Plague

Discover stories from the Bible in a way not yet told.

Lucifer causes a plague with the potential to change the entire biblical narrative.

A scientist develops nanobots that can monitor one's vital signs, report metabolic factors, and target abnormal cells such as cancer and other troublesome diseases—all without the need for repeated blood samples. The technology is thought to be the next step in mankind's evolution. Yet with great potential comes the potential for great harm. Others have hijacked the technology for a nefarious scheme to target those of Jewish descent, and this brings Bible prophecy to the brink of being a mere fairy tale. Can what the Bible teaches be changed to fit a new agenda?

Does Lucifer finally have the technology at his fingertips to get the upper hand in the ultimate battle he has been trying to win for so many ages? Or does God show his touted prophecy cannot be deterred?

Coming February 2023

(BEFORE FINAL EDITING)

SAMPLE CHAPTER FROM
THE LUCIFERIAN PLAGUE
PART OF THE ADVERSARY CHRONICLES SERIES

The Luciferian Plague

CHAPTER ONE

New Assignment

Raphael looked at Mikael as they appeared in the laboratory. "Are you sure this is where we are meant to be?"

"This is where Ruach specified."

Both walked around numerous lab benches filled with various chemicals, flasks with colorful liquids being mixed with the use of magnetic stirrers. Some benches were filled with microscopes and other equipment. Petri dishes were displayed next to the microscopes, apparently ready to be viewed by someone.

Fume hoods lined the back wall; each had some type of experiment in progress. Some contained metric balances, others distillation apparatuses, with a few in use, and others were closed with their lights on but apparently vacant of activity for now.

"And what does Lucifer have to do with this place?" Raphael asked as he investigated one of the microscopes briefly and then looked around at various items displayed.

"Ruach was not very specific," Mikael said as he also turned periodically, seemingly intrigued by the scientific apparatuses in use.

Raphael turned and looked at Mikael and smiled. "Now there's a shocker."

Mikael smiled. "Apparently all will become clear as we explore this place. Remember, this is the twenty-first century. There is much more technology for Lucifer to use in his diabolical schemes."

Raphael turned up the corner of his mouth. "Well, that definitely gives one something to contemplate." He shook his head. "Seeing all he has devised over the centuries, with very little technology, I don't even want to think what he may be contemplating this time."

"Look at this side of the lab," Mikael said as he walked beyond the lab benches to what looked like three padded benches with a monitor at the head of each.

"Looks like something one would see in some type of infirmary."

Raphael nodded. "Yes, it does seem out of place considering the rest of the room." He turned in a three-sixty. "Where is everyone, anyway? Should we look elsewhere or stay here?"

Mikael shrugged. "Ruach was not too specific. He just said to observe."

"And we haven't encountered Lucifer himself yet either. Seems as though we're on a different type of mission this time."

At that moment the door opened. Two individuals entered the lab. One was carrying a beagle.

ERABON PROPHECY TRILOGY

Come read this exciting trilogy where an astronaut, working on an interstellar gate, is accidently thrown so deep into the universe that there is no way for him to get home.

He does, however, find life on a nearby planet, one in which the citizens look very different from him. Although tense at first, he finds these aliens think he is the forerunner to the return of their deity and charge him with reuniting the clans living on six different planets.

What is stranger still is that while everything seems so foreign from anything he has ever experienced . . . there is an element that also feels so familiar.

Available now!

THE STELE PENTALOGY

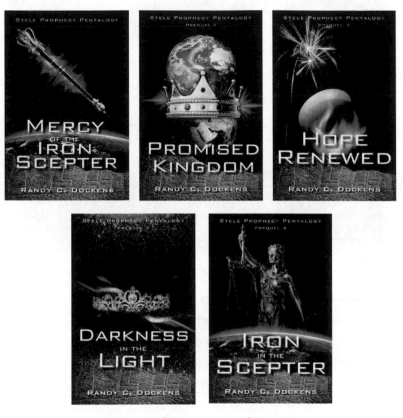

Do you know *your future*?

Come see the possibilities in a world God creates and how an apocalypse leads to promised wonders beyond imagination.

Read how some experience mercy, some hope, and some embrace their destiny—while others try to reshape theirs. And how some, unfortunately, see perfection and the divine as only ordinary and expected.

Available now!

THE CODED MESSAGE TRILOGY

Come read this fast-paced trilogy where an astrophysicist accidently stumbles upon a world secret that plunges him and his friends into an adventure of discovery and intrigue . . .

What Luke Loughton and his friends discover could possibly be the answer to a question you've been wondering all along.

Available now!

THE ADVERSARY CHRONICLES

Come read this exciting series where the many schemes of Lucifer are revealed and unfolded. Journey from when his pride first manifested itself separate from God's will and started our world down his same path, the path of choice, to a path that seems could change even the prophecy of Scripture as we know it!

His schemes are always more devious than they first appear, with consequences that go far beyond what one would think. Despite his aims, he finds that God's unchanging promises always prevail no matter how well his schemes are crafted. Yet many are lost in the wake of Lucifer's lies.

The stories are as old as time but told in a new and exciting way. You don't want to miss them!

The fourth book of the series will be available February 2023!

Why Is a Gentile World Tied to a Jewish Timeline?
The Question Everyone Should Ask

Yes, the Bible is a unique book.

Looking for a book with mystery, intrigue, and subterfuge? Maybe one with action, adventure, and peril suits you more. Perhaps science fiction is more your fancy. The Bible gives you all that and more! Come read of a hero who is humble yet exudes strength, power, and confidence—one who is intriguing yet always there for the underdog.

Read how the Bible puts all of this together in a unique, cohesive plan that intertwines throughout history—a plan for a Gentile world that is somehow tied to a Jewish timeline.

Travel a road of discovery you never knew existed. Do you like adventures? Want to join one? Then come along. Discover the answer to the question everyone should ask.

Available now!